The Big Open

by

T.H. Bear

International Standard Book Number 13:
Softback 978-1-60452- 173-3
eBook 978-1-60452- 174-0

International Standard Book Number 10:
Softback 1-60452- 173-2
eBook 1-60452- 174-0

Library of Congress Control Number: 2021937174

BluewaterPress LLC
2922 Bella Flore Ter
New Smyrna Beach, Florida 32168

http://www.bluewaterpress.com

I have long wanted to do something
for my grandsons
Andrew Ryan Rodriquez
&
Devon Smith,
who years ago I gave the name Buckshot.

This book is for them, with
affection, from Grandpa

Appreciations and Recognitions

First off, I would like to thank Tammi Elbert 640 Rachelle Rd. of Washington, MO. for allowing me to use her picture of Apache on the front cover of this book. He is a beautiful animal captured in the full spirit of his glory.

I also would like to thank Devona and Steve Porter, Innkeepers of the 1840 Tucker House Bed & Breakfast, for allowing me to make reference to their home. It is a wonderful place to stay and I sincerely hope when I'm in Louisville again I will be able to stay there and enjoy their hospitality.

If you wish to do the same you may contact them at

Devona and Steve Porter, Innkeepers
2406 Tucker Station Road
Louisville, KY 40299-4529
502-297-8007
888-297-8007
www.tuckerhouse1840.com

Once again the illustrations herein are the work of *Rose Evans* one of the most talented artist and simply good person I have ever had the pleasure to meet. You may contact her at

Rose E. Grier Evans
(386) 365-3057 rosegrierevans@gmail.com
http://roseegrier.wix.com/roseegrierdesigns

I know you will be happy you did.

Acknowledgments

I also would like to say this story is entirely fiction and does not in any way reflect an actual occurrence.

History does indeed give us such names as the Hunkpapa War Chief Gall as well as the Oglala Lakota War Chief. Crazy Horse. There was indeed a General William Clark and Confederate Generals Sterling Price, Robert E. Lee, Nathan Bedford Forrest, Henry Sibley, and of course, Richard Lucian Page who was a Brigadier General in the Confederate States Navy during Mr. Lincoln's War. Also, there were Union Generals Lyon, Butler, and Crook and the infamous George Armstrong Custer all spoken of herein as recorded in history. However the main characters are purely images of my imagination and are not based on anyone who ever lived, and the events told here of and about them never happened.

I also wish to say I try very hard, through innumerable hours of research using both the Internet as well as traveling to my story locations and spending untold hours in their local libraries in an effort to make my tales as historically correct as any piece of fiction can be.

Too, I go to great lengths attempting to use the correct jargon as well as the conversational sentence structure common to the people of a particular location, race, and religion, of the times.

Someone once asked me were my books politically correct and I answered, "Yes. They are politically correct for the time and location of the story." In this case the common American in the 1880s.

I try very hard to give each and every reader something they find enjoyable. I know some read for pure pleasure, some for educational reasons, some as assignments, and some to find fault. Once again I must say in order to please everyone I sometimes, and very cleverly I think, intentionally leave a word misspelled, or a comma in the wrong place, or even a sentence that is less than perfect, in order to please these Grammar Troopers who need desperately to find fault with other's work. So when you see these little mistakes just smile knowing that they were strategically placed there to please the Grammar Troopers.

Introduction

This tale entitled *The Big Open* is a continuation of the lives of a few of the characters who played a part in the trilogy, '*The Owl Hoot Trail*'.

To fully understand all the events the reader would do well to first read these previous three books; however, this has been written in such a manner that this is not a necessity, rather a suggestion, He that hath eyes to see let him see.

The Big Open referred to in this novel is that stretch of the Red Desert in Wyoming lying south of the Big Horn Range and bordered on the west by the Great Rocky Mountains encompassing the continental divide, and on the east by the Laramie Range of the Rockies.

It is mostly treeless, save for the scattered cottonwoods and willows that manage to survive along the very few river banks, and the ever-present, short, but hardy sage-bush.

Except during the thaw in the early summer, water is scarce, and many of the rivers and streams are dry with little more than sand until the snows come again, and it is from this condition that Powder River derived its name.

Just a small notation here. Never have I found the word *The* placed in front of Powder River. It always is, in the nineteenth century as well as today, simply referred to as Powder River.

The wind is as common in the Red Desert as the coming of morning and night, rarely dropping its velocity below fifteen miles an hour and almost always out of the southwest. A cold and bitter wind during most of the year, but a hot burning wind throughout the month of August, night or day.

Grass is scarce, but what's there is buffalo grass mostly, which the wild steer could survive on, if not cropped too closely.

The Indians were the first to call the area between the Elk Mountains[1] and the Wind River Valley, *The Big Open*.

It was the Mormon travelers who named it *The Red Desert*. A term later picked up by the railroad workers laying the tracks for the Union Pacific which crosses its lower section, and to this day on all official maps, it is so marked.

Nonetheless, most of the cowboys and sheepherders who lived there then and today accepted it as it really is, *The Big Open*, and it is here the guts of our story is played out.

---

1 Elk Mountains: Indian name for the Big Horn Mountains.

Chapter One

On The Santa Fe Trail 1849

Pacing Bear watched for a long time as the three wagons sluggishly crept along the trail that led to the Spanish settlement called Santa Fe. *'Oxen are slow,"* he thought. *'Too slow for a man, they are even too slow for a good woman. I will never understand why the white-man puts up with a creature that moves so slow. It is just one more sign that the whites are a poor excuse for a human man and have an inferior mind.'*

Cory Loren and his brother Juda, and his brother's wife's sister and her husband, Carl Moody, had left the train when the wagon master demanded they stop at Bent's Fort. However, it was common knowledge there was an outbreak of cholera at the fort, thus the Loren and Moody families continued west on their own rather than take a chance of the dreaded disease.

Late on the following day, their wagons stopped and they made camp for the night along the south bank of the Arkansas River where clear water and grass was abundant.

Watching their camp just reinforced the old Comanche's conclusion that the whites were the most ignorant of all two-legged creatures.

Pacing Bear was not leading a war party, his seven braves were hunting antelope when they came upon the Loren wagons sluggishly lumbering along, but it would have been foolish to let such an opportunity pass them by.

The oxen were as big as a buffalo although not nearly as tasty, but neither were they so difficult to kill, and each wagon also trailed one or two horses and a cow.

The travelers were all walking along beside the wagons, since Conestoga's had no prevision for a teamster to ride, as did the smaller schooners, save the single small slide behind the left front wheel. Unfortunately in dry dusty times anyone riding there would be eating more dirt than a gopher could dig, and it was almost always dry dusty times on *The Big Open.*

Their walking made it easy for **Pacing Bear** to see how many people traveled with these two wagons. He could also see only the three men carried long guns. *'It will be a simple matter to relieve the plains of these invaders and bring home meat and horses at the same time,'* he thought, as he lay on the ground peering over the slight rise at the unsuspecting pilgrims no more than two hundred paces away.

The moon rose a little after ten that night and being in its last quarter it was only faintly seen due to its task of penetrating a thin layer of high status, but it was more than adequate for the Comanche.

Slowly one by one, they led the white man's horses off some three hundred yards to the edge of a little arroyo south of Loren's wagon. There the animals were divided into two groups, a little less than a quarter-mile apart and the Comanche spanceled them with course hair rope then waited for the dawn.

Pacing Bear made the suggestion he would go over to the north side of the wagon camp and the others would wait, out of sight, near the hobbled horses, three to each group. It seemed a good plan and everyone agreed after all, Pacing Bear was taking on most of the danger as it would be him who would be closest to the camp and he would be alone.

Just as the eastern horizon was changing from a deep purple to a light blue they watched a tall man roll from beneath the lead wagon and stand. Stretching, he turned and looked about. Finally, it became obvious he missed the horses as he suddenly called out.

The braves were too far away to understand Cory Loren's words, even had they known his language. It mattered not; they knew what he was saying for very quickly others could be seen also moving from under the wooden monsters looking all about, then one pointed to where the horses now were grazing, not more than fifteen yards from the shallow ravine where Indians lay in wait.

The man who had awakened first threw his hat to the earth and yelled something and immediately the other two men began walking out towards the animals. After a short distance one of them returned and picked up his gun and then hurried after his brother-in-law, but the other man had continued a steady pace straight towards the horses with only a loosely looped rope in his hands.

When Juda was some thirty feet away he suddenly stopped. He had spotted the braided horsehair ropes hobbling the animal's feet, and he froze. He looked first to his left and then to his right.

Hears The Wind Talk saw the man suddenly turn to run, but it was a foolish defense, for he drew his bow quickly and let fly an arrow.

The tin point, made from a discarded coffee pot, entered Juda's left rib cage and buried itself to the fletching. He screamed and fell to his knees but stood again and tried to run on as he yelled at the top of his lungs.

At first, his companion did not realize the significance of this and thought he was calling to the horses, but when he saw his brother-in-law fall, he suddenly dropped his rope and cocking his flintlock he quickly aiming it at Stone Mountain who was now rising from where he had been hiding.

The shot went high, but it did achieve one thing, the pilgrims were now alerted and Cory Loren stopped what he was doing and ran to the front of the Conestoga where he had leaned his rifle and began pouring fresh powder into the fission pan[1] as fast as he could.

Carl Moody had no time to reload before Wolf-Lays-Down hit him in the back of the head with a stone club bursting a large hole in his skull.

Pacing Bear was now across the river and slipping up to the backside of the wagon which hid the last man's body, but not his legs, and there he waited. Finally, the report of the rifle thundered across the plains and he immediately rounded the tongue and drove his iron tomahawk into the man's right shoulder blade as he was desperately working at ramming another ball down the muzzle.

Cory jerked his head back as far as he could when the sharp blade cut into his back. His hands went up and the rifle fell at his feet and he slowly began to lose control of his legs and would have fallen, except for the strong left hand of Pacing Bear holding him upright by a lock of his curly blonde hair. However, this lasted only long enough for the knife in Pacing Bear's other hand to remove the trophy, and then he screamed his victorious cry and pushed the dying man forward, holding the scalp high for his comrades to see.

Two of them were doing likewise to the men who now layout by the horses, but the other redmen were racing rapidly

---

[1] Fission pan: A Flintlock rifle had a frizzen (striker) and pan cover made in one piece where the spark first ignited a fine powder which in turn ignited the powder load in the barrel.

towards the wagons where the terrified women stood frozen by the scene they had just witnessed.

Two of the woman succumbed to 'The Fate Worse Than Death'[2] they were put through in the next few hours, but one survived, and she and the four children were taken captive and tied on a long rope with each one's neck looped in such a manner that should one fall, it would trip the others.

All of the animals were led away and the wagons abandoned. Wolf-Lays-Down wanted to burn them, but Pacing Bear said the smoke might attract others and they had all they could handle presently with the slow-moving oxen and the captives.

A year later in Taos, during the trade fair of 1850 between the Comanches and the Mexicans, Connie Loren was traded to a wealthy Don in exchange for a fine palomino stud, but the children who were of the age had been integrated into the band.

---

[2] Fate Worse Than Death: A Victorian phase for rape of a captive woman.

Chapter Two

Jacque Louis Laramie Patay

Laramie Patay[1] was still a boy, little more, however, he had seen much in his short life. The day he watched Reb Brown, the man he had come to love as a father, ride away from their home in Montana, a loneliness swept over him like none he had ever felt before, save perhaps when he realized his mother had been taken captive by the hostiles.

Clifford 'Reb' Brown[2] had his own life to live, the boy knew this; he had fought his fight and had never shucked a task in his long and arduous drive to find the man who had murdered his wife. He had been a man's man in the true sense of the word as Laramie knew it, and the lad hoped he, too, could in some small way achieve the structure he had learned made up this almost God-like figure of the Georgian.

That day as he watched his hero ride the strangely spotted stallion on a course that would lead him south by south-east, Laramie knew he would probably never see Reb Brown again

---

[1] Laramie Patay: Introduced in The Owl Hoot Trail, Book Three, *The Long Trail.*
[2] Reb Brown: The main character in The Trilogy *The Owl Hoot Trail.*

and doubted if either would ever know of the other's life beyond this day. Nonetheless, Laramie was determined he would live a life that would make this man proud to have known him, should Reb Brown ever hear of him again.

He stayed there with Otie James and his family for almost three years, working hard, striving to be a good man, and saving all the money he earned, never expecting anything to interfere with what seemed like the life that was set in place for him to live out. However, during the last week of August while in Copperpolis he overheard a man talking loudly, in the *White Mountain Saloon,* about a blonde woman who was the squaw of an Assiniboine buck at Fort Belknap, up on the Milk River.

Most of the others just brushed the tale off as whiskey talk; they all knew no Indians were allowed to keep whites in this day and time, but not so Laramie Patay.

Immediately the long-buried hope of finding his captive mother suddenly rekindled and Laramie moved closer to the drunken miner.

The next morning after helping with the chores, he gathered his poke and asked an audience of his adopted family. "I know Reb told me my mother is dead and I have never questioned that a single minute until yesterday. However, a man in town said he saw a blonde woman living with the Assiniboine at Fort Belknap and I just can't let it be. I must go and make sure it is not Me-ma, non."

He could see tears building in Ginny's eyes and the last thing he wanted was to cause any form of grief to these people, the only family he knew. Nonetheless, the lure of his long, gripping venture pulled at his heart and he had no control over it.

"I'm sorry. I do love you all."

"Will you come back?" she asked as she drew a quick breath through her nose.

"Oui, I'll be back," he said, although he was not sure that it was the truth.

Blackcat stretched forth his hand, "Good luck boy and remember you will always have a home here."

"Thank you. I feel that, too," he said and then looking over at Otie he just nodded.

It was hard to leave Blackcat and Ginny, they were his new parents, but during the last year, he and Otie had drifted apart. Otie had become a little bossy, a little cold, almost as if he resented Laramie being there. Otie would always be his friend, sort of a half-brother, but it would not be so hard to leave him, at least not at this time.

"Come on, I'll ride a ways with you," Otie said, and then he turned to go and saddle a mule.

While Otie was in the barn, Laramie walked to the grave of Black Band and removed his leather hat. "I know old friend, you understand why I must do this. Reb told me she is dead and I have no doubts but what that is the very truth. Yet I also must follow any reasonable lead, just in case Monsieur Mouton had lied to Reb about her being killed," he said, looking first at the small mound of earth that had gradually shrunk from it's original height to where were it not for the wooden marker, no Whiteman would have recognized it as a grave. His gaze moved up to the deep blue sky above and finally back to the mound. "I must do this, Non?"

Before he could say more, he heard the sound of the mule's shoes ticking small stones along the path. Nodding a last farewell to the spirit, he replaced the flat top hat on his head and drew tight the rawhide line beneath his neck, before turning to meet his approaching friend.

Chapter Three

Buckshot Gunter

Buckshot Gunter[1] had been only ten years old the day he watched Reb Brown ride from the stage stop at Estherbrook along the Florida/Georgia line.

There were tears in his eyes that morning even though he fought them strongly. He did not want his hero to ride off where he might never see him again, but neither did he want Reb Brown to see him cry. Mr. Reb had called him a little man and a little man he would be.

Nonetheless, his heart was heavy with the loss, so much that he had never gotten the image out of his young mind. An image burned deep in his memory, an image of the tall thin man riding off into the misty grayness that foggy morning on the new horse Mr. Sam[2] had given him.

---

[1] Buckshot Gunter: Introduced in The Owl Hoot Trail, Book Two, *The Withlacoochee Renegades.*
[2] Mr. Sam: Sam Brooks introduced in *The Owl Hoot Trail, Book Two, The Withlacoochee Renegades.*

Over and over he had told himself that one day he would go west and find Mr. Reb and help him kill John Tidwell[3].

Every now and again Mr. Sam would receive a letter, brought by the stage, penned in ink by Reb Brown and he would always share the news with the others who lived at Estherbrook. The epistles came fairly often the first few years, but gradually they slowed and finally stopped altogether.

Dog days[4] were in full swing when he made up his mind to leave.

The afternoon before his departure he had been over helping Mr. Sam with the changing of the team and he was asked by Miss Esther to bring in a bucket of water from the well.

During the past few years, her hands would at times become swollen and they were starting to twist around the finger joints which made carrying the heavy bucket painful.

Buckshot did not mind helping her. He thought of her as a very pretty woman even though she was the oldest woman he knew. Of course, he had known Granny Keeling and she was older even than Miss Esther, but Granny had died three years past.

That day as he lifted the water bucket to the table for her, he casually asked, "Has Mr. Sam heard any news of Reb Brown?"

"No son, not in a couple of years. The last letter had been posted in someplace called Coulson, out in Montana Territory; wherever that is," she replied, and then she looked above the fireplace at the heavy wood mantel that had been cut from a huge cypress tree. "I think it's over here somers'," she said, but when she looked she could not find it. "I just know Sam put it here somers'. I'll have to ask him when he comes in."

------

3 John Tidwell: Introduced in *The Owl Hoot Trail, Book One, Gold In The Red Desert.*

4 Dog Days: A time in late summer where in the south it was said the heat drove the dogs mad and the big rattlers went blind and they struck at everything that moved.

'Montana Territory.' The words brought visions of mountains covered with white caps not unlike the picture he saw once in a book where all the little houses had funny curved roofs and everyone wore strange clothes. *'I have saved thirty-eight dollars and four bits,'* he considered. *'I might just have enough to get to Montana Territory.'*

Late that night after everyone was asleep, he slipped out into the darkness and easing a rope halter around Ananias' head, he led the mule off.

Ananias was very old and no longer used to work around the place. Mr. Sam said Ananias was in mourning 'cause his teammate Sapphira had died. Buckshot figured if that was so, the old red mule mourned more than a natural human would have over a mate.

In reality, Buckshot didn't believe that a mule could have such feelings for another mule. He figured the skinny crow bait was too old to earn his keep anymore and Mr. Sam was just being nice to him for times long gone.

'It won't be like stealing if I wus to take Ananias, since he ain't good for nothing but munching on the green summer grass in the big pasture,' he thought.

Although he could read and write, Buckshot's handwriting had never been good and only those who were used to it could consistently understand his scratching. This did not bother him, writing was not a man's talent anyway; a man must know how to figure and when it came to figures, none were his equal. Even Mr. Sam could not do his figures with pencil and paper as fast a Buckshot could do them in his head. Of this he was proud.Still, this night as he scratched out the note explaining why no one would be able to find him come the morning, he suddenly wished he could write a little better, for when this was found he would be miles away from the people he loved.

Chapter Four

Ryan Rodriguez

Ryan Rodriguez had been born north of Tucson, some fifty miles, to a Shoshone squaw who was working as a cleaning woman at the ranchero of Francisco Vargas, a very wealthy Don who had in his employment over thirty men. Many were riders keeping track of the vast herd of longhorns he brought north with him from Sonora.

At the time of his birth, the Vargas Empire was unchallenged by the Americans. His vaqueros were all well armed and equally well experienced in fighting the Apache, the common foe of both cultures in southern Arizona.

It was from one of these Vaqueros' seed that Ryan had been conceived, though not from some casual encounter by two strangers in a back room of a canteena. Rather by two lovers who would remain together for as long as they both lived free.

Wah Ha Two Muah or Two Moons, had been raised on the reservation at Fort Washakie in central Wyoming and had been educated in the Indian school there. It was there she had known the young army Lieutenant Ryan Peters and with a childhood crush on him, she always carried a tender spot in her heart for the tall dark man, and thus gave her firstborn his name.

In his youth, Ryan had followed his older cousin around much like a puppy follows an older dog. Carlos didn't mind, he liked little Ryan and he liked being the child's hero which was the first time in his life anyone had paid him so much attention. That had all come to an end when Carlos[1] rode north with his father Gilberto Rodriguez and older brothers[2] never to return.

---

[1] Carlos Rodriguez: A vaquero working on the Circle Rocking AR ranch in Wyoming, see *The Owl Hoot Trail Book Three, The Long Trail.*
[2] Rodriguez Family: See *The Owl Hoot Trail Book Three, The long Trail,* Chapter Five.

Chapter Five

Quigley Hancock

Quigley Hancock was not a boy. In fact, some who knew him wondered if he had ever been a boy. From anyone's earliest remembrance he was a man. At an age some would have called him a child, he was thought of as a little man.

His father called him a little man the first time he saw his son nursing on his mother's breast and from that day forward he was so thought of, and so treated by Cader Hancock. Of course, his mother, Jestern, had other feelings for her firstborn, but such were kept inside her, save what she shared with little Quigley during their tender moments.

Quigley Hancock was born near Louisville, Kentucky on September the first 1838, which happened to also be the day his famous uncle[1] died.

His parents did not choose this location for his birthplace, in fact, he was not due to arrive for another three weeks according

---

[1] His famous uncle: His mother's sister Judith was married to William Clark of Louis and Clark fame.

to Jestern's calculations, but the journey had been unusually strenuous on all of the passengers and especially on her.

Hazael and Nancy Tucker, Louis and Addie Brown,[2] and Cader, also had learned to hate the travel by coach hours prior to their arrival at the small log cabin where the last changing of the team was supposed to take place before they would finally arrive in Louisville.

The Concord may have been a discomfort to the others but had become far more to Jestern. It's never-ending rocking to and fro, interrupted all too often by sudden jolts when the iron tires found the remains of stumps uncovered by years of beating by untold numbers of hooves on the clay road. And on this day, a horrendous storm swept through the valley of the Ohio leaving behind a thousand uprooted trees as well as crevices cut deep in the pike where rivers of rainwater sought an escape to flatter ground.

Soon after their arrival at the Stage Stop it became obvious that they would not make Louisville that night. The storm had sent a cloud of twisting hell through the countryside taking with it half of Swift's barn and all of the replacement horses.

The team was exhausted and the wind and rain still pounded throughout Jefferson County, and the night was approaching rapidly, although darkness had surrounded them since shortly after the storm broke.

The small log home of Chester and Helen Swift was not normally used as a stopover for drivers or passengers, rather a place for a simple change of the team, but on this night it would suffice for both and gratefully so.

No man really wants to be near his wife when she enters the later stages of labor, for it is the only time he is likely to feel guilt over his manly act, but Cader had no choice in the matter. Moments before her screams became nearly constant, hail the

---

[2] Louis and Addie Brown: The parents of Reb Brown, See The Owl Hoot Trail Book Two, 'The Withlacoochee Renegades'.

size of walnuts fell upon the stage stop and no one dared to venture from the protection of the strongly constructed roof Chester Swift had labored so long in building.

The morning broke clear and clean, with only narrow and distant streaks of white high above, to otherwise hide the blue sky.

Hazael was the first of the passengers to venture out of the cabin and upon seeing the beautiful morning he called out, "Nancy Jane, you must come quickly."

His wife, who had been up most of the night assisting with the birthing, was in no way ready to be beckoned by such a spirited voice, but after wiping her face with a borrowed apron and straightening an unruly curl that refused to remain at any location on her head save to hang in front of her right eye, she turned to the door and walked towards her husband.

"Look at this beauty, listen to the birds singing praises to the Lord, and there, do you see Ole Mister Groundhog up and surveying his territory," Hazael said with enthusiasm as he pointed towards the brown varmint sitting on his haunches atop a stone fence some seven rods distant.

"You know this land has good trees, it is high and dry, has good water and clay from which a fellow could make his own bricks, and there, do you see that limestone? It could be used by an industrious man to construct the foundation of a fine house."

She was tired, she was weary, and she was hungry but she dearly loved Hazael Tucker and she could feel the zest he was radiating and quickly she too began to ingest closeness to this piece of God's green earth. "Yes my husband, it is a beautiful morning, in a most beautiful part of this world. We must return here someday when I have had more rest so I can truly enjoy its beauty."

The six passengers who shared that stormy night with Chester and Helen Swift would part company the next day never to see one another again. Louis and Addie Brown would soon be on their way to South Georgia where they would spend the remainder of their lives. Cader, Jestern, and their 'little man' would find themselves in Arkansas within a year, and one year to the day of this separation Hazael and Nancy Jane Tucker would return to purchase this small log house and some eight hundred plus acres surrounding it, upon which they would build '*The Tucker Plantation*'[3].

There among the barns and outbuildings, the stables and slave quarters, the corrals and hog pens, they built a glorious home of solid brick walls, poplar floors, with seven fireplaces and gorgeous, seeded-glass windows, a home that would stand for centuries.

---

3 The Tucker Plantation: is still today a place of beauty and a contribution to Louisville. For more information see www.tuckerhouse1840.com or contact the Inn Keepers Devona and Steve Porter at 1840 Tucker House Bed & Breakfast, 888-297-8007.

Chapter Six

Fort Belknap

Laramie Patay never reached the height of his hero, nor had he enough to eat to develop what one might call a large man's stature. Rather, he was some above average in height nonetheless three inches shorter than Reb Brown and wiry as a twisted cedar that held to life on a mountain ridge where huge boulders were more common than soil. But he became just as hard and steadfast in his beliefs as had Reb Brown.

One of the beliefs Reb Brown had instilled in him was the need for possessing good weapons and the ability of both swiftness and sureness in their use; there was never a time he did not strive to achieve that standard.

He had saved his money and in the spring of '78 traded the Open Top Colt Reb had given him for a new revolver. The trade had been both bitter and sweet. It had been hard to part with something that had been given to him by Reb Brown, but remembering the importance Reb had placed on having both handguns and long guns chambered for the same cartridge, a few months later he bought one of Mr. Winchester's new carbines that shot the same 44 centerfire as his new Colt.

However, the very morning he rode east from Copperopolis, he had stopped by Coker's store and bought back his old Open Top and placed it along with a box of 44RF shells in his saddlebags. This move left him short on funds, but somehow that old revolver seemed to be a part of Reb Brown himself, and Laramie just didn't feel right about riding off leaving its future care to some stranger.

Fort Belknap was not a real fort, not in the sense most imagine a fort to be. It was rather a collection of buildings erected mostly by troops with a few civilian stores scattered among them somewhat like Fort Laramie had been. However not nearly so well built, nor as large, and it in no way reminded Laramie of the home of his youth and namesake.

Among Belknap's buildings was the sutlers store wherein the local Indian Agent plied his trade and it was in front of this building the lad tied his cayuse to the hitching post.

John Oscar Chancy had brought his Mary Elizabeth west from Illinois with a Mormon wagon train but had had words with one Porter, a man of high authority within the Church, but low respect for other's rights.

Porter had taken a shine to the beautiful Mary Elizabeth and had made it known should something happen to Chancy, he would be the one to take her as a wife.

Realizing were something to happen to Oscar Chancy it most likely would be at the hands of Porter himself. The couple departed from the group at old Fort Casper and moved north, first into the Black Hills shortly after the Deadwood Camp was established, and then to Mercerville. However, when the opportunity to take over the sutlers store at Fort Belknap came his way, he quickly took his wife and headed north.

John Chancy found the store at the military headquarters just to his liking, but Mary Beth did not totally share his enthusiasm.

They had a good life. Chancy worked hard and provided her with all the necessities a woman could ask for. Nevertheless, there was something about the vastness of Montana that gave her a feeling of uneasiness, of smallness, a feeling that she was so insignificant in this brown country. Late at night, after he was resting peaceably beside her, she often wept, longing for her green homeland so far away, and the family she had left behind.

When the lad walked into the store his eyes required some adjustment from the brightness of the outdoors to the darkness of this structure and its low hung roof.

It wasn't until she spoke did he even realize he was not alone. "Good afternoon young man, may I help you?" she inquired as she studied the intruder. *'He is an odd-looking one, hair as light as a flaxen horse and skin as dark as a Nakoda.'*

Laramie was startled at the sound of her voice and a cold chill ran up his spine before he looked upon her face. *'I do believe she is the most beautiful woman I have ever seen,'* he thought as he stared at the dark-haired woman who seemed to appear from nowhere.

The two stood only a couple of yards apart, each studying the other, neither quite sure what to say next, as each mind questioned the person before them.

'He is young with a kind face, but nonetheless hard and strong,' she thought. *'I wonder if he is a breed.'*

'Although she is dark, she could not be an Indian, no Indian ever was so beautiful, and she is tall, as tall as Miss Bea Desmond[1] and no Indian woman is that tall,' he considered.

Finally, she again spoke, "Well?"

"I, er, I was looking for the sutler," he stammered as a reply to her question.

"My husband is not here at the moment, perhaps I can help you."

---

[1] Bea Desmond: See *The Owl Hoot Trail Book Three The Long Trail, Chapter Six.*

"I er, I don't know."

He now realized he was stammering and the very idea gave way and a cloud of embarrassment swept over him. Finally, after taking a deep breath, he gathered himself and finished. "I have come from Copperopolis. I heard there about a woman living with an Assiniboine buck, a white woman."

She thought a few moments before replying, "I know of no white woman living with any Nakoda."

"I was told she was here at the Fort, a woman with light hair, like mine," he added touching the strands of hair escaping from his hat.

"No, I don't think so," she replied shaking, her head slowly. She could see her answer distressed him greatly and she wondered what such a woman meant to him. "Why do you ask?"

He ignored her question and turning, he looked about the store. Now that his eyes were fully accustomed to the dimly lit room, "Mee'be your husband knows her."

She started to tell him it was very unlikely her husband knew any woman who lived with the Indians near here that she too did not know. Yet somehow she felt such a statement would bring more stress upon him, and for reasons she did not understand, bringing stress upon this young man was something she did not want.

"Perhaps he does. He is up on 'The Milk'; he will be back before sundown if you would like to ask him."

"Yes, I would like that very much," Laramie said back nodding his head before he turned and started for the door. Just before he reached for the rope latch he hesitated and turned back, *'I wonder how old she is, not much older than me. What a looker,'* he thought before he said, "Merci Madame," and touched the front brim of his latigo hat.

She looked at the door for several seconds after he had closed it behind him and wondered at the mysterious lad.

Chapter Seven

The Cost Of It All

Buckshot had been right about more than one thing, Ananias for example. The animal was truly an old mule and by the time they could see the train station in Quitman the old fellow simple sat down on his hunches for a few moments looking ahead before he mustered a strange noise from deep inside his throat, and then he slowly eased on down, then rolled over, and died.

The idea of him dying took Buckshot totally by surprise. He had never dreamed that the trip from Estherbrook Stage Stop to Quitman would kill the animal and suddenly he felt awful.

He knew Mr. Sam had a strong affection for the old mule and the last thing on earth he wanted to do was cause Mr. Sam grief.

After some consideration, he decided it best not to say anything to anyone about the dead animal at the top of the rise, especially of it being him who rode it there.

The ticket clerk said the fare from Quitman to Thomasville would be four dollars and two bits, which totally floored Buckshot.

He had no idea of the cost of living anywhere except at Estherbrook and there, of course, all it cost was to do the chores assigned to him. Turning, he started for the door with his head hanging in such a manner his chin was only an inch from his chest.

Orville Brooks had seen the expression on the boy's face change from excitement to gloom when he quoted the price of the fare. Although he was often confronted with disappointment from the poor whites in the area upon learning of the cost of rail travel, there was something about this young man that touched him.

He hesitated to speak, he knew he should not do so, he knew he could lose his job for the very idea, but just before the lad reached for the brass handle that would open the door and remove him from Brooks' life, perhaps forever, and he called out, "Young man."

Buckshot stopped and slowly turned back to face the thin man in the white shirt.

"If you are here at 6 pm precisely, I may have an extra ticket."

"Thank you, Sur, but I can't afford it."

"You can afford this one," the man said and again he looked about making sure no one was close enough to hear his statement, even though there was no one in the station at the moment, save he and the boy.

Buckshot nodded his head and then he walked out. *'Gee if it cost so much to get to Thomasville, how much will it cost to get to Montana?'* he wondered. *'I had better not go anywhere else in this town. I had better stay right here and wait for that train.'*

There he stopped and sat down on the hardwood bench just outside of the door. *'I guess I should just go back to Estherbrook, but what will I tell Mr. Sam about Ananias? I can't go back there now; I can't tell him about killing his mule.'*

So instead of doing anything, he just sat there on the bench with his cased rifle in his lap and his legs swinging beneath the bench.

That evening he watched men and women board the westbound, however, if any of them noticed him they gave no indication. Still, he waited and watched the big clock atop the courthouse some distance away.

Finally, after it was apparent all who were boarding the train were on board, the long arm reached the 12 and the clock began chiming out the hour, only then did he open the door of the depot.

"Come quickly," the man said and once more looking about he asked, "Where do you want to go?"

"Coulson, Montana," Buckshot replied.

"Well, that is a little beyond my jurisdiction," Brooks replied as he began punching out holes on a string of yellow tickets. "However, these will get you as far as Atlanta. You must change trains a Thomasville and try not be too conspicuous."

"Yas Sur," Buckshot replied, not completely sure what conspicuous meant.

"Now hurry along and never tell anyone where you got these tickets."

Buckshot nodded his head and started for the door, but just before he opened it he turned back, "I'd admire to know your name."

"Orville Brooks," the agent said, and then immediately regretted it.

"Brooks? Do you know Mr. Sam Brooks over to Estherbrook?"

"Why yes, I do. He is my cousin."

"He is my friend," Buckshot replied smiling "You Brooks' sure are a fine bunch a' folk."

"Yes, well you skedaddle on now before you miss the train."

Chapter Eight

Harshaw Arizona

Ryan had never wondered about his name. It was simply his name, and things of that nature never enter a boy's head, that is until that day when Mr. Tecum Harshaw himself asked him what a half breed was doing with a good Irish name.

Ryan had never liked Mr. Tecum much anyway, he was too much a big shot and much too rich, but he owned *The Hermosa Mine* which was the mainstay of Harshaw, mainly because the mine employed 150 men and a 20 stamp mill.

Only because of it there were boardinghouses, hotels, corrals, blacksmith shops, stores, and saloons, 30 of them in fact. Other structures too, and because of all of this, Ryan had a job, the first one he had ever had, other than helping on the Vargas Rancho. Nonetheless, he did not forget the snicker Harshaw had given him nor the insult he considered it to be.

A day in the mine was hot and dusty and he labored long and hard, but there was little relief from the misery upon coming topside. The Arizona sun beat unmercifully on the dry desert sand driving the temperatures above the 120-degree mark until the darkness arrived. Then when the treeless terrain had nothing to hold in the warmth, quickly his skin was covered with chill bumps in the cold night air.

It was an unending hostile atmosphere, but he knew little else from the day he was born, except when his mother would take him to the high country. Unfortunately, these excursions to the north ended long ago.

That night the tall, lean lad had trouble sleeping. The small wooden 6X6 box he used to sleep in seemed to offer no protection from the cold and he was awake enough to overhear the voices of the two men who ventured nearby.

"I tell ya Carlson, that no good rich bastard deserves it."

"Yeah, only how we gon'a get away?"

"I got two horses stashed yonder just over that rise. Got two canteens on each saddle, be plenty to get us across the border into old Mexico."

"I guess," his reluctant companion replied.

'They are sure up to no good,' Ryan thought, as he threw back his blanket and peered out between the slats of his box, but he could just see an outline of one of the men who was crouched next to the wall of Henry Watson's store.

Ryan was sure the other man was near, but he could not locate him now that they had stopped talking.

Slowly and ever so carefully Ryan lifted the end of his box which served as its only entrance or exit and slipped out.

He felt a chill of danger as he eased along past more boxes being used by other miners for the same purpose; still, it all seemed rather exciting at the same time.

These two men were about to commit a crime, of that he was sure, what crime he did not know, and really did not care all that much. It was the opportunity to witness the action that was the lure to him.

Finally, he found a place where he could see the man well, crouching beside the store wall, and there Ryan stopped and waited.

His wait was not overly long, for soon the sound of heavy boots being applied on the boardwalk was clear in the night air, boots approaching with force and determination.

Tecum Harshaw outright owned nine of the thirty saloons in the little mining village. He also was the silent partner in one other, as well as that of Henry Watson's store. This fact was only known by, Henry, Geneva, Henry's wife, and Tecum. In fact, it was Tecum's relationship with Geneva before she married Henry that had been the sealing of this partnership.

John Swelley, Geneva's brother also worked for Harshaw although not because of any dept Tecum felt to Geneva, rather because John Swelley was the biggest man in the area and the job he had been assigned was well suited to his size. Every night he went to each of Harshaw's saloons and collected the profits of the evening and carried them to a drop shut in the side of Harshaw's office.

There the money bags fell directly into a very large safe located in the basement. The chute was too narrow for a man to enter, and so angled, should a boy attempt it he would be found in the safe the next morning when Harshaw opened his office.

On this night, as Swelley stepped from the wooden planks, that made up the boardwalk in front of his sister's store, onto the hard-packed soil, a long slim blade was expertly slid into his side only a quarter of an inch beneath his rib cage, the point of which pricked into the very bottom of Swelley's pumper.

John felt the quick pain, but he had no idea the extent of his injury. Instead, he backhanded his foe with such force he literally lifted Lazarus Ross from his feet and knocked him back to within a yard of where Ryan hid.

The boy looked down at the twisted face of the man who lay there, stunned for a moment, before the big man was again upon him.

Carlson Webb now crunched himself even lower behind an empty whiskey barrel as he too watched the fracas taking place.

Ross finally was able to pull the 31 caliber Colt from his waistband and cock it, but John blocked his aim with another blow to the face and the shot went wildly up over his head and through the window above.

The second shot also was a miss, but by now Swelley's strength was failing and slowly he released his grip on his assailant. Ross rolled the big man off him and staggering to his feet he grabbed one of the money bags and charged straight out into the street, disappearing between two buildings on the other side.

Ryan, having never seen Webb, now rushed to Swelley's side.

"Mr. Swelley, Mr. Swelley, can I help you?"

At that very moment, Geneva leaned out her now open window and looked into the dark alley below.

Gazing up at the lad, John recognized him and he gasped. "Rodriquez, help me," then he gave up the ghost.

Geneva heard her dying brother speak, but his last two words were so weak she could not understand them and she screamed loudly the single word she had heard—"RODRIQUEZ."

Suddenly, much to his surprise, there were several men coming at a run toward him and the dead man. Again she screamed this time saying, "There, there he is, the Rodriquez boy. Get him."

Ryan twisted his head at her, but the sound of the approaching boots was more convincing to him at the moment than the screams coming from overhead and he turned and bolted to the east.

A quarter of a mile away was a shallow gulch used to deposit garbage and other unwanted waste of the camp and it was, although a very unpleasant place to be, the salvation of his escape.

Ryan lay there atop the rotting waste and watched the many torches that were now moving about the dark areas of Harshaw, being lead by one Carlson Webb, who swore he saw the Rodriquez boy grab one of the money bags as he fled the scene.

Ryan lay there for a long time thinking as soon as it was light he would return and explain everything. However he suddenly realized he had never seen the face of the man who really killed John Swelley, and the only name he had heard was Carlson. He did not know if that was the man's name or the name of his accomplice, or if it was a first or last name.

Eventually, he remembered the two horses that had been spoken of, and since he was already halfway to them he turned and headed over the little rise.

Chapter Nine

The Arkansas Avenger

Quigley Hancock spent his birthday in a room over the saloon on River Street in St Louis.

From the very earliest times, he could remember his mother talking to him, he recalled she so often spoke of her older sister Julia, who had married the famous General William Clark.

He had heard over and over for so many years the wonderful achievements The General had done for his country and he even had read some of the transcripts about the first journey any white men took across western America. Stories that as a youth had inspired him, and perhaps instilled the wanderlust he found burning deep in his soul.

Now at forty-one these inspirations had dulled some and their brightness was but a dim flicker among his goals, but the curse of the wanderlust still gripped his inner thoughts to the point he rarely had much control over it. Nonetheless, one of the goals of his early life had not been erased, that being to visit the gravesite of his famous uncle and this day he would do that very thing, along with the other, being his visit of the final resting place of General Sterling Price, which lay in Bellefontaine Cemetery not that far away.

He dressed early and washing the night crud from his mouth with a long draw on an almost empty bottle of rye, a righteous century standing silently beside the washbasin.

Next, he looked out through the dirty windowpane at the muddy river moving slowly, yet ever steadily, southward.

It was the first time he had ever been in Saint Louis, but it certainly was not the first time he had seen the river, not by a long shot. The muddy Mississippi and the equally muddy Missouri had played a large part in much of his life during the last seventeen years, sometimes by choice and sometimes not.

To say he had a fondness for the rivers would be stretching the expression some, but still, he appreciated them, understood the necessity of them, and used them when needed.

Next, he rolled his black coat in his bedroll and tied them tight with a couple of latigo straps. Finally, satisfied they would stay secured until he needed them to be loosened, he turned and looked at the bed before he reached into the pocket of his vest and retrieved a two dollar gold piece and dropped it on the table beside the pitcher.

Walking to the bedpost he took his rig from where he had hung it the night before and slung it over his shoulder. After opening the door he gave the bed first and then the remainder of the small room one last glance, then he closed the door behind him.

There was some conversation going on downstairs but he couldn't make it out and figured it was the ole darkey who cleaned up, talking to someone, or perhaps just talking to himself, neither was worth wasting his time on and instead of heading down the stairs he turned and walked the length of the narrow hallway to the door located at the back of the building.

Before opening it he strapped on his rig and adjusted the holster where it rode well on his right hip and then he lifted the Colt slightly and let it fall back to its resting place.

Quigley Hancock was not like most men in the west, he was taller and much broader in the shoulders. Unlike his compadres, he was neither slim nor wiry. His narrow waist was a result of hard work, not lack of food and this weakness sometimes gave him heartburn, especially when he wore a heavy revolver, and all too often the belt would simply slip from his slim hips and drop to the floor when he walked. As a result, when gambling, as his profession had become of late, he wore a shoulder rig, but today he planned to ride and a hip rig better suited his needs. *'If only I can get to the livery without walking out of my belt,'* he thought.

Gambling had not always been his means of livelihood, in fact up and until a couple of years before he would have never given poker a second thought, but a stray bullet had caught him in the upper shoulder and his gun hand had been left almost useless for several months, and there was little demand for a Pistolero without a gun hand.

Not many people knew the name Quigley Hancock, however *'The Arkansas Avenger'* not only was well known but often spoken with reverence and fear. He had not intentionally chosen this alias, rather it chose him, and once there, stuck like a Texas tic on a Missouri milk cow.

Late in the war, he found himself assigned to the 4th Arkansas Mounted Dragoons under General Price's Command in their struggle against the overwhelming odds and supplies of the invaders.

Quigley was a third sergeant in Company B and had been given orders to scout the area around Moscow, seeking to determine an accurate number of General Steele's command. However, before he got near Moscow he found himself and his two companion's cut off by a Company of Kansas Cavalry supporting two infantry battalions near the Cornelius Farm.

Seeking shelter and a place to hide, they located an old, abandoned barn, at least it looked like it was abandoned. However, they soon learned it in fact housed the Stebling family, who also were hiding there.

Adam Stebling was in his fifties and suffering from consumption, he also walked on a wooden peg below his left knee, a memoir from his days in the army during the war with Mexico.

Mrs. Stebling, Adam's second wife, was ten years his junior and a strong-bodied and strong-willed woman. With them, they had two daughters Dora 18 and Altha 14, as well as eight-year old Albert, and a loyal Negro they called Josie.

Quigley would learn during the next forty hours that Adam Jr. and Andrew were away serving their state.

Sergeant Hancock had been given provisions for three days when they left, but such provisions were in reality only enough for a man to sustain health for a single day. Normally it would have been plenty as they knew the Yankees were well provisioned and all they had to do was take what they needed from the corpses of the men in blue who had the misfortune to cross paths with the three scouts. Now they were nine instead of three and with little hope of scrounging more while those Kansas boys were camped in front of their hiding place.

Finally, on the third night, he made a decision to slip out past the pickets wearing Hanna Stebling's dark shawl. It had been a good choice to make his move when he did for soon after he had walked past the sentry, on the pretense he was headed for the bushes for a duty call, a bugle sounded assembly and everyone began to move about.

However, just as they were ready to move out, the lieutenant gave the command to fire the barn.

Quigley watched in horror as several blue clad men rushed to the old structure with pine torches in hand.

The screams of the girls were the first to be heard and later those of the others seemingly trapped in the loft.

Quigley was over a hundred yards away, still, he could readily distinguish the voices of the women from that of any man and yet when they tried to escape the inferno they all were shot down including Josie.

After this night never again did Quigley Hancock give mercy to any man who wore the uniform of a Federal, and his actions soon brought about the alias *'No Quarter Quigley'*. Later when they started calling him, *'The Arkansas Avenger'*. It stuck and for the next decade, he was so known.

On the night of April 13, 1864 after Price had disengaged and allowed Steele's men into Camden, Third Sergeant Hancock was seen easing out of camp on a coal-black mount.

Corporal Enslow, who never liked Hancock to begin with, smiled at the thought his immediate supervisor was deserting.

He started to alarm Lt. Gaston but decided it would be better to wait and let him be absent from roll call at dawn. That way none of the men would look down on him for agglutinating to the old grudge.

What Enslow did not know was Quigley Hancock was not deserting; he was on a one-man campaign to eliminate as many of Steele's Bluebellies as he could, especially those of the 6th Kansas Mounted Rifles.

The night was mostly dark with only a quarter moon and the first Federals he encountered was a pair of sentries on picket duty overlooking the Ouachita River.

Below he could see a steamer tied to the bank with the gangplank down and many bales of cotton stacked, ready to be loaded come first light. *'This will have to be taken care of, but first I have duties nearer the town,'* he thought.

For most of his life Quigley had not been a patient man, he was full of energy and it needed an escape. However, on the night he watched pretty young Dora Stebling screaming as she ran from that burning barn, only to be gunned down by two troopers using revolving carbines, he learned the art of patience. This art he would hone to a sharpness some would call perfection.

On this night he lay patiently not ten feet from the two men talking of home and the women who waited for their return; of the lousy no account Sergeant who put them on picket duty when the others in their outfit were warm and dry in the newly occupied town; of the lousy food they had been issued since they left Little Rock; of what they planned to do when they returned home.

All of this Quigley listened to as he lay in the damp grass remembering the Steblings and his two men who died with them.

Of course Charlie Ware and C. J. Hill were Confederate soldiers and even though they did not deserve to die in the manner they did, nevertheless they were soldiers. The Steblings were not in any way a part of this war except as victims, and they were not causalities of war. They were victims of murder and the murders wore uniforms of blue and served under a guidon of the State of Kansas.

The first of those who would earn Quigley his alias was an exceptionally tallboy from New York State.

Thomas Hankins had not been at the burning of the barn a few nights before. In fact, he had thus far never fired his weapon in anger, having only arrived as a replacement the day before they marched from Little Rock to Cornelius' Farm.

Nonetheless, Thomas Hankins had one fault that would be his death calling, and that was a small bladder. Every thirty minutes or so he needed to relieve the pressure and as he strolled away from Cole Macon's presence to a little privacy just down the bank a few steps he walked straight past Quigley Hancock.

Most men would have found it difficult to have reached forward and slit the throat of a man who stood six foot three inches, but not so Quigley Hancock. The truth was, he stood two and a half inches above the New Yorker, and found it quite a simple gesture to place his left hand over the mouth of the surprised boy, a split second before he swiftly twisted his wrist and sliced his razor-sharp Sheffield Toothpick from just under one ear to an equal location on the opposite side of Tom Hankin's neck.

There was a slight gurgling sound for only a second or so and then Quigley slowly lowered him to the bank making sure his head was downhill.

"What's taking you so long?" Macon called out. "Yous get to thinking about that girl yous wus a talking about?"

His last statement was more of a laugh than a true question and he was still chuckling when he saw the tall man walk up the bank. The fact that the tunic was not fully buttoned and that it seemed too small in the shoulders did not register to him, there in the misty darkness as the man approached, and it wasn't until he felt the terrible bite as the point of the 14-inch narrow blade sliced into his right ventricle did he realize the man before him was not Hankins.

Thomas Hankins' trousers had fit him well, even though the coat had not. However, in the effort to undress him the dead man's cap had rolled down the bank and now to complete his new uniform Quigley removed the blue kepi from Macon, as the man stared at him with cold uncertain eyes while the last of the blood drained from his brain.

The killer also reached over and removed the black leather belt that carried Macon's cartridge box, before he picked up the new Colt Carbine and started walking towards Camden.

The sight of the fire was seen even from their camp as he rode back just at dawn. His new blue tunic and cap were tied behind his saddle.

As he passed him, he gave the disappointed Corporal Enslow a slight nod of his head.

Lem Mathis noticed the bloodstains on his butternut shell jacket and the new blue pants he wore, but what grabbed his attention most was the four red leggings that swung from the saddle, not unlike an Indian would display scalp trophies.

The next day, April the 16th 1864, while Quigley Hancock slept peaceably fifteen miles west, Captain Lang was explaining to Colonel Judson how every man aboard The McNeese Rex was killed, and the steamer burned. Along with over a hundred bales of precious cotton that had already been promised to General Lyon.

The next engagement between the grossly outnumbered boys in butternut and those who had invaded their land, took place only a few miles from the Federal headquarters in Camden, at a little place called Poison Springs.

The Federals had foraged throughout the area stealing any and all corn they could find from both Confederate stores as well as civilian farms and were en route back with their loot when they were cut off by a force of Texas, Arkansas, and Missouri Cavalry along with a troop of Confederate Choctaw Indians also wearing mostly gray.

The greatest loss to the boys in blue was suffered by the First Kansas Colored, who were sacrificed by their white commanders in an effort to save their artillery pieces.

The Choctaws were swift to sweep upon the wounded colored soldiers and relieve them of their wiry hair and other body pieces.

Quigley was not interested in killing the wounded; he considered them a waste of his time as they would most likely have died anyway without proper medical care, which the retreating Union army failed to leave behind.

Quigley was far more interested in the living Yankees who had escaped, especially those of the Sixth Kansas Cavalry.

That night once more he was seen slipping from camp on his black stallion. This time Corporal Enslow had no thoughts of telling anyone, he had seen the red leather leggings Sergeant Hancock had returned with, knowing there was only one place where he could have gotten them, and that was within the enemies own camp. This night he decided it best to keep his thoughts to himself for fear of Hancock's revenge falling upon his own neck some night as he slept. *'Besides'*, he thought, *'the Yankees will kill him sooner or later.'*

A year after the fight at Poison Springs, General Lee surrendered in Virginia; a few weeks later Forrest experienced his only loss of the war after his troops had exhausted all their ammunition over in Alabama. Joe Johnson finally surrendered in North Carolina and Sterling Price led his bewildered force into Mexico rather than surrender.

Quigley Hancock had similar ideas although he saw no point in going to Mexico; instead, he recruited a few of the boys who had worn the butternut, that no longer had homes to go to, and started out for Kansas.

Chapter Ten

The Brown Brothers

By August of 1866 when the Sixth Kansas finally disbanded, Quigley Hancock had learned a great many names and locations where these men were likely to be found after being mustered out.

The first to succumb to his postwar revenge, however, was not officially in the Sixth. He was one Corporal Adams Brown and his brother Thomas, both freedmen who lived near the mouth of Drum Creek on Osage land, at the northern boundaries of Indian Territory.

Brown came to the area on the promise that those who had fought against the traitors would be given land originally promised to the Indians. He had brought with him his younger brother and two women.

The Brown boys were born slaves near the town of Pulaski, Illinois to a wealthy corn farmer. However, in February of 1863, upon hearing that Father Abe had freed the slaves, the three brothers up and left their master.

George Newsom quickly sent a pack of dogs as well as a large posse led by the sheriff of Pulaski himself after them.

The three were soon caught and brought back to the Newsome farm where they were bound to the rear wheels of the large wagons Newsom used to transport his crop to the river.

Their protest went on deaf ears about being freed by the president and a sickening feeling swept through Adams when the sheriff explained that Lincoln's Emancipation Proclamation did not apply to slaves in the states loyal to the union.

They each received twenty lashes by the expert hands of Carl Tucker, Newsom's overseer.

The next time Adam and Thomas slipped away their little brother choose to remain on the farm.

This time they were substantially more cunning in their venture and escaped all the way to northern Kansas before being caught.

Their captors this time were none other than Ransom's Raiders who offered them a choice, return to Illinois or join the outfit. A year later Adams was a corporal in the First Kansas Colored assigned to the Sixth Kansas Cavalry.

Quigley had learned that Adams Brown was in one of the infantry units at Cornelius Farm. He was not sure Brown was actually at the burning of the barn and subsequently the murders of the Stebling family, but that mattered little to him. Both of the Brown brothers were escaped slaves; they both were among the Kansas Volunteers who were in the area, and thereby both deserved to die. It was as simple as that.

Quigley had, by this time, twelve men riding under his command, all former confederate dragoons[1], and all with a huge grudge burning within their souls.

Adam Brown was returning from the creek with two barrels of freshwater tied to the sides of a wagon when he spotted the riders approaching.

---

[1] Dragoons: Cavalry Troopers.

At first, he thought them to be Osage, who were not at all pleased with his presence on their land. However, when they drew nearer he saw each was setting atop saddles, and knowing it was not the practice of the Plains Indian, he immediately abandoned his wagon and fled along the creek bank.

He hid with his face down as the line of horses passed him, and then worked his way back towards the crudely constructed shelter he and his brother had put together a mile away.

He was still some distance from them when he heard several reports of pistol fire, and knowing Thomas only had a musket, realized his brother was under attack.

As all men do in Indian Territory, he had carried his own rifle, a Springfield 58 bore, with him that morning and he hurried along towards the obvious battle at or near his new home with the musket in hand.

The last quarter mile was over open land and although he could see the riders leaving to the east with the two women laying belly down over the saddle horns of a couple of the horses, he could not see his brother and therefore flattened himself against the hard land and waited until he could no longer hear the sounds made by the hoofs, only then did he slowly rise and walked cautiously ahead.

There were no windows and only one door to the shack, and this was on the opposite side from which Adam approached the structure.

Flattening himself against the cottonwood logs he waited and listened. Eventually, he heard sounds coming from either inside or on the other side of the house, of which he was not sure. Still, he waited and listened, finally he realized what he was hearing was the low chanting of Thomas singing Rock of Ages.

Adam immediately came around the shack and shuttered at the sight before him.

In the open door, Thomas was standing on a small, empty nail keg. The keg was atop the only chair they had, and one of its legs was slowly boring itself into the earth. Around his neck was a coarse rope and this was attached to the roof above. When the leg moved again it would spill the chair and Thomas' keg would fall away thereby hanging him.

Carefully Adam leaned his musket against the wall and reached for his knife as he approached his younger brother. "Easy now Thomas, I'll have you free in just a second. Don't you do nothing to disrupt that chair."

Quigley knew there was supposed to be two former Federals living there and he figured it was only a matter of time before the other showed up. Therefore, he told Murphy to take the men on back to their camp and he would catch up with them later.

There was one thing Quigley Hancock admired about the Sixth Kansas and that was late in the war, they traded in their revolving carbines for Sharps, and it was one of these he had long ago taken from a boy in blue who no longer needed it. This morning he had the same carbine in his hands at the moment.

The large conical slug struck Adam squarely between the shoulder blades and Thomas looked in horror as his brother fell forward, knowing full well the force would upset the chair beneath him.

Quigley Hancock walked forward and using water from the bucket there beside the dead Adam he poured several ladles of the cleansing liquid down the bore of his rife before he drew a cotton patch, he had cut from a shirt no longer needed, through the barrel. Looking in from the breach end and being satisfied with his work he slipped another paper cartridge in the chamber and closed the action before mounting and riding off.

Chapter Eleven

The Drake Constitution

One of the best things that happened to *The Arkansas Avenger* and his men were the events that had taken place on opposite sides of the state of Missouri.

On April 10 in Saint Louis, Missouri's Second Constitution, known as the Drake Constitution, was adopted.

A group of politicians, known as "Radicals," favored the emancipation of slaves and disfranchisement of persons who were sympathetic to the Confederacy during the war. The Radicals included an "Ironclad Oath" in the new constitution to exclude former Confederate sympathizers from the vote and certain occupations, severely limiting their civil rights

Right after the war's end, in Lexington, 28 former Missouri Volunteer Dragoons rode in to meet with Captain Rodgers to discuss the terms of surrender. After they were assured they would receive the same conditions offered by Grant to Lee's men, they were attacked by a Wisconsin Cavalry detachment.

It was never learned if this was a chance occurrence or a planned trap by Roberts. Nonetheless, it sealed the fate of this bunch and opened an avenue of escape for Quigley Hancock.

The only rebel shot that day was a seventeen-year-old boy from Clay County named Jesse Woodson James.

He was able to fight off his attackers killing two of them before he made his escape through a wooded area with a ball in his chest, but he would not die from this. He would return and form the most recognized gang of revengers ever recorded in American history books.

When this gang of Missouri raiders began to hit Union Banks and Union Trains the local newspapers went wild; either as haters or sympathizers. Nonetheless, both sides rode to glory and riches on the news the boys were making for their printing machines, and it was from just such an article in the staunchly Republican *'The Kansas City Daily Western Journal of Commerce'*, Quigley got his brainstorm.

They had described the tall well built Cole Younger and shorter and much thinner Jesse James as the leaders of the gang and suddenly Quigley realized that with little more than that knowledge, someone unknowingly could mistake Duke Murphy and himself for Jesse and Cole.

Soon thereafter, each time the boys ran short on funds, they would hit a bank or a stage, and even a couple of Atchison, Topeka and Santa Fe Railway trains, never failing during such robberies to call out the names of either Jesse or Cole at a time it would surely be heard by others.

They too were careful to always rob only Union owned businesses and often leave a small portion of their plunder to those who had been loyal to the south during Mr. Lincoln's war. Although the business of robbery was not his profession, feeding and supplying a group of men cost a lot of money at any time, and especially so in the south after the war.

Another thing that Quigley made sure of, was he and his men always wore Federal uniforms on all assignations and robberies, a small gesture that proved more than once to be life-saving to him and his men.

During the years following the killing of the Brown brothers, Quigley very carefully, with a lot of time and research, eliminated at least fifty three former members of the Sixth Kansas Volunteers and another eleven men who either were with one of the marked individuals at the time, or who were sought out for some other crime committed during the war against noncombatants.

Although in all cases where a robbery was the course of the day, he continued leaving those who witnessed the offense with the belief the crime had been done by the James-Younger gang.

However, when it came to assassinations he made no bones about why these men were being murdered, often to their very wives as they pleaded for their husbands' lives.

On these occasions, he pretended to be no one other than himself and seldom were he or his men dressed in Blue, and these times only added fuel to his reputation as, *The Arkansas Avenger.*

Chapter Twelve

Lieutenant Scott

It was during one of these raids, a tragedy occurred that would come to change the course of Quigley's life forever.

They very carefully, after months of study going through many documents containing the post muster rolls of the various Kansas Troops, located a Lieutenant Stanford Scott who had commanded a troop of cavalry at Cornelius Farm back in 1864.

Quigley did not know the name of the lieutenant who had given the order to fire the barn and subsequently gun down the family as they tried to escape. However, he had seen him and would never forget what he looked like sitting there atop his big bay with drawn saber, while the blaze of the flaming barn bathed his face with a golden light, and always this man had been his number one goal.

'Hopefully tonight we will find him,' he thought as the squad of seven men approached the Scott spread on the outskirts of Verdigris City in late April.

Duke Murphy and two other men rode the Leavenworth, Lawrence & Galveston Company train into town and there rented a buckboard, supposedly to bring back a load of wheat from a farmer near the border.

Quigley and three men lead the seven horses to a place he had located some two miles from the Scott farm. There they had waited for their colleagues before moving forward on fresh horses.

Dressed in union blue, they stopped at the short fence in front of the small soddy and called out, "Lieutenant Scott, I have a message for you."

The hour being near eleven and quite dark, the sleeping couple was slow to rise, and Miles Abbey said rather loudly, "Let's just torch the blame thing."

"No," Quigley replied. "There may be women and children in there. I'll not be a part of that sort of thing."

Momentarily, a flicker of light was seen coming from inside, followed by the glow of a coal oil lantern being turned up.

"Who are you?" came the voice from inside.

"Captain Norris. Nineteenth Kansas Cavalry. Sir, I need to speak with you."

"What about?"

"This is something I can only converse with Lieutenant Scott and no one else. Until I'm sure you are him I must keep my message silent, but I assure you, sir, it is most important."

The door opened slightly and they could hear a woman's voice saying, "Don't go out there, Stanley."

Gradually it opened more and finally, a short man stepped out with a lantern in one hand and a long gun in the other.

"I'm Stanley Scott, what message do you have for me?"

Quigley looked keenly at the man, he was about the correct build for that murdering Lieutenant back at the barn, but he seemed a little short and truthfully, Quigley was not sure about him. *'His face just doesn't look quite right, and his hair seems a little light,'* Quigley thought. *'Nonetheless whether or not he was that same lieutenant, he was a dirty federal officer and this record alone is enough to kill him.'*

"Are you former Lieutenant Stanley Scott?"

"Yas, I was during the war," the man replied, but suddenly his statement was interrupted when the lantern slipped from his firm grip, and in trying to catch it without burning himself, he unintentionally pointed the shotgun at the Troopers, who were still mounted only seven yards away.

Within a heartbeat, Miles Abbey sent him to meet his maker, with a revolver ball to his forehead.

The sudden report startled the horse he was riding and suddenly Miles was atop a bucking bronk, which caused the other mounts to also begin to jump about.

By the time Quigley had his horse calmed down, the door to the cabin was fully open and a woman in her nightclothes was running out to her dead husband.

She flopped down and began sobbing as she held his shattered head in her lap. "You dirty rotten Yankees," she screamed. "Why won't you leave us alone?"

Duke quickly shouted back, "Lieutenant Scott has been killed because of his crimes against southern people during the war."

"What?" she screamed as she suddenly looked up at the men on horseback.

"He is a southerner, we are both southerners. He was a Lieutenant in the Seventh Louisiana Cavalry, he didn't do no crimes again our own people."

These words hit Quigley like a hot iron. *'Could she be telling the truth? Could I be wrong?'* he thought. But then Duke shouted again, "He weren't no such. He was a Yank."

"You lying bastard. You murdering bastard. Don't you ever call him no Yank, not after all he suffered for his state," she screamed and reached for his gun.

Immediately, Quigley saw the arm extend of the rider beside him and he spurred his mount so it would jump, bumping the horse next to him and the shot went high over the flat roof of the log cabin.

"Come on. Let us go before we have to kill her, too," he commanded and turning, he rode off into the safety of the black night.

When they reached the buckboard they dismounted. The ride there had been in silence and this was not broken for more than a minute. Finally, James Roberts said, "I don't know. We wus so sure about him."

"She's lying. He was a yank. We found him on the record where he mustered out at Fort Leavenworth back in '66."

"Mee'be, but she seemed so certain. I don't know," another added.

"Well, if she is telling the truth, we are no better'n those we are seeking out," Duke finally said. Then he turned to the tall man who was removing the McClellan and replacing it with his Tennessee Ranger saddle. He asked, "What do you think, Boss?"

"I'm through thinking on this matter. I will know the truth before I speak on the subject again," Quigley replied, but he never looked at Duke as he spoke, rather he looked off into the black air and into his memories of that woman's face that had stared with so much hate at them.

Chapter Thirteen

Fort Bowie

Ryan found the horses just where the man had described and knowing he may be pursued he rode one and led the other throughout the long night and well into the morning, stopping only to give the animals water and to change from the one he was riding to the one he was leading.

Finally, from atop a small rise, he saw the outline of the Butterfield Road snaking its way across the desert floor ahead.

Realizing he had covered the seventy-plus miles in a little over ten hours, he himself was amazed at his accomplishment and he thanked his father for the many nights they had ridden together on the Vargas range, guiding themselves by the stars.

This past night he had picked out a bright one that seemed to twinkle a beckoning to him and never let it out of his sight. The ordeal had proved worth it, and now he was reasonably sure no one could catch up with him.

For the first time, he removed the saddles from both horses and watered them before he tied a hobble rope to their front legs. Then after drinking the last from his canteens, he laid down and fell asleep in the shade of a large barrel cactus.

It was two hours before the shade offered by this great plant vanished leaving him to the mercy of the sun, which had now risen almost straight overhead.

He shook the sleep off and stood looking about. One of the horses stood a few yards off, the other was nowhere in sight. *'Damn, I must not have made a good knot.'*

He knew the stage station was not far away, he just wasn't sure if it was to the east or west.

Finally, his stomach began a constant and irritating complaining effort so he surrendered and began searching through the saddlebags the robbers had prepared for their own escape.

In the first, he found a roll of brown paper which contained a dozen strips of jerky, a set of long johns, much too large for him, and a silver watch which had the image of a beautiful light-haired woman. He realized he should not be caught with such an identifying object, so he tossed it aside.

In the other side were more clothes and a box of cartridges, but since he had no gun he also dropped them in the sand before picking up the other bag.

The side that appeared to be the fullest again contained clothing, but these were more his size.

Although Ryan was young he had inherited his father's height and stood over five feet ten inches and was still growing, of course at his age, he was still quite thin.

These clothes he would keep. In the other side he found a kerchief tied in a knot, upon opening it, he discovered seven gold eagles, the most money he had seen in his whole life.

Extremely pleased with his new fortune, Ryan saddled the gray gelding and started down towards the road ahead.

He was a little over halfway when he heard the sounds of the approaching stage. It was evident the team was tired as the driver was continually cracking his whip over the heads of the six up encouraging them on.

Teddy Nichols had seen the lone rider descending the hill to the south, but he knew he was too far away to present any real threat if in fact, he was alone. The station was only three miles ahead and just over the little rise so he kept cracking the whip and the team kept pulling on up the grade.

With the sight of the Dragoon Mountains far away to his left, Ryan Rodriquez made a decision, *'I will follow it; the station must not be far.'*

The old Butterfield Station at Apache Pass with its strong rock walls was still being used by Wells & Fargo Company and it was here the young half breed would come to rest for a few days.

It was also here he would meet a man who would lead him north, away from the dry desert, the only land he had ever known.

Chapter Fourteen

Riding The Rails

Buckshot had not been as fortunate as Ryan, he had not found saddlebags with gold coins, and he had not even found an animal on which one could place saddlebags if one had the money to buy such an animal or the money to feed it.

Buckshot Gunter had ridden the rails to Atlanta where his luck seemed to run out.

For sixteen days he lived off the remaining money he had from his savings. When this ran out he began to slowly starve.

His health had been good and perhaps this was the only reason he survived without food for so long.

There were times when his pain was so great he hid in dark corners and wept, but he was determined he would die before he would steal.

Mr. Reb Brown had told him once, those who never tell a lie and never steal will be blessed by the Lord, and he had promised Mr. Reb that this was the way he would live, and he was determined to so live it. He hoped borrowing Mr. Brook's mule had not been stealing.

Mayor Calhoun began a paving project of Atlanta's streets in the fall of 1879 and this was the first work the young boy was able to find after his cash ran out.

The job was simple, but labor-some and almost degrading to him. He had to carry water to the men and mules that were working at laying the bricks on the streets, a labor he considered much below his intelligence level.

He had asked for a job, hunting the nearby fields and thickets and providing food for these workers but he was only laughed at and offered the job as water-boy.

Considering his condition, he accepted it hoping for advancement before long. Such was not the case and his wage of one dime a day did little more than keep him alive.

As fall began to descend on north Georgia he began to worry about freezing during the winter months.

Finally one exceptionally cool night in early October the north wind came rushing into the yard where he had gathered enough discarded boards to make a small shack near the tracks. The storm destroyed his shelter.

Out of fear and desperation, he found a door unlocked on an empty boxcar and there he went to avoid the biting wind and eventually fell asleep. Only to be awakened sometime before sunup by the swaying of the car as it traveled along the narrow tracks.

Realizing he was moving at several miles an hour in a direction he had no idea of, the thought of a dime a day seemed very prosperous and he said aloud with no one to hear, "Oh Lord, what have I done? How will I survive without my job?"

Chapter Fifteen

Delano

On Friday, October the third, 1879 *The Wichita City Eagle's* headlines boldly questioned;

Is Any Loyal Unionist Safe?

The article continued;

> Now that the Demarcates have intimidated Congress into repealing the Reconstruction of the Traitor States will anyone who gave their oath and blood to preserve the Union not be subjected to fear of their lives as well as the lives of their families and property?
>
> Especially those Freedmen who have come to Kansas escaping the bonds of slavery.
>
> The whole state of Kansas is being all too often overrun by Texas cowboys, prostitutes, gamblers, pimps, and dead beats of every kind, but when whole communities of people who have exited here to Kansas to live free now shrink in fear of the treachery of these demons who boldly ride our highways without fear themselves of capture or retaliation for their crimes.

> People in townships like Nicodemus disappear
> from their own streets with the setting of the sun
> and cringe in fear behind bolted doors praying
> that they be spared a stray shot fired by one of the
> James gang won't penetrate their hearts, or they
> be lynched without mercy by the devil himself
> cloaked as the infamous 'Arkansas Avenger'. This
> most cowardly of all creatures who sneaks through
> the night bringing death and destruction to any
> Freedman or other man who loves the Union.
>
> I challenge our government to seek out this
> treacherous demon with a guide-on of 'No Quarter'
> and destroy him and his band of cutthroats so
> decent women and children may once again walk
> our streets without fear.

Quigley read with interest the article. *'I never been to Nicodemus in my whole life and the only niggers I ever killed since the war, was the Brown brothers back some thirteen, fourteen year ago. That bastard's got some nerve, maybe I ought to pay him a visit while I'm in town.'*

He laid the paper down and walked over to the bottle sitting on the single dresser and poured himself a short drink before looking through the cloudy window at the dusty street below. *'Sure looks like a cold wind is blowing down there, wonder if a storm is brewing?'*

He made a fist and released it several times and then raised his right arm and worked it in slow circles three or four times before placing the palm of his other hand on his shoulder and massaging the ball, *'I'm not my old self yet, but I sure am a lot better than I was for a while.'*

He then slipped his short-barreled Colt into a shoulder holster and strapped it on before covering the rig with a dark brown vest. In the right front pocket of this, he added his makin's and in the other pocket, he dropped the 41 Remington.

Looking into the dirty mirror, which swiveled from two thin towers above the dresser, he made sure the presence of the derringer was not easily recognized. Satisfied, he adjusted his wide-brimmed hat and turned to the door.

At the top of the stairs he gazed upon the floor below, even at this early hour, the saloon was busy. Chucky, the bartender was drawing a couple of schooners from the dark oak barrel that was sitting atop the back-bar. Eve, the skinny saloon girl who worked the floor during the daylight hours was waiting for Chucky to finish.

What appeared to be an out of work buffalo hunter was losing his last dollar *Bucking the Tiger*[1], and three men were sitting at a single round table. The two with their backs to him he could not see, but he recognized one of the trio to be Taylor Fletcher, another professional gambler who had drifted into Wichita about a week before on the Santa Fe.

Quigley did not care much for Fletcher; he had an air of sneakiness about him, the kind of man that gave gamblers a bad reputation. Another man who was very recognizable was Mansfield Cornell, Wichita's Town Marshal. *'Just like the dumb bastard, sitting with his back to the door,'* Quigley thought as he ingested the scene below.

Cornell had never given Quigley any reason to dislike him, save the fact he readily announced he had served with the 100th New York at Morris Island, South Carolina where, according to Cornell, they repelled several rebel attracts.

He was not a big man; in fact, he was unusually slim and were it not for the heavy black frock he was never seen without, one might miss him altogether on a dark night.

Still, Quigley had long since learned it was best not to be conspicuous when the law was around, so instead of descending to the floor below, he turned and exited *Lipperts* through the back staircase.

---

[1] Bucking The Tiger: Playing Faro.

Four hours later Quigley was sitting at a table in Ed O'Kelly's *Red Irish Saloon* **in** Delano[2] playing stud with three losers, when the obvious concussion of a strong explosion shook the earth and shattered the front windows.

Everyone jumped at the sound and a scream was heard from the upper story moments before the naked Rose McLaglen ran from her room and looked wild-eyed at the floor below.

Quigley realized he was holding his Colt some moments after the blast when everyone was heading for the front of the saloon trying to locate the source of the explosion.

A dull glow of red could be seen across the river in downtown Wichita, but the other buildings hid the actual location.

His first thought was someone inexperienced with explosives had tried to blow the safe at *The Kansas National Bank*, but within a few minutes a stunned boy of about 18 suddenly appeared and looking in through the broken window shouted, "Someone done up and blow'd Mr. Murdock's newspaper office all to smithereens."

Within seconds the faro dealer added, "It had to be *The Arkansas Avenger*. I knowed Marshall Murdock was an idiot fur publishing such a' editorial."

Quigley gathered his winnings and headed for the door. The walk back to *Lipperts* was crowded as it seemed everybody who lived in Sedgwick County was suddenly out investigating the explosion.

He stopped at Douglas and Main and seeing Cornell rush past, he detoured around Woodman's Grocery via the alley, then on to his hotel room.

After gathering his possessions he dropped a twenty-dollar gold piece on the dresser, and once more left by the backstairs heading straight for *Johnson's Stables* where he had his horse boarded.

---

[2] Delano: Wichita's especially wild and woolly area west of the river.

As far as he knew, no one in Wichita identified him as *The Arkansas Avenger* and he wanted it to stay that way, and that is precisely why he decided to make himself scarce when Cornell began looking for anyone who fit the description of The Avenger.

He could have easily proved he had nothing to do with the explosion; there were several who could swear he had been in O'Kelly's for hours. Still, he felt uneasy about even having to do that.

A man who was average size would not easily come to mind but a man who stood taller and broader than most anyone around stuck in one's memory, and not only did that description fit him, it also fit *The Arkansas Avenger.*

'The Younger brothers have been in Stillwater Prison for nearly three years. I guess nobody can blame this on them and word has it the James boys are in Texas or Tennessee, depending on who you talk to, but I suspect they are really not so far away,' Quigley thought, as he rode north towards Ellsworth.

'As much as I hate it, I must admit there is some justice in it all. For years I have been able to place the blame of our robberies on them. I guess this being blamed on me is fitting.'

That night as he lay beside his small campfire on the south bank of the Smoky Hill River his thoughts returned to that terrible night six months before when following a good lead, it led them to the wrong man.

After that terrible night, Quigley immediately began rechecking his information and eventually came to the realization that indeed they had killed the wrong Lieutenant Scott.

Soon thereafter he disbanded his gang and encouraged each to learn the lesson he had and end their revengeful careers.

For a time Duke Murphy rode with him, but that partnership was dissolved after they had hired their guns to a Texas cowman who had been having trouble with border raiders as soon as he crossed the Cimarron.

On this occasion, twenty well-armed Jayhawkers jumped the herd during the night.

They had the beeves bedded down after a long and difficult crossing, and everyone was exceptionally tired and in need of rest.

However, Quigley and Duke had not hired on as cowboys, rather as protectors and thus were riding night herd when the raid occurred.

The first indication there was trouble was when Duke lit a smoke and was promptly toppled from his saddle by a rifle slug in the chest.

The twenty-odd men came upon them out of a draw and attempted to scatter the cattle, but fortunately, the 1400 steers were as tired as the punchers and did not develop into a full-blown stampede.

Other night riders were able to contain most of them while Quigley went after the raiders. He knew for sure he dropped two of them because their bodies were found after daylight, but it was this night that he, too, had caught one in the upper arm which caused him to drop his revolver and therefore also drop the pursuit.

Now as he lay there watching the twinkling of the stars he made a decision, he would return to Verdigris City and do what he could for Scott's widow. *'Something I should have done months ago.'*

Quigley Hancock and Duke Murphy

Chapter Sixteen

The Chancys

Laramie Patay returned to the sutler's store an hour before dark as the woman had suggested. His day had been spent mostly waiting to see the commanding officer of the fort, only to receive no news that would assist him in his search.

John Chancy was a tall man, at least it seemed so to Laramie, and he had a very strange manner in which he had his hair cut, but the lad was not there to criticize or judge the man, he only wanted to get answers to his questions.

Likewise, when John saw the boy tie up his pony in front of their store, he began to size up the young man Mary Beth had told him about. He judged Laramie Patay stood near 6 feet and weighed little more than 145 pounds.

His short flat-brimmed leather hat hung carelessly down his back, held fast by a latigo string around the neck. His buckskin shirt sported a line of long fringe across his chest and along each sleeve giving water an easy escape route on those rare occasions when it rained on the plains.

His trousers were pale blue, not so different from the common issue of the military, save any sign of a ribbon or other piping running down their side to identify the branch of service they were issued to. His boots were simply knee-high moccasins laced and tied with more rawhide latigo.

The boy's face was dark, almost as that of the native, but the long yellow hair hanging to his shoulders expelled any thought of him being Indian.

Around his narrow waist, tightly cinched, was a wide black belt that surely had been issued to some soldier somewhere, but the holster that housed the revolver certainly had never been in a quartermaster's depot.

Ingesting this all, John Chancy immediately judged the lad to be a scout or tracker. However, he also saw the kindness, despite obvious concern in his face, which was the same trait Mary Beth had detected earlier. For some reason unknown to him, the sutler wanted to help the boy.

"My wife tells me you are seeking information about a white woman living among the Indians here," he said, extending his hand in a common gesture.

"Oui, my Mee-ma. She was taken by Cheyenne or Arapahoe in '76, south in Wyoming. Taken from the Deadwood Stage."

"I do seem to recall that," John said, turning and looking over at his wife as he nodded his head.

"There are no Cheyenne or Arapahoe in this part of Montana, what makes you think she is here?"

"A man, a miner in Copperopolis, told me he saw a woman with hair like mine here last winter. She was with an Assiniboine; perhaps traded."

John could tell there was a pleading in the boy's statement and although he had no real news to give him, he wanted desperately to help in some small way.

"I know there are no white women among the Indians here. Perhaps north in Canada, but I don't think so there either. I did hear that there was a woman living south in Wyoming with a buck. She is reported to be a white woman, but I know nothing of her hair color. It is only hearsay and then perhaps two or three times passed over, but they say she refuses to leave her man and hides out when the army comes near for fear they will take her away."

The boy nodded his head accepting the news, then before he turned he asked, "Do you know where in Wyoming?"

"I do not, but he who told me of this is a Blood[1] who is called Coutu Wolfchild. He comes here to trade, but there is no telling when he will return, these people keep no schedules."

"Do you remember when he was here last?"

John nodded his head a couple of times and then replied, "I believe it was in May, just after the big thaw. Everything was very muddy then. I would suspect he will be in before the winter winds come again."

"He doesn't live on the reservation?"

"Yes and no. He is a hunter," John said and raised his shoulders. "Do you have a place to stay?"

Laramie shook his head, he had not even thought about such.

"There is a shed outback. We use it for storing pews[2] in the winter but it is empty now, it will keep out the wind," he said and then shook his head slightly before adding, "Mostly."

The lad wasn't sure about this offer. Even though the man had appeared to be kind, he realized he was in a strange settlement among unknown people, to let his guard down for a few hours, perhaps a few seconds could result in his being robbed or worse. He was just about to decline the offer when the woman spoke. "If you will stay, you will be welcome at our table for dinner," then after a small pause she added, "Tonight."

There was something about her that had touched him the first moment he saw her, something besides her striking good

____

[1] Blood: One of the three distinct tribes within the Blackfoot Nation.
[2] Pews: Mountain Men called their fur pelts pews.

looks. She had a good heart, this he felt deep inside and if she asked him to stay, he was sure she knew nothing of evil plans.

"I have a' elk shoulder stewing in the back, with potatoes and a few wild onions."

Laramie first looked out across the dirty street only a few feet away, and then to the floor near where he stood, and finally into her eyes. Removing his hat he spoke, "Oui, I would be most proud to share your table." Then he returned his hat to his head and added, "First, I must attend to my horse."

"Good," she said, and without further a' due she disappeared into the darkness at the rear of the low roofed store.

"There is a livery, Jack Jensen's place. It's just up the street, by the blacksmith's shop," John suggested.

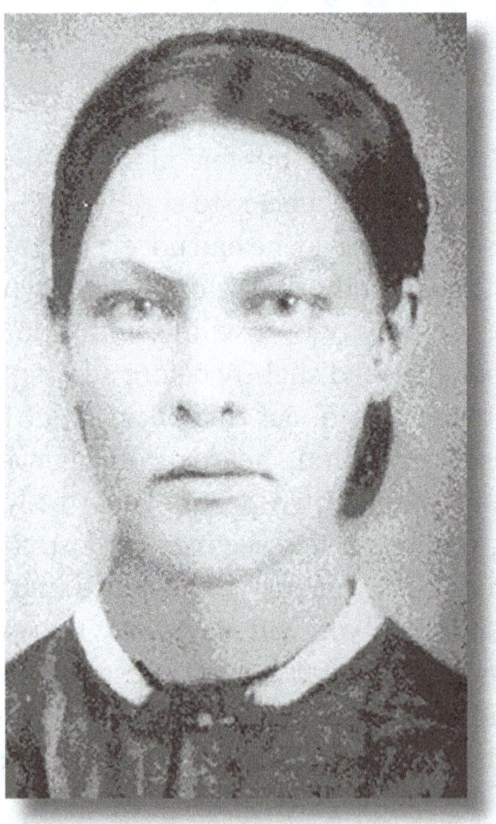

Mary Elizabeth Chancy

Chapter Seventeen

Mariah Scott

Mariah Scott was born in Shieldsborough, Mississippi in the fall of 1858. Her father, Louis Roux was the owner of the sawmill in Kiln, which served to secure his family's future, but it was his hotel at *The Bay* where he and the family lived.

Being the owner of one of the two hotels on the beautiful bay in Hancock County where wealthy plantation owners from the Natchez River Valley and some of the upper crust from New Orleans, came to escape the stress of daily life among Southerns in the antebellum days, gave him the prestige he was sure his bloodline was entitled to.

Unfortunately, this wonderful life came to a crashing halt when little Mariah was five years old.

Captain James Alden turned to the seaman standing close by and said, "Weymouth, swing her as close as you can, but remember we have a 17-foot draft."

"Aye-aye, Captain," replied the coxswain as he spun the large wooden wheel and the USS Boston slowly began to make a sweeping turn where she would come within four hundred yards of the tall, white, structures facing the gulf.

When satisfied their sweep would be as he planned, Alden turned to his favorite quarter-gunner Hank Wilkins and yelled, "Clear the shore of the aristocrat's cottages."

"Aye, Captain. Can do."

The first shell fell short, landing in the shallow bay some seventy yards from the beach.

Mariah who had been playing in the white sand, under the supervision of her mammy, Anna Mae, looked up at the huge splash.

The second shot had been corrected some and it exploded against a palm and sprayed the area with hot steel. It was this shell that sent the sliver through Anna Mae's right side into her liver.

Without the slightest display of fear for herself, she charged forward and fell upon Mariah protecting the little girl with her large body.

The USS Boston continued shelling the resort area for twenty minutes. Finally, after viewing the total destruction of all the structures within sight, Captain Alden mashed his long glass together and turning to his First Mate said, "Cease all firing, clean and case your guns, and take us on to Mobile Bay, Mr. Ittell."

"Aye-aye, Captain."

Michelle Roux, Mariah's mother was in the kitchen supervising the preparation of the noon meal for the twelve guests who had fled New Orleans after General Butler's men ransacked the city.

The third shell from the Boston and the first fired from her 10-inch gun landed squarely in the dining room, killing everyone on the ground level floor.

Louis Roux had been at his sawmill at the time of the shelling and knew nothing of the carnage for several hours.

Later he would take his daughter to his mother's home north of Jackson and then despite his exemption from conscription, due to the need for the wood planks his mill produced for the cause, he joined a guerrilla group operating under General Forrest in central Mississippi. When the war ended Louis Roux did not return and was never heard from again.

Nineteen-year-old Mariah met Stanley Scott in New Orleans in the summer of '77 while she was there with her grandmother. He was a fireman, tall and handsome with carefree blonde bangs that all too often fell forward almost covering his right eye. She immediately was infatuated with him and before the summer was over, realized he had stolen her heart.

Although he was twelve years her senior, he was polite, well educated, came from one of New Orleans's older families, and he had a kindness about him, and a strict sense of responsibility that ran deep in his soul.

At the age of fifteen, when superintendent Rev. Linfield resigned from 'le Lycee Scientifique et Militaire de l'Etat de la Louisiane'[1], Beneficiary Cadet Sergeant Stanley Scott did likewise and volunteered to fight for his state, and served proudly until being captured when General Page, commander of Fort Morgan,[2] was forced to surrender on August 23, 1864. Thereafter Stanley Scott spent the last horrible months of the war at *The Rock*[3] near Chicago.

When Mariah returned with her grandmother to what was left of their once-proud plantation, then a simple boarding house on the Natchez Trace, her heart remained in New

---

[1] le Lycée Scientifique et Militaire de l'Etat de la Louisiane: Louisiana State Seminary of Learning & Military Academy, now LSU.

[2] Fort Morgan : A fort at the mouth of Mobile Bay, Alabama.

[3] The Rock: A Union prison in Chicago where food and other of life's essentials were deliberately refused to the Confederate prisoners. It had a higher death percentage than did Camp Sumter near Andersonville, Georgia.

Orleans. The following January after a short illness, Geraldine Roux succumb to the fever.

Mariah, being the only known relative, immediately sold the property and headed south to wed Stanley Scott.

Using what money she had received from her grandmother's estate, they left Louisiana to begin a new life on the frontier, buying the sixty acres, from an Osage man who thought more of the Whiteman's whiskey than he did his people's heritage.

The newlyweds settled down to build a strong cabin and introduce the fields to the cutting edge of a plow.

Unfortunately, this happiness came to a sudden end for Mariah just as had her childhood happiness when the midnight riders murdered her new husband.

It took Quigley three days to ride from Ellsworth to Verdigris City near the border of Indian Territory.

There he took a room in *Evie Fold's Boarding House* giving her a week's rent in advance and lodged his gelding in *Davis' Livery.*

He went first to the only saloon in town, a one-room shack that was little better than a Tiger, and dropped a Morgan dollar on the counter before taking the bottle and a glass to a table near the opposite wall. There he sat down and poured two fingers of the bad-tasting whiskey.

Half an hour later a woman he judged to be in her late twenties, came in through a door in the back wall. She walked up to the man behind the plank bar and they talked shortly and then Quigley saw the bartender nod his head in the direction of where he sat. A moment later she turned and looked at him. Immediately she walked over and in broken English, she asked, "You buy drink for Caesar?"

'Caesar hell, she's a' injun squaw not no Roman prince,' he thought, but instead of saying so, he opened his palm and moved his hand toward the other chair at the table. *'A saloon*

girl might know as much as anyone else around here, and is less likely to talk about it afterward,' he reasoned.

Within half an hour he had filled her glass three times and his own only once and with her 125 pounds versus his 240 the alcohol had saturated her brain quite thoroughly while he was still barely feeling its effects.

"Come on," he said. "Let's go and find a nice place to hide."

"Me got place," she said, and started to get up, but her legs failed her so he reached over and assisted her by placing his large hand under her armpit and lifting her to her feet.

"You don't take too long Caesar," the barkeep yelled as they started out the back door.

Upon re-entering the world of lightness, Quigley saw directly behind the bar an old army tent, and it was towards this she was generally headed. "Your tent?"

"Ugh," was her only reply.

Inside, he saw a bedroll on the dirt floor and a small table with an overturned chair lying beside it, nothing more. She headed for the bedroll and began unbuttoning her dress.

"How much?" Quigley asked.

"Two dollar gold," she stopped her undressing to reply.

"No, one dollar silver," he suggested.

She looked at him for a few seconds, "No gold?"

"Gold only for information," he said back.

This brought a strange expression on her face as she twisted her head and tried to focus on him. "What this information?"

"A man," he paused a moment. "Named Scott was killed here a few months back. You remember that?"

She shook her head and then continued her struggle with the bone buttons on the front of her brown dress.

"If you don't know," again he paused before he added, "no gold."

Again she stopped and gave him that same twisted look. "You got gold?"

Quigley reached into his vest pocket and lifted out a ten-dollar eagle. "You know about Scott?"

She looked at the coin and then at the tall man who was holding it between his thumb and forefinger. "I no know him."

Quigley dropped the coin back in his pocket.

She wet her lips with her tongue and then said, "I know his woman."

"Tell me about his woman," he said, and again retrieved the gold piece where she could see it.

"She live Osage land. She good woman. She no trade for gold, you best trade with Caesar."

"Is she still living there? After her husband was killed?"

"She still live there. She plant maize in season of planting moon," the woman replied, and then again began working on the buttons and without looking up she added, "She no trade for gold with you."

Finally, she was able to get all of the buttons undone and she opened the dress exposing her nakedness, only to see he was gone.

Apache was not an accurate name for the big gelding he now rode. Although he was a brown and white paint, he was much too tall for an Indian pony. Nonetheless, Apache was what Quigley named him and that was what he answered to.

The next morning when Quigley mounted him, he seemed anxious to get out in the open air once again and he danced about with vigorous anticipation of their ride.

Quigley always hated the fact he had been cut before he bought him. The thought of not being able to pass along some of his greatness gnawed at the man's soul, but he had found him too late and the damage had already been done.

The ride from town to the Scott farm took slightly less than an hour. He first located the little grove of cottonwoods where they all had met that night and then the path to the farmhouse he had to follow again, although it was perhaps the most difficult ride he had endured since the war.

Stopping beside the small hewn cabin, he looked to the field ahead. The stalks of corn were two and in some cases three feet high with little or no weeds seen between them. *'The whole field looks as professionally worked as if half a dozen experienced field hands had taken it on as a personal project, that is all except at the very west corner where two or three large rocks remain. Those rocks are allowing the growth of unwanted vegetation,'* he thought.

Then it was there he spotted her. She was working on her knees pulling at the thorny vines.

Quigley watched her for a full two minutes before he conjured up the courage to call out, "Hello the Cabin."

Her head lifted almost immediately and she seemed uncertain as to where the sound had come from.

Again he called out, "Hello the cabin, may I come closer?"

This time she turned and looked back at her home where the rider now was seen.

At first, when she heard the sound of a human voice she thought it might be Indians. Although she had never been bothered with them and on occasion a freshly killed deer was found hanging from the juniper tree beside her cabin, a sure sign they had been by and offering a sign of friendship or respect, she was not sure which.

Nonetheless, marauding savages were not uncommon this close to The Nations, as well as marauding white renegades headed south escaping the pursuit of the law.

Her holed straw bonnet hid her face from the light of the sun and finally, she used the back of her hand to lift the wide brim where she could better see. "Who are you?"

"My name is Hancock. Quigley Hancock."

"What do you want?" she said slowly standing and brushing her gloved hands against her thighs attempting to dislodge the clay that was clinging so desperately to their leather hide.

"I would like a word with you if you are Mrs. Scott."

"I am," she said back, not feeling any less frightened. Although substantially more angered at herself for allowing a strange man to approach her so, without her realizing his coming, and also catching her without her shotgun.

For months after Stanley had been murdered, she had not ventured a step from her front door without the old single barrel, and still, when she went anywhere, it was always beside her on the wagon seat.

However, only Tuesday past she had gone into the field without it and when she realized her mistake, she just continued with her chores and thereafter while working in her field, she had not bothered lugging the heavy gun along. Today she regretted her foolishness.

She now walked forward across the field carefully meandering so as not to damage a single stock. Finally, when she was a few yards from where he sat, she removed her hat and with the sleeve of her blouse she wiped the sweat from her young brow and again asked, "What is it you want, Mr. Hancock?"

He looked down and ingested her image, *'She is so young. Young enough to be my daughter,'* he thought gazing at the woman. Her light brown hair was parted in the middle of her head. Her eyes, also brown, were kind, but tired and strained and her face was dirty yet beautiful. She was both taller and thinner than he remembered, *'At least thinner,'* he thought.

"I have come to make you an offer on your land," he said.

She slowly shook her head, "My crop is not in yet, there is no way either of us can determine the value until then. I don't understand you, Mr. Hancock."

Quigley took a deep breath and then forced himself to look away from her, back to the field from which she had come. "I am willing to offer you top dollar, prospecting that the crop will be a good one."

Once more she raised her arm and shaded the sun from her eyes with her hand as she tried to look at his face. "Why would you do that? There is other land here's about that can be bought for less."

"May I get down?" he asked, returning his Stetson to his head.

She paused for a moment and then taking a deep breath said, "I think it would be better if you did not Mr. Hancock. I don't believe you. I don't trust you."

Quigley nodded his head in an understanding manner, "Very well, Mrs. Scott. I will obey your wish and bid you a pleasant good day." He then pulled slightly on his left rein and Apache turned his head and started off in the direction they had come.

Mariah immediately rushed inside and open the breach on the Stevens making sure it was loaded.

That night she slept restlessly wondering about the strange intruder. The next morning, when she awoke to the sound of her rooster crowing, she slowly rose and without bothering to dress, headed outside to gather the yard eggs she hoped to find scattered about where her four hens nested.

Billy, her mule, gave her a strange call, but she paid him no mind until she turned back and saw there over in the far end of her field a horse standing. Immediately she hurried back inside dropping the two eggs she had found and closed and bolted the heavy door.

Her next move was to grab the Stevens and drop the small porthole Stanley had cut in the window. The sun was shining across the field and there was a light fog lying near the ground mostly hiding the animal from her.

After a couple of minutes, she was able to see some movement there in the corner where the hated rocks were, but almost immediately, the fog thickened and blanketed this corner of her property from her view.

On she waited, hoping, praying, finally she decided if she was to be killed she would not die in her nightclothes and closing the trap she carefully laid the shotgun against the log wall and turned to her crudely made armoire and took her brown work dress, but there she stopped and instead she took her yellow sundress. Looking at it, she remembered the last time she had worn it was a week before Stanley was killed, and a tear began to build. She fought it back and nodded her head, *'Yes, if I am to die today I will meet Stanley in my yellow dress.'*

After slipping it over her head she returned to the window and again lowered the porthole. This time the fog had lifted some and once more she could see the dim outline of the horse standing there. She eased the long barrel out of the small opening and took careful aim at that corner of the field, but then shook her head, *'It is much too far for this, and besides how many times did Stanley tell me not to put the barrel out far enough someone could grab it and pull it out through the hole.'*

Quickly she jerked the gun back inside and then she bit her bottom lip and pondered her situation.

She had no timepiece, she had never needed one. She got up when her rooster announced it was time and she went to bed when the sun went down, other times during the day were just times between these events.

This morning she wished she had a timepiece. She remembered her father saying fog usually lifted by nine o'clock. *'I wonder how near it is to nine now?'* she questioned herself. *'Maybe fog in Kansas is different than fog in Mississippi?'* she thought and then turning to see where she had put her extra hulls she again wondered, *'It was foggy yesterday morning, now how long did it take for it to lift?'*

Finally, she looked back out and there suddenly was the wisp of a breeze and the earth cloud began to twist and in moments it vanished before her and she could clearly see the paint horse across the field and there nearby was a man on his knees.

She blinked a couple of times to clear her vision and then narrowed her eyes as if to see better before she gasped.

She threw the door was thrown open with such force it shook on its hinges a second before she marched through it with shotgun in hand.

Halfway across the field, she yelled, "What the hell do you think you are doing?"

Quigley stopped his digging and looked up at the woman marching as straight as he remembered the Yankee infantry doing at Shiloh back in '62.

He remained on his knees, but took his left hand and removed his hat, then wiped his brow with his sleeve.

When she was a few feet away he said, "I saw you had some unsightly thorny briers here and thought I would lend a hand while I waited for you to wake up."

"Wake up. I've been awake since the rooster crowed. Been aiming this shotgun at you ever since."

"Well, I'm obliged you didn't fire it, you might a' hit Apache there and I sure do fancy that horse."

"What the hell are you doing here?"

"Like I said, I'm just lending a hand."

"I don't need no help."

"Don't you Mrs. Scott?" he said back in a most non-threating manner.

Slowly she lowered the Stevens and she too wiped her brow. "I don't understand you, Mr. Hancock. If you think coming around and digging a little in my field will somehow get me sweet on you, you are so wrong."

Quigley raised his hands, palms out to her before he replied, "I assure you, ma'am, I have no intentions of that nature. In fact in a small way you remind me of my own daughter." It was a lie, he had no daughter, but somehow it seemed the proper thing to say to reduce her fear and her questions.

She shook her head and turned back to her cabin before she said without looking at him. "Oh hell, do you want some breakfast?"

"I brung you a dog. He's just a wisp right now, but soon he will be bigger and then he can warn you about strangers like me coming up in the night."

She looked back at her cabin where he was indicating and spotted a small black and tan puppy sitting there looking out at them. *'Why I didn't see him when I came out I'll never know.'*

Mariah Scot

Chapter Eighteen

Mendoza Haeckel

Both Mendoza Haeckel's Mexican mother and German father would have hung their heads in shame had they only known the dreaded plague their son would bring to the high plains.

He arrived in Wyoming in the late spring of 1874 with a dog and a mule-drawn wagon to settle in what would later be known as Somerset. It was his forty-second year on this earth and many wished he had never made it past forty-one.

At age fifteen, during the war with the United States, Mendoza had been given the unpopular assignment by his Captain of herding a flock of 900 sheep to feed the 20,000 troops of El Presidente Antonio de Padua María Severino López de Santa Anna y Pérez de Lebrón, who was advancing on the American defenses at the hacienda of Buena Vista, a few miles from Saltillo.

The boy watched from afar as General Pedro de Ampudia's attacking troops overran several defensive positions, but darkness comes early in February and thus halted the attack and soon the night became strangely quiet while the Mexican soldiers dined on roosted mutton and the American troops went hungry.

However, with the same enthusiasm, dawn brought on another attack.

Ampudia, confident that he would enjoy the warmth of the hacienda that night, sat atop a magnificent black stallion observing the action as his forces swept forward, however a flanking charge led by Col. Jefferson Davis and a determined artillery barrage under Capt. Braxton Bragg saved the day for the Americans and Santa Anna withdrew the next day, turning to meet a reported invasion force headed for Veracruz.

Although Mendoza Haeckel witnessed the death of over 2500 men during those three days, he likewise learned that a single man and a good dog could herd more sheep than twenty good vaqueros could do with half that number of the wild beeves that roamed the country.

From that day on he would be a sheep-man and this was the shameful plague he would bring upon Wyoming.

Mendoza also arrived at Fort Bowie with a little over 3000 sheep the very morning Ryan Rodriquez rode in from the south.

Ryan had, since the moment he had awakened that morning, noticed a strange smell in the air, but it was not until he saw the dirty ragged-looking flock following the strange wagon did he realize the odor was that of sheep.

Mixed feelings were soon apparent at the fort and little village close by. General Crook was relieved to see fresh meat for his troops, but the agent, a man named Tiffany, who depended on beef deliveries from Texas to keep his store stocked, was outraged.

"These damn varmints don't graze, they sweep. There won't be enough grass left where they have been to keep ten steers alive, let alone the number we need to keep fresh meat here year-round."

And although no man outranked Crook in the military of the South-West, Tiffany was a civilian employee of the Department of The Interior with strong political influence in Washington and within two weeks of his arrival Haeckel and his sheep were ordered out of Arizona.

Late that same afternoon a U.S. Marshal by the name of O'Neil arrived with a telegram in hand calling for the arrest of one Ryan Rodriquez on the grounds of murder and robbery in Harshaw.

When the band of sheep moved slowly out of apache country Ryan rode with them, leaving no tracks for the law to follow.

Sean Hennessey and Zeb Sapp moved into Wyoming in the summer of '78 with a small herd of beeves brought over the pass from Oregon. After selling them in Green River, they quickly squandered their profits and found themselves out of money and out of work. Finally, that October they had managed to get to Laramie and were hired by Hiram Kelly to help drive a small herd up to the Chug[1], where he had a ranch and trading post.

They were a strange pair, for never had two men seemed so different and so hated by one another, yet stayed partners until the reaper separated them.

Hennessey was from Philadelphia and came to California around the horn[2] arriving in the summer of 1861 only to quickly be conscripted[3] into the service with the 1st Infantry, California Volunteers and marched east into Arizona to meet the Confederate challenge there. Private Hennessey constantly complained it was impossible to be conscripted into a volunteer outfit, but his argument fell on deaf ears.

---

[1] Chug: Chugwater Creek is a tributary of the Laramie River in Southeastern Wyoming.

[2] Around the Horn was a common expression meaning one had come west on a sailing ship from the east coast around South America's tip Cape Hone, and up the west coast to California, usually San Francisco.

3 Conscripted: A common term used in the 1800's meaning drafted into service.

Sapp, originally from Kentucky, had been one of the California Copperheads that raised so much trouble before California joined the Union.

Later he began holding up gold shipments for the Confederacy until one day, he and his band decided they needed the gold more than Richmond did, and thereafter turned pure bandit.

Hennessey stood slightly less than six feet tall and was slim and weathered. Sapp barely was five foot eight in his boots and was built like a bulldog. His dark hair was so thick he had trouble keeping a hat on, where Hennessey was mostly bald by his thirtieth birthday. Nonetheless, they rode together on Kelly's range.

Karl Siebold homesteaded on a water hole north of the stage road between Mormon Crossing[4] and Independence Rock in the spring of '77 and soon had a sizeable herd of beeves on The Big Open he claimed as his personal free-range, and as a result often in dispute with the vast holdings of the CY spread.

J. M. Carey and his little brother had little use for Seibold and the feeling was mutual.

Carey had warned Seibold to stay off CY land. Seibold quickly spread the word he would destroy any beeves he found with the CY brand grazing on his land.

Although the *K—S*[5] would never be in the league of the CY, or for that matter several others in Carbon County, he still had become a sizeable rancher by the winter of '79. However, it was Seibold's next endeavor in his fight with the bigger outfits, especially the *WT*,[6] that would drive him to do something that would bring a hated and heretofore unseen disaster upon the German's head.

The *WT* was owned by not only one of the wealthiest men in the territory but Paul Somerset also claimed he had relation, by marriage, in the White House.

---

4 Mormon Crossing: Later was named Casper.
5 *K—S*: The *K—S*, the brand of Siebold's ranch.
6 *WT*: The Running *WT*, the brand of Wallton's ranch.

On the morning of March 8th, despite the temperature hovering at twenty below, the rail workers at Rawlins offloaded a complete car of strangely constructed and very heavy boxes into the six waiting wagons before they reconnected the empty car to the eastbound.

The arduous trip from Rawlins to the *K—S* over frozen grown took three days. However, due to an unexpected early thaw, by Good Friday Karl Siebold was digging holes for his fence posts and by April Fools Day Wyoming got its first taste of Joe Glidden's 'Devil's Rope'.[7]

Paul Somerset swore the first *WT* steer he lost to the wire would be the signing of the death sentence on Siebold.

Most of the other large ranchers in the Territory felt the same. Nevertheless, steers were to become entangled in the wire and all too many times this resulted in large sections being cut and left open.

Siebold was determined to hold his ground and to do so he imported seven Line Riders from Missouri, three of which were rumored to have ridden with *The Arkansas Avenger.*

Three of the others were former members of the Missouri State Guard under Bill Anderson, and the last was Tom Todd, son of George Todd.[8]

When word of Siebold's Line Riders reached Somerset he declared war on the German.

However, this didn't bother Siebold, he knew his men were worth more than thirty of Somerset's ranch hands and he had another card up his sleeve that would put the icing on the cake for central Wyoming.

October 17th found Siebold in the small village of Casa Blanca, New Mexico where he met a full blood Laguna Quantum Pueblo who was returning from the celebration at Saint Mary Margaret's mission.

---

7 Joseph Glidden: The inventor of barbed wire as we know it today once called The Devil's Rope.

8 George Todd: One of Quantrill's Lieutenants.

His Spanish name was Gilbert Pacheco, however, he had just received his Cane of Authority making him a member of the Tribal Council; this resulted in a new name of his people for him translated in American as Small Turkey.

Siebold found the man as friendly as any he ever met and was pleased to accept an invitation to share a meal at his home.

During the evening Gilbert informed his guest of the sheep herd that was stopped a short distance away, and the next morning led him over and introduced him to Mendoza Haeckel.

This unexpected rendezvous resulted in a business arrangement between Siebold and Haeckel where the rancher agreed to buy every head he could deliver to his ranch in Carbon County, Wyoming, as well as give Haeckel a permanent job there as the foreman of his sheep herd. For the remainder of his life, Siebold would remember and be thankful to the friendly Pueblo, Small Turkey.

The idea of going to Wyoming was met with great enthusiasm by Ryan for he knew it was Wyoming Territory that his older cousin Carlos had gone some years before.

Chapter Nineteen

The Ohio River

Buckshot watched over and over as the train stopped for wood and water but he had no idea where he was or which direction he was headed.

Once as they stopped in a town he started to jump, but he saw the bulls headed his way checking for free riders and he slipped out of the empty car he had been riding and climbed atop the train where he rode until the cold became too great to withstand. Then he dropped down through the small vent door into a car mostly filled with bales of cotton.

Later when he tried to open the side door of this car he found it to be locked on the outside. Now unable to reach the opening in the top where he entered, he realized he was trapped.

He tried to move the bales around so he could climb up and get out, but the swaying of the train was such that he could not arrange the heavy bales by himself, so he settled down and waited. *'At least I'm not freezing anymore.'*

For two days and two nights, he waited among the cotton bales. Sometimes the train would be stopped, but more often it was moving and he finally determined he must be headed north.

The gray overcast days offered him no sun to judge from but on the second day, he saw through a thin crack in the side that the landscape was covered with snow, and some had actually collected on the door so he could gather a little to ease his thirst.

On the third morning after he entered this car the train stopped in a large town. Buckshot could see there were several other train cars also stopped on other tracks and he hoped somehow he could escape, for he was becoming quite weak from lack of food and water.

It was near noon when finally he heard men talking and eventually the sounds of the lock being opened. He crouched low lying as far back as he could on the top of the last bale hoping they would not see him.

Whitey Hogan had lived in Owensboro all of his fourteen years, and since his father hired out as a coal heaver on a rear wheeler and never returned, he had brought home a large portion of the food his younger sisters ate for the past two years.

His mother worked in the cannery, but her wages simply were not enough to feed them all and pay the rent, so Whitey helped.

He had a job working for Mr. Greene driving one of the smaller delivery wagons from the docks to the markets. Still, it took a little more than what he made to readily keep food on the table, thus he had learned to supplement this by lifting one or two items from each of the markets he delivered to.

He didn't take much, not enough for them to really miss it, but by taking a little here and a little there by the end of the day he had enough.

Unfortunately, this day he had been seen slipping an orange into his pocket and Clarence Johnson had paid dearly to have the fruit shipped all the way from Smyrna Florida up the Mississippi and then east on the Ohio to Kentucky. Therefore he had no intention of letting the little thief get away with a single one.

Before Whitey knew it he was being dragged from his delivery wagon by three of Johnson's men who quite obviously intended to beat a little law and order into him for his crime.

However, the one thing Whitey was better at than stealing was squirming and before they really knew what had happened he was loose and running for all he was worth.

The three were ordered by a furious Johnson to bring him back or not return themselves, and in these times when jobs were so hard to come by, they were making full steam at overtaking the fleeing lad.

At the same time only a few blocks away, two railroad bulls were in hot pursuit themselves after a stowaway, and the two escapees were headed on a collision course.

Buckshot really did not understand what the big deal was; he had simply tried to get in out of the cold and then was unable to get out. He tried to explain this to the man with the hickory club, but when he drew back his arm the boy gathered all the strength he had left and dove between the man's legs and was up and running for all he was worth by the time the Bull had turned around.

Just as he rounded the corner passing a tall wooden building he saw the river ahead and his only thought was to run there and jump in, but before he reached the edge, Whitey run full force into him, spilling them both. They each looked at each other quite surprised and then at the pursuers which were approaching now from two different directions. Finally getting his wits about him he said, "Come on," and Buckshot followed.

Thankfully, his new comrade knew the docks, and they both were able to hide out until things quieted down.

"Where are you from?"

Buckshot saw the canteen at the other boy's side and needing fluids badly he nodded towards the small tin bottle.

Whitney, realizing what was meant by the gesture, handed the canteen over to Buckshot.

Eventually, after drinking all that was left in it he replied, "Florida."

"Oh, that's where oranges come from ain't it?"

"I don't know. I never seen no orange one. But we do have blackies down-home. Mr. Sam had one who worked fur him fur a spell."

"No. An orange. It's like a ball. You eat it."

"Oh, I never seen one of them neither."

"Boy, you sure are ignorant."

The statement cut deep, but he guessed the boy was right. "Yeah, I reckon I am, but I can read and write and to figures in my head."

"If you can read, you ain't ignorant," the taller boy said and smiled. Buckshot felt better now and smiled back.

"Say, what's your name?"

"Buckshot, Buckshot Gunter. What's yours?"

"Whitey Hogan."

"Glad to meet you, Whitey Hogan," he said, holding out his hand like he had seen so many full-grown men do.

"Say, can you drive a wagon? It's just a one-horse rig."

"Sure. I can drive a team," Buckshot answered proudly.

"Good. Come on and help me out."

When they were back within sight of Clarence Johnson's vegetable market Whitey said, "See that delivery wagon there, the one with the white sides?"

"Sure."

"Well go over there and get in it and drive it around the block for me. If anyone stops you just say Mr. Green sent you to pick it up."

Buckshot looked at the wagon and shook his head, *'Why don't he just go over and get it?'* "We ain't stealing it are we?"

"No. It's mine but the man who owns that market was who was chasing me and I can't go back there now, and Mr. Greene owes me money that I'll never be able to get if'n I don't bring back his delivery."

"Why were they after you?"

"'Cause I took one of his oranges."

"You mean you stole it."

"Alright, I stole it. So what?"

"I don't hold with stealing," Buckshot said, but then he remembered it was this boy who helped him escape from the railroad bulls and surely saved him from jumping into the cold river, "but I will go get the wagon fur you."

"You will? Gosh, thanks."

Buckshot remembered how Mr. Reb Brown would often raise his arm as a gesture when he was walking away and he did the same thing now, walking towards the white delivery wagon.

He did not stop to talk to anybody, he simply picked up the weight and placed it back in the front boot and climbed up on the seat and reached for the reins.

"Hey, who are you?" the tall skinny man yelled.

"Mr. Greene sent me to get the delivery and finish making the rounds."

"Well, you tell Thomas Greene he had better fire that little thief or he can stop delivering here, and if I ever catch him I'll give him a lesson he won't soon forget."

"He done fired him fur not coming back with this here wagon," Buckshot said, as he dropped the long leathers on the back of the tired old mare.

That night he stayed with the Hogan's and ate his first full meal in several weeks. After the others were asleep he and Whitey made their plans.

"Every boat needs a ship's boy. Some will even take on two, and if you can read and write, I'm sure we can get a job."

"Wow, do you think any a' them boats goes to Coulson, Montana?"

"I don't know, but I wouldn't be surprised."

"Wow."

Chapter Twenty

A Fall Crop

Quigley had been unsure about her fall crop of corn producing, but here it was the first of December and he was delivering her last wagon load of corn to Verdigris City where she was getting top dollar for the produce coming in this late in the year.

Their first week together had been strained to say the least. She distrusted him immensely. However she couldn't place just why, he asked for nothing, worked from daylight to dark and seemed totally happy sleeping on his bedroll out in the small barn.

No matter how much she insulted him or how often she scolded him, he took it without so much as an angry reply. Still, at times when she said something she knew herself was out of place, he had frowned but said nothing back. After the third week, she stopped trying to run him off.

Not once had he made any moves on her and as he had said the first day he treated her like he would have his own daughter.

By Thanksgiving, she hoped he would not leave anytime soon.

They spent Christmas day together cooking and laughing and enjoying each other's company and it was the first time since he arrived, she asked him to eat with her in her home.

That winter after her crops were in and sold, he began hand hewing logs to wall her barn, replacing the sod there. It was the first of February before he had all of the walls finished and really wanted to get to work on the roof, but on the morning of February the forth he found Mariah weeping and when he asked why she simply turned and walked away.

Thus this day he did not work on the barn, rather just did small chores and tended to his horse.

She did not come back out until late in the afternoon. Just as the sun was slipping steadily behind the western hills, she opened the door of the cabin. Stepping out she said, "This would have been my first wedding anniversary."

Suddenly he felt the moisture building in his own eyes, the first time that had happened since he watched Dora Stebling shot, sixteen years before.

Quigley stayed at the Scott farm throughout the winter and just as the spring was blossoming with the promise of fine weather, he finished her barn and replaced the roof on her house.

However, after her early crop was just popping from the earth, as they sat on the little porch enjoying the cool of the evening he said, "I'll be leaving come morning."

"Oh, where are you going?' she asked, looking out over her fields not understanding the meaning of his words.

"Got a' be moving on," was all he said in reply.

Suddenly a huge lump began to swell in her chest and the pain of it hurt fiercely. "Why?" she asked fighting back tears.

"It's time," was all he gave her.

Mariah until this moment, had not thought a single moment about her feelings for this man, other than she knew her dislike for him had vanished within a week after she met him.

She came to realize she had become very dependent on his strong back and levelheaded thinking. Now suddenly the thought of him not being there was almost unbearable. *'I feel the way I felt when Stanley died,'* she suddenly realized.

"No. You can't leave me. I need you. Who will help me gather my harvest? Who will protect me from the Indians?"

Quigley didn't answer right away, he was having a hard time finding the words. Not that there was any truth to her arguments, *'Hell, she can gather her own harvest, or hire a nigger helper or two, and surely no Indian would harm her, all them around here like her and respect her.'*

"I took the liberty to enter your home while you wus out to the little house, and I left you a small bit of money. It ain't much, but it's mostly all I have. I want you to keep it fur me 'til I return. I'll be traveling and have no place to properly hide such. I want you to use from it as you need, consider it yourn 'til I come back."

"But why are you going? You don't have to," she said, now she couldn't help it, her words were truly sobs and the tears were flowing down her cheeks and she suddenly knew she was deeply in love with Quigley Hancock and had never realized it before this moment.

Quigley knew this day had to come sometime. He realized he should have left long ago, but he kept finding some excuse not to.

However, he realized his departure was a must if this girl was ever to find another husband. No young man dared to come courting with him there, and although he had never so much as touched her other than what was necessary when two people worked side by side day in and day out, others thought differently.

The people in town thought differently, and Mrs. Comings, the storekeep's wife, had more than once dropped a slight word here or there on the subject.

The first time, he had returned her comment with a hard stare and she felt a cold chill run the length of her spine. Still, she was a meddlesome woman and such can never leave a body alone when they think they can uncover another's business.

This last time she had made some comment about the arrival of children, and that had been it for him.

His reply was cold and harsh but truthful, "Mrs. Comings, you are hunting in the wrong patch a' woods. Mrs. Scott is a lady beyond reproach, not one to have her virtues talked about behind her back, especially by miserable old witches who most likely never has enjoyed the love of a man."

"Well, I never," the woman said and turned quite red.

"Yas Ma'am, that's what I thought," Quigley answered, getting in the final dig. Then he touched the front brim of his wide hat and left the store.

The Comings woman was not the only one who had made some comment close enough for him to hear. Once while in town not long after he began staying at her farm, he had a hankering for a drink and had stopped in Archie Thigpen's, only to have a drunk ask why a purty thing like Mariah Scott was satisfied bedding down with an old dog like him. It took three men to pull him off the drunk and later he heard the man may never fully recover from the beating, something he worried little on.

"After word gets around a' me being gone, they'll be those who will be coming trying to court you," he said, looking over at the hound who was now scratching his long ears. "I caution you, not to marry up until you find one that fills that empty hole in your heart the death of your husband has caused."

He then took the small piece of cedar all that was left of the stick he had been whittling shavings from, and placed it in his mouth before he spoke again. "There is enough money there so you should not feel the need for such from a man. Wait until the right one comes along." When finished with his statement he stepped down to the ground and patted the dog a couple of times and then with affection rubbed his head.

'The right one has already come along,' she thought, as she watched him walking away.

That night she did not open the blue neckerchief lying on her table. She did not even look at it after first noticing it there, but the next morning after she had found the hen eggs and knew for certain he was gone, she went back inside and sat there at the table for a long time staring at the bundle before finally, ever so slowly, she untied the thick knot and laid back the folds of the cloth, and then she gasped.

There were numerous coins, mostly gold double eagles and a large roll of gray backs tied by a small white string. Suddenly she once again burst out crying only this time she did not hold back and the dog outside looked in wonder at the howls that were emerging from the log cabin.

Chapter Twenty One

The War Begins

During the spring round-up both Sean Hennessey and Zeb Sapp were able to secure jobs with the *WT* outfit and move north into central Wyoming. They liked their new job, liked the comfort of having more riders around, and working with a bigger outfit offered in Indian country. And they liked the better grub Somerset insisted his men get. Nonetheless, it was still a job of riding line in barren country on cold nights and hot summer days.

The idea of being involved in a range war carried a touch of excitement for Sapp, especially since their side outnumbered the opposition three to one. Then there were the riders from the other big outfits along The North Platte that hated barbwire as much as the *WT* did.

The first confrontation came in late March when Blaine Sedgwick followed a maverick down a little draw that ended in the dry wash called Powder River. He had just gotten a rope around the critter when the presence of others was felt at the back of his neck. Whirling, afraid Indians had come upon him, he dropped the lariat, only to see two other mounted cowboys stopped atop the bank watching him. "Oh wow, you scared a year's growth off me. I thought sure injuns were upon me."

"You a *WT* rider?" Miles Abbey asked.

"Yeah, been after this here stray fur nigh on two miles, but the little fellow was sure a slippery one."

"You be on *K—S* land."

Blaine looked around and then back, "I don't think so, this here is Powder River. It's the boundary and I'm still in the middle, ain't on *K—S* land yet," he said back with a little smile hoping this was all some sort of joke, and at the worse, a threat.

"And I see you're trying to steal a *K—S* calf. I do believe that's what they call rustling, ain't it Luffman?"

"Yep."

"Now look here, this here is a maverick, he ain't wearing no brand, not *K—S* nor *WT*. Suppose he could belong to either 'cept I just chased him for more'n a mile from back yonder, that makes him *WT* fur shor."

"Nope. He's *K—S* and you been caught rustling stock, that's a hanging offence only, there ain't no trees near 'bouts so I reckon we'll just have to shoot you."

"Now wait here a minute, Mister, I never ______," Sedgwick stopped talking when he saw the man slowly remove a rifle from a saddle scabbard.

'Son-of-a-bitch, this ain't no place to die, not here in this dry riverbed with no one around. I never even got to______.'

The 45-slug hit him full in the left breast ending his thought, and he looked down at the blood squirting in long gushes from the hole, every time his heartbeat, and he smiled and said, "Funny." It was the last thing he ever said.

Shelly McCrery and Eddie Thorbs were the ones who found him. Blaine was still on his horse sitting mostly upright by the assistance of a stout sagebrush that was tied to the saddle in such a manner his body could lean back on it. His shirt had been sliced several times and he had been scalped.

"Injuns," Thorbs said, as they lowered him to the ground. But McCrery wasn't so sure. I lost $20 to him last night in a poker game and I seen him put it in his pants pocket and it ain't here. Now, what would injuns do with Whiteman's money?"

"Doe-no," Eddie replied, thinking hard on the subject.

When Paul Somerset heard about the incident, he had McCrery and Thorbs and six other men ride back to where they had found Sedgwick. From there they backtracked him to the riverbed.

It was quite obvious the boy had been killed and butchered there, evidence was everywhere from deep stains in the sandy soil to dozens of boot prints around where the body had fallen. However, they could not find a spent shell, no matter how much they searched, until finally, Buford Gillyard found the discarded 45-60 case mostly buried where Abbey's horse had stepped on it after it had been ejected.

Somerset took the spent shell from Gillyard's gloved hand and studied it a few seconds and then slipped it in his vest pocket before saying, "Siebold is responsible for this and he will pay." Then he mounted and led the men back to his main ranch house.

That night he sent riders out to deliver messages to several of the other ranch owners in the Platte River Valley notifying them of a meeting being called at his place two nights hence.

"We got ourselves a range war. We all knew it was coming when that no account Kraut unloaded Devil's Rope from the U. P. and now it's started. He's done killed one of my line riders and tried to make it look like the injuns done it, so I want to know what we aim to do about this?"

John Carey, being a Texican, had never liked Somerset much. Something about the harshness of his Yankee upbringing always seemed to show through anytime he got a chance to stand on a soapbox, and this night he was standing high and shouting loud. Still there was truth in Somerset's words. Siebold should not have brought barbwire to The Big Open. It was sinful and there was no denying that fact. *'This is open range and it will be a hundred years from now,'* Carey agreed in his mind, although he did not say so to Somerset.

"Judge, you organized the Wyoming Stock Growers Association, can't you kick him out?"

Carey knew all the eyes in the room were on him now as the others also wanted to know his answer and he carefully studied his options before he answered. "No. I don't see how we can do that. We have no proof he did the killin', no real charges against him. It ain't again the law to fence in land as long as it cannot be legally claimed by others. What we need is some definite proof, then we can get at him."

"Hellfire, Judge, they scalped the boy," Somerset yelled.

"Somebody did. Just who, no one here knows and that's just what I mean," Carey replied sternly.

"Well, I know, and I'll do something if the rest of you won't," Somerset said just as sternly.

"Don't do nothing that will bring the law down on the rest of us Paul," Greg Searight said.

"The law! Hell, in Wyoming we are the law, and you all know it," Somerset shouted back.

The Dry Basin known as Powder River after a light snow

Chapter Twenty Two

Driving a Herd North

Moving along over the open range had never been much of a problem, even in the high country, but when they would get in timber it was laborious to keep the sheep together, even with the dog working hard. As much as they tried to cut around it, at times they had to go through timber.

Snow drifts were also a problem but staying on the western slope helped a great deal, for the winds never laid on this side of the divide.

They lost a few to deep snow, but not nearly as many as they could have. Nonetheless the going was slow, and by April they were still in Utah moving steadily along.

Ryan had long ago lost his sense of smell as far as the sheep were concerned; in fact, they smelled no different than Mendoza or the dog he had named Nombre Bola because the white fuzzy pup reminded him of a snowball, or he himself for that matter.

The people they encountered along the way would not have agreed. In fact, there was the small village of Fillmore, Utah that refused to let them come through, which caused a three-day delay when they had to go to another water hole several miles out of their way.

Most of the people in Utah were not so unfriendly and although they often were asked to leave one or two behind as a tax for using the grass and water, the Mormons treated them pretty well, much better than some of the other so-called Christians they would encounter as they made their long walk north.

Keeping as close to the mountains as the spring drifts would allow, they skirted most of the camps, especially Salt Lake City, before turning east towards Wyoming.

They lost a little over a dozen to drowning while crossing Bear Creek on the narrow road when the U.P. engineer amused himself by repeatedly blowing his whistle terrifying the sheep, but this was not the greatest harm he would do to them.

There was a posse of some ten armed men waiting west of Evanston with full intention of turning them back and would have, had it not been for the unexpected arrival of Andy Botkin, a U.S. Marshal from Montana who had been injured and was en route to Omaha for medical treatment on the next train. Upon seeing the happenings Botkin ordered the train stopped whereupon he busted up the unauthorized posse and sent the sheepherders on, advising them to avoid Evanston and as many towns as they could.

Ryan did a lot of growing in the seven months he moved north with Mendoza Haeckel and his sheep. It was a kind of growing not noticed by those who simply saw a person from time to time, rather a growing one would notice when they were together for long periods. A type of growth that takes place in the head more so than in the rest of the body.

The boy who had hidden in the shadows by Henry Watson's store and watched Lazarus Ross kill John Swelley had died somewhere along the trail and the young man who walked beside his horse along the narrow riverbed between the gigantic canyon walls leading into Wyoming was somehow a different fellow, a better fellow, a young man rather than a boy.

Mendoza spoke both Mexican and German quite well, as they were the languages of his parents. However, he had learned long before that to trade on an equal base in America one must be able to speak and understand American, as well as know the minds of the American people. Often, he would talk Mexican, but listen in American and this had proved very beneficial to him.

After taking a liking to Ryan and learning to trust the boy, he decided he should also teach him to speak American. That is not to say Ryan had no use of the American language, for he certainly could converse with most Americans, but his use of the language was sketchy.

When he spoke the language, he still thought in Mexican and Mendoza knew that would be a great handicap if he was to remain here in the north. So before they had reached Utah, the older man began working every night with Ryan, teaching him this new and most difficult way of talking.

Ryan was not new to languages. He, like Mendoza, spoke both the languages of his own parents, Mexican and Shoshone and he could understand and talk a little American. These former learnings were a great help as they worked at it.

Three nights after leaving the U.P. tracks, they cut a trail to the northeast. While camped along a muddy little creek, Mendoza rubbed the ears of his dog and gazing at the windblown desert ahead, he imagined the short sage bushes to be an army of men coming to assist them in their struggles. He smiled at this thought. Finally, he spit a stream of tobacco juice and spoke, "Ryan, see the soldiers?"

"No miro Soldados."

"We are now in America, we must talk American. Now, do you see the soldiers?"

"I see no soldiers," Ryan said back.

"Very good. You are learning well, but remember what I have told you. It is as important to think as it is to speak a language," he said.

Then looking back at the open plains covered here and there with drifts of snow, he pointed out at the little shadows and added, "See the little bushes, they make me think of soldiers."

Ryan then understood why his friend had asked the question and he nodded his head in the moonlight, although he failed to see the resemblance of soldiers to the squatty sage bushes.

Wyoming's Big Open

Chapter Twenty Three

The Lady Denver

Whitey Hogan knew riverboats, he had lived around the docks for as long as he could remember, and his father had shipped out more than once and returned to tell tales of fun and adventure on the river.

Whitey never understood why he failed to come back that last time, but the thought of working on a boat had been his dream for a long time. The fact that for some reason his father failed to return never influenced the lure the river held for him.

He would have gone before were it not for his devotion to helping his mother and little sister, but now that old man Clarence Johnson had labeled him a thief over the theft of a mere orange he had no choice. Or at least that's what he told himself that morning as he and Buckshot signed on *The Lady Denver* as she filled her belly with dark-cured and fired-cured tobaccos of the finest quality.

Whitey had asked for a job as a coal heaver, not because he wanted it so much, rather because that was what he remembered his father always was, and it was the first thing that came to mind when the boys approached Captain Marsh.

The short stout man in the long black coat studied the two lads before him and immediately pegged them as runaways, but that really didn't bother him so much. He had been a runaway himself back in '27 when he shipped out on *The Lady Pittsburg* and had found the river to be a good life, except during the war when his boat had been confiscated by the government to run supplies and soldiers down to Memphis and Vicksburg.

'The taller boy seems like he might just make a coal heaver eventually. It surely will take some time though to build enough muscle on that skinny frame, but there is possibilities. I don't know about the little one though, he's a might shy for such,' Marsh thought before he turned to Buckshot and asked, "And just what job do you want, Shorty?"

"My name's Buckshot, not Shorty, and I'd admire your job."

"Why you are feisty for such a little guy, and I don't know if I can use you or not," the captain said then he looked back at Whitey, "I'll give you a try though."

A lump suddenly erupted in Buckshot's throat, *'I guess I should a' let him call me Shorty,'* he thought before he heard Whitey saying, "No, we come as a team, he don't get the job, I don't either."

"Well, I'll be, you both are a might feisty and a little sassy too, and I don't reckon I need either one of you then."

"Suits me," Whitey said back. "I doubt this bucket a' rotten timber will make it to Saint Louie anyway."

Buckshot turned to his friend and said, "No Whitey, you take the job, I'll find some other way to get to Coulson."

Captain Marsh suddenly squinted his eyes and looked strongly at the boy. "Coulson, you say? Why do you want to go to that God-forsaken country?"

"I got my reason and that's where I'm going."

"You know, I changed my mind, I can use both of you. If'n you can shovel coal as well as you can sass, I'll give you a try."

The coal was loaded from a rail car on the riverfront spur to wagons and then brought aboard where the haulers shoveled the black gold into the hold and waited for the next load. During this time between wagons, Buckshot watched the tobacco being loaded and stored on the main deck, but it was brought aboard by a long boom on which were fitted large block and tackles with ropes the size of his forearm. It was bundled in bales of various sizes much like cotton. He took interest in all he was observing, wanting to know as much as he could about any and everything so he could somehow get different duties, for in short order he found the life of a coal hauler was not to his liking.

Captain Marsh walked up just as they finished with the last wagon and turned to Ramsey Cook and asked, "How many bales we take on?"

"Well, there was 63 a' the two hundred pounder's and 81 a' the hundred pounder's and 92 a' the sixty pounders' so_____," he said looking down at his little pad and began working with his pencil.

Buckshot without hesitation said, "26,260 pounds or thirteen tons."

"What?" questioned the captain?

"We took on 26,260 pounds or 13.13 tons according to his figures, but he's wrong, one a' the little bales fell into the water yonder," he said pointing at the dark object floating near the front of the boat next to the dock.

"It's 26,360, Sir," Cook said.

"He's wrong, he don't do his figures so good," Buckshot said back using his dirty sleeve to wipe the sweat from his forehead.

Marsh looked at the confident boy and then back at his man, "Check your figures again Cook," he ordered sternly, but without anger.

The man looked irritated and then began to run his numbers again. When he finished, Marsh saw a strange expression come over him and then he started again only this time much slower. Finally he looked up to the upper deck where the Captain now stood looking down at him.

Sheepishly he said, "26,260."

"How many tons is that?"

Again, he took his pencil and began dividing until he looked back and said, "Thirteen point one three tons sir."

Marsh looked back at the boy and squinted his eyes, "How'd you know that?"

"I heard him say to you."

"No, I mean how did you know how much the total was?"

Buckshot lifted both shoulders and then let them drop before he replied, "Figures come easy to me." Then feeling a little embarrassed added, "But I ain't so good at writing my letters." He felt as if he should somehow correct his boast with a shortcoming.

Marsh then asked, "If a fathom is 6 feet and we have a draft of sixteen feet and the river is three and a half fathoms decreasing at a rate of one foot every quarter mile what does that tell you?"

Buckshot blinked his eyes a couple of times and then said, "You better reverse your course pretty damn soon or you will run aground," he paused and then added, "in just a bit over a mile."

"Come with me," he said and then turned and walked back out of sight.

The Lady Denver, a two-deck side wheeler with the pilothouse on top of the second deck was owned by *The Coulson Packet Line*. She had originally been constructed as a three-deck passenger liner but when taken by the military they converted her by removing her second deck altogether so large pieces of equipment such as naval guns and other stores could be carried, and after the war, Sanford B. Coulson, known along the Missouri as Sallie, convinced his brother John to leave her that way utilizing her tall main deck to haul goods and retaining only the upper deck for passenger service and to keep her on the Ohio and Mississippi due to her deep draft.

Of course, Buckshot knew nothing of *The Coulson Packet Line* or the fact Coulson, Montana was named after John Coulson who based his Missouri River operations out of there. However, the captain had not failed to hear the boys' comment and he, of course, knew all about Coulson. When the boy reached the pilothouse, Captain Marsh turned to Mossy, a darkey that had been with him since he first began on the river, and said, "Take him down and get him clean and then find some clothes for him to wear. I think we have some makin's here."

"Yas Sur," was all the faithful old man said and then placing his large hand on Buckshot's shoulder he spoke, "Com' ons and wes gits you clean fo' da captain."

Chapter Twenty Four

Suitors and Freedmen

Mariah Scott felt like her heart had been torn from her body once again just a few weeks short of a year since she buried her husband. At that time, she was convinced she would never love again, marry perhaps as she was young and a young woman has certain needs, but she knew she would never love again, could never love again, and then along came this mysterious Quigley Hancock out of nowhere who was her strength for so many months. He had helped her in so many ways that looking back, she doubted she could have made a go of the place without him. The strength he possessed, he displayed, he gave her, had so affected her that she had fallen deeply in love with the man without her even realizing her true feelings and now he, too, was gone from her life.

He had been right about her corn, right about her need to repair the cabin roof before the snows came, right about the dog, right about her mule, right about just about everything.

Now he was no longer there and just as he had said, it did not take long before Judd Alden showed up.

Judd was a young man, only a year older than she, and he was strong and well-built and quite handsome, and she was tempted when he offered to help her with her farming, but he was too good to be true, too pretty to be true. His idea of a day in the field began after a hot breakfast and ended when the sun got high, he was quick and fancy on his feet and could make a fiddle sing or cry, depending on the tune he was stroking.

Mariah went to the barn dance with Judd after the Confederate Memorial Day Services. On Sunday following, they had dinner on the grounds and church all around, but Quigley had been right about Judd also. What Judd wanted was not to toil in her fields, he would rather play house after half a day's work was done. She soon made up her mind, even though he helped her forget Quigley for a little while, she really didn't need Judd Alden after all.

Next came Brother Will Maynard, a Mormon farmer, who needed a younger wife to help the aging mother of his children do the work on his own spread, and who was extremely harsh to her when she turned down his kind offer.

After Maynard stopped arriving every day shortly after dawn, she saw a brave sitting on horseback just in the shadows of the big cottonwood down on the bank of the Verdigris River at the very edge of her land.

Although he never once did anything that could be said he intended to do her harm, it was he who worried her the most. He never got close enough for her to identify if he was Osage or some other Indian, but when she would see him, she felt weak and exceptionally vulnerable.

One morning as she carried her shotgun in one hand and a bushel basket in the other, she said aloud, "Oh Quigley, why did you leave me?" Then she dropped to her knees and burst out in a sobbing fit. Finally, when she again gained control over her emotions, she looked over and the Indian was gone. Although she kept watching for several months, after that day she never saw him again.

Once more she planted late in the summer in hopes of a warm fall and her gamble paid off. This year she was able to hire a family of freedmen who had come west from Grundy County, Tennessee and had tried to make it on their own, but never having made decisions for themselves before, they made a couple of bad ones and ended up losing most everything they owned.

Mariah allowed them to camp their wagon down near the river where the woman and children made a home in the old ambulance while the brothers helped her with her fall harvest.

Once more her luck ran true, for in less than two days after they had the fall crops in, a cold wind brought a sleet and ice storm as the country had not witnessed since '68. The ice became so thick most of the trees in the country, which wasn't that many, had their limbs broken, and the stock on the open range had their feet frozen to the point many simply fell off before the animals died.

Mariah's fall crop brought a premium due to the hard winter and by spring, she had paid off all her mortgage and had bought the 160 acres joining her to the north.

When the ice storm hit so severely in November, she had Josh and Seth bring their wagon up close to the cabin to give them more protection from the terrible wind and before it was over, she had both families with their six children living in her home, trying to stay alive.

Closeness of this nature brings out the good and the bad in others as well as oneself and although she had little use for Seth's wife, Bonnet, Mariah got along with Anna Mae as well as if they had been sisters and both men were God sent to her fields come spring.

Mariah convinced them to each homestead on land adjacent to her own only across the river so they would have full water rights in the area. The first two years she paid them to work her land thereby providing them with the cash to buy the necessary provisions to build the structures to complete their obligations on their homesteads. By the third year, their oldest sons were big enough to work in the fields and the three families helped one another.

Although there were nights when that demon would sweep down and depress her, all in all having Josh and Seth and their families nearby eased her need for a man and she slowly began to accept the fact that she most likely would be a widow for the remainder of her life.

Chapter Twenty Five

Coutu Wolfchild

Laramie had taken a job as a bronc buster for the army in order to stay at the fort for the remainder of the summer and into the fall, in hopes of learning anything about this white squaw who rode with a redman.

The army would often buy a hundred or more green broke horses from the ranches in the area, or at times from a horse trader. But these animals were not nearly ready to be turned over to troops and it became his job to break them down where a trooper could begin their training as a mount for the cavalry. This took up most of his time during the daylight hours and he was so tired that, his after-dark hours were mostly spent in the loft over *Jensen's Livery.*

In September a string of Blackfoot that Coutu Wolfchild belonged to came in, but he was not with them. They told Chancy he had gone south with relatives for the winter and they had no knowledge of when he would be back.

This news was hard to take for Patay, he had hoped this lead would be a good one. Whether or not it would lead him to his mother was not the point, he had to run it down and find the truth or falseness in it one way or the other. Finally, when he had turned over the last cayuse to the army, he stopped by Chancys' store for provisions and to tell them of his gratefulness for all they had done for him. Mary Beth tried to talk him out of going, but he had made his mind up that he would head south to the Yellowstone where, somewhere this Coutu Wolfchild was supposed to be.

Just as he was leaving, a buck and two squaws entered the store. When he passed them on his way ou,t one of the women reached up and tugged his long hair and said something to her friend in their native language. He couldn't understand what she had said, but whatever it was the other agreed by nodding her head several times.

John could speak the language just enough to get by. Most of his trading was done with the universal language of the plains, that being sign language by using the hands. However, he heard the words Otahko Aakíí and he stopped Laramie. "Wait, wait a minute." Then he immediately began to ask her what the woman had meant. Finally, he nodded his head and thanked her and when he walked over to Laramie, he had a smile on his face. "She said your hair was like the hair of an Arapahoe woman she had seen near here two summers ago."

"Arapahoe, does she know where this woman is now?"

"In the land of the Arapahoe on the lower Big Horn River."

"The Lower Big Horn?" he questioned.

"Yes, in Wyoming, in the Wind River Range."

"Oh my God. Yes, it was Arapahoe who took her so long ago, it must be Mee-ma. It must be."

The excitement in his voice was beyond imagination and he turned to Mary Chancy and saw she had tears in her beautiful eyes, expressing her gladness for him. "God ride with you Laramie Patay. I will pray every day for your safety."

"Pray I find Mee-ma."

"I will pray for that, too."

Chapter Twenty Six

Wichita

Quigley Hancock knew he must leave Verdigris City before he had to kill someone. These people were mostly settlers from the northeast, abolitionists sent here before the war to assure Kansas remained a free state and they did not have the upbringing of gentlemen, or ladies for that matter.

'No respectable lady would have made such a comment to me about Mrs. Scott as Mrs. Comings had, especially in the presence of others. Perhaps a drunk might have blundered out some question, but never a lady.

'There are just too many in these parts without proper respect for others and I'm not one to abide with such for long, so I'm moving on.' At least that was the reason he told himself for parting.

Wichita was the first place of any size he came to after leaving Mariah's home. He needed supplies and a job, but what he wanted was to be taken drunk and enjoy the benefits and sorrows of the event.

He had abstained, for the most part, of such while living at the Scott Farm and now that he was through with that, he intended to get back down to some serious living. So it was no surprise that without any real thought his cayuse seemed to end up at the hitching post in front of *The Red Irish.*

"Well, if it ain't me ole friend Quigley Hancock," were the first words out of Ed O'Kelly's' mouth upon seeing the giant of a man block the sun that was trying to slip in past the swinging doors.

"Hello, you Big Mic," Quigley said back.

"Where the hell have you been? I ain't seen you in nigh on a year, maybe two."

"Been farming," was all Quigley said back as he strolled up to the bar.

The Irishman let out a loud laugh, "A fool-hoeman me ass, the day'll never come when Quigley Hancock turns in his Colts for a plow but have it your way. It ain't polite to ask such, so you will be accepting me apology and letting me buy you the first drink," he said. Then turning to the red-headed, freckled face woman beside him and saying, "Be giving me friend a glass of the good stuff."

Quigley, using the point of his thumb, pushed the brim of his hat up giving him a better view of the saloon's contents, and turning so he could see in the big mirror, that hung on the back-bar, he smiled and replied, "Sure, the first, but not the last."

They each downed the caramel-colored liquid and then Quigley said, "Ed, come on and let's get a table, I want to talk to you."

The saloon owner looked over at the only empty table and then to the occupants of the table next to it and then made a suggestion, "C'mere to me office, the atmosphere in here is bollocks, if you get me drift."

Quigley himself now looked over at the five men playing poker at the table and raised one eyebrow before looking back at his friend, "Alright, if you say so."

Just as they entered the back room, Ed said, "If you'll be so kind as to close the door, I'll be getting us another."

"Who are they?" Quigley asked, knowing he needed to say no more.

"Law Daugs. Kansas Law Daugs. Been here some six months, requested by the mayor and sent with authority by the governor to keep the Texas Cowboys in line when they hit town.

"If you be asking me, they have damn near killed Wichita as a shipping point. Holy Shmoly, Cowskin Crick is mostly abandoned and most of me old customers have taken to driving their herds to Dodge nowadays.

"I don't understand, 'em Texas boys is what made this whistle-stop in the first place."

"Well, it all started a year or so back when *The Arkansas Avenger* blew up the newspaper office. That damn Murdock printed up a first-page editorial on the lad and the next thing a body knows his whole damn office is nothing more'n a pile of splinters. So Murdock appeals to the Governor and he sends them down here to catch the Avenger and pretty soon that damn Pastor Shaw done stirred up the, let me t'ink, they calls themselves *The Respectable Women of Wichita*, and them bitches starts a temperance league which Murdock gives top billing and before you know it, them Law Daugs are assigned here permanent-like."

Quigley listened quietly while Ed ran on and on about how the whole affair has ruined his business and that now they have even taken to harassing the saloon girls in town and trying to get them run out of the county. "If it weren't fur Delano being across the river, I guess they would a shut me down, too."

"Did they catch them?"

"Catch who?"

"Them that blew up the Newspaper Office."

"Catch *The Arkansas Avenger*? Hell no, not in your lifetime me lad," the red-faced man said looking down at his cluttered desk and slowly shaking his head. "Naw, they run in a few but none of them was The Avenger, he's one slick gun-toter. I heard it said he was seen on the eastbound what was pulling out at the very moment Murdock's printing press went blasting through the roof."

"So, they know what he looks like finally," Quigley threw out to see what he might snag.

"Yeah, I hear he's as skinny as a rail about six foot tall with dark sandy hair and a thick mustache. Eyes so gray they seem to penetrate a body,"

"Gee, that sounds like what I heard Jesse James looks like."

"You know, come to think of it, I think I've heard the samet'ing. What'll you know about that? Do you be supposin' *The Arkansas Avenger* is really Jesse?"

Quigley looked hard at his friend and then asked, "Was there anything in this Murdock's paper about the James boys?"

O'Kelly thought a moment before answering, "Mm, you know, I do believe there was, well what do you know?"

"Well, Ed, has the temperance league run all of your Soiled Doves out a' this camp?"

"No, we still got a few."

"Got one with yellow hair?"

His Irish friend let out another "Mmm," as he thought a moment or two and rubbed his palm around on his chin. "Well, you might say Ginger has yellow hair, kinda dirty yellow but she's uglier 'n sin. We got us a lass here that is so pretty she'll make you want to marry her. She's a schoolteacher from back in Tennessee somewhere's and just comes out here in the offseason to make some real money. A young thing as pretty as they come, long brown hair and nice, too.

Quigley thought a moment and realized he could have been describing Mariah Scott, so he said, "No, I want one with corn silk hair."

"Aye, but mind me, come the morrow you'll be wishing you had spent your money on Susan. She is not hard like most of the scarlet sisterhood and she'll fag like no other."

The next day while Quigley was playing a game of stud in *The Red Irish,* he overheard two men sitting at a table next to him talking about a big outfit in Wyoming hiring gun hawks to help control the rustling problems.

As soon as he got a chance to turn in their direction without it being obvious, he looked at them, *'Hell the two a' them together might not be as old as I am,'* he thought. The very notion was depressing. *'Hellfire, I'll be forty-two come next September, an old man for someone in my profession. Most of those who rode with me are done gone under, either to a bullet or a hangman's noose, 'cept for Brazos, he succumb to the consumption.'*

His thoughts were interrupted by the two girls coming down the stairs, which attracted the attention of most everyone there. Clara, the one he had been with the night before, was having trouble with her dress and she suddenly just stopped about halfway down the stairs and said something to her companion and then lowered her dress to her waist exposing her ample breast to any and all who were looking while the other girl corrected whatever was wrong. Then in a gesture to the howls and hoops of the crowd below, brazenly Clara shook her shoulders causing her mammies to shake also, which brought on another loud applause. Satisfied, she lifted the top and the other woman secured the ties behind her neck before they continued their cavalcade down the stairs.

'She is uglier than sin,' Quigley thought, looking at the pockmarked face of the woman. Her hair was not yellow as he had requested, but neither was it black or brown or red, something in between that could pass for yellow if a man really wanted it to. *'At least she didn't remind me of Mariah,'* he thought and then realizing his thought he suddenly became angry with himself.

Later he couldn't remember why he had become angry, but he did remember the name *WT* as the outfit in Wyoming who was hiring and the next morning, he was in the telegraph office sending a wire to the Foreman of the *WT* Ranch in Cheyenne.

While awaiting an answer, he took a room at *The Texas House*, a large rather well-kept hotel across the toll bridge in proper Wichita. However, an unfortunate event took place on his third day in town. While returning from *The Rock Island* depot, where the telegrapher was located, he was immediate across Douglas Street from *The Kansas National Bank* when three men came running out and headed for the horses a fourth was holding for them. Before they could get mounted, a man in a white shirt with a black vest came out of the bank and fired a small handgun at the trio and at the same time, yelling about a bank holdup.

The rider who had been holding the horses lowered a single barrel shotgun and blasted the bank teller off his feet. Within a couple of seconds, a man was suddenly beside Quigley who began firing his revolver at the bandits. This, in turn, caused one of them to return his fire, only he did not single out which of the two men standing there was his enemy, or he simply was a bad shot, for his second round took off Quigley's Stetson and without time to think, his own Colt barked, and the horseman fell with a 45 slug to his chest.

The man who had attracted their attention was still firing as the other bandits rode down Main crossing the tracks and out of sight behind a steam locomotive that was just pulling up to the depot.

"That's good shooting, Mr. ______," the other man said letting the question lay.

"Hancock, Quigley Hancock," he said back. As he dropped the spent round to the boardwalk and replaced it with another loaded case, refilling his chamber. Quigley had never been one who practiced the theory that one should let his hammer rest on an empty chamber, he had learned during the war that in a firefight a man needed all the cartridges he could get and back in those days he often carried several revolvers. Instead, he simply set the cylinder so the hammer rested between caps and later when he bought his 45, he found the rims on the cartridges to provide a perfect valley for which the firing pin to rest, and thereby eliminating the need for an empty chamber. Of course, he also considered a man who would drop his revolver unworthy of owning one, so the matter was closed in his mind.

"I Am Deputy Meager. I appreciate your assistance, Mr. Hancock."

"He shot at me first," was Quigley's only reply and then he picked up his hat and in examining the hole he ran his thick finger through it and held the Stetson up in that manner for others to see.

The next morning *The Eagle* again printed a front-page headline about him, only this time few could have showered more praise about how he had been the only man to kill one of the ten-man gang that robbed *The First National Bank* of over twenty thousand in gold.

Twenty thousand in gold, why that would weigh over six hundred pounds and I only saw three men ride away and they sure weren't carrying no two hundred pounds apiece. Either the bank lies or the paper lies or was it taken by those other six invisible bandits that the paper reported were involved?'

The Eagle also identified the dead man as 'Cimarron Jac' one of four brothers wanted for other offences in Kansas.

That same day Quigley received a reply to his telegram, saying Mr. Somerset was in Dodge City on business and would not return until the first of the month.

'Hell, Dodge ain't that big,' he thought and asked about the next train west.

Chapter Twenty-Seven

Dodge City

That afternoon Apache was riding in an Atchison, Topeka and Santa Fe animal car bound for Dodge.

It took him three days to locate Somerset, but finally he found him in *The Phoenix Club* where one could enjoy the pleasures a man desires in a manner a man of his assumed stature deserves. It was a little to highfalutin for Quigley's liking, but he figured it fit Somerset.

In an assuming manner the rancher looked up at Quigley.*'Although he is looming, he appears too old to be the kind of man I need.'* "I'm sorry Mr. Hancock, I've already hired all the men I need, perhaps if you were in Cheyenne later on, I might could use you," Somerset said, not even giving Quigley the courtesy of rising from his chair when he spoke.

"Obliged," Quigley replied as he touched the brim of his new hat before he turned and walked back and out the door. *'I need some air, that place is filled with folks that could use a good dose of Calomel, for they sure are afflicted with the flux.'*

That night Quigley witnessed something that caused him to wonder about the future of Kansas lawmen. He was playing draw in *The Saratoga Saloon* when a boy dressed in the outfit of a Texican became quite drunk and drawing his old revolver shot twice at the head of the Buffalo that hung over the mirror behind the back-bar, missing it both times. Almost immediately a man who he later learned was Jim Masterson, walked up behind the kid and said quite loudly, "I'll take that pistol."

The drunken cowboy whirled around and stuck the long barrel of the Kerr in Masterson's belly without saying a word.

Quigley could see the hammer was cocked and at any second he figured there would be a new grave in Boot Hill this time tomorrow.

"Who are you?" the boy asked, while swaying about on unsteady feet.

"I'm Marshal Masterson, and you are under arrest for having a firearm north of the Deadline."

"What? What's a deadline?"

Luckily for both men the barkeep, used this talking time, to get within sticking distance of the cowboy and in short order he placed a well-aimed blow across the back of the lad's head with a leather covered jack. Immediately, the blood splattered all about and the unconscious Texican's knees buckled and he collapsed on the floor. However as he fell, his gun fired and the 44 ball splintered the hardwood floor between the marshal's boots.

At that moment another man also dressed in the array of a Texican rose and started for the two men who were dragging the bloody boy out. "Where you going with him?" he demanded.

"He's going to the calaboose," Masterson replied steadfastly.

"Like hell, he's going to the Doc's office 'afor he bleeds to death," and in a flash of an eye, the man was holding a short barreled Colt pointing it at the lawman.

Quigley looked at the revolver, it was obvious someone had cut it down for the barrel was the same length as the ejector housing and there by removing the front sight. Quigley had seen revolvers altered in this manner before. They usually belonged to a point shooter and those who practiced this were quite good at up to some fifteen feet, but rarely could they hit anything much over that. Nonetheless at close range, he knew they were deadly, and for many a year, never understand exactly why he did what he did next. It was totally against his nature, these men were southerners, the law here was quite obviously not, and Yankee lawmen had never been an ally of his. But still he stood and slipped his own Colt into the back of the new offender.

"Friend, you don't want to kill that no account Yankee. It'll only get you in a passel a' trouble and most likely in a noose."

The Texan slowly lowered the hammer on his revolver and let it swing down and over, now only holding it by the trigger guard. He then lifted it so Quigley could take it from him, not wanting it to fall to the floor.

"I don't want your gun mister, just didn't want you to do something that you would regret later."

"Well, I do," Masterson said, and he reached for the cut down Colt and jerked it from the man's hand.

"Obliged Mr. ___________, what is your name?"

"Hancock," was all he received as an answer, but it immediately alerted the Texan.

"Quigley Hancock?" he asked.

Quigley looked at the man and, wondered if he knew him from somewhere and deciding he did not, nodded his head as an answer.

Suddenly he could see hate form on the man's face and he never stopped staring back as they forcibly led him away.

"Take them both to jail, and Charlie, get Doc to see about that kid's head," Masterson said.

The second morning after, as he was eating his breakfast in the dining room of *The Dodge House,* he saw Somerset and two other men come in and take a table near the window. *'Surprised to see you in such a lowly place as this,'* Quigley thought,' but he said nothing and returned his attention to his steak.

Before he was finished, the door between the lobby and the dining room opened again, and he saw three men enter. Immediately he recognized two of them to be the Texans from the other night, the one still had a wide white bandage around his head with his sombrero[1] hanging down his back, they all three were healed[2]. *'I guess they ain't too impressed with Mr. Masterson's law against carrying north of the tracks,* he thought. *Well, that's alright, neither am I.'*

Immediately upon seeing him, the man he had to interfere with that night bumped his elbow against one of the others and getting his attention he nodded at Quigley. Then they all three started towards the empty table next to him.

Normally a man would not have taken this as a threat, but Hancock had not survived the past twenty years without being able to recognize things others would have thought nothing of.

Quigley knew his gun hand was not as quick as he had once been, the shoulder wound had left its mark. Not that he had failed to recover the full use of his gun-arm, for he surely had, but the speed he once possessed had not returned after taking that bullet. He also remembered the speed with which the Texan had pulled his short barreled revolver in the saloon that night.

Quigley himself had a short barreled Colt, not a cut down one, rather the newest issue without an ejector housing at all. He carried it in a cross-draw rig he had a saddle maker in Wichita do for him. Unlike most cross draw holsters that carried the gun on or about the left hip this one was designed to ride only a short distance to the left of his buckle and the stock was angled down and to the right giving him a good chance of getting a grip on it in the least amount of time, even so he knew

---

1 Sombrero: Usually refers to a hat preferred by a Mexican Vaquero, but could also be any large, brimmed hat designed to keep the sun and rain from one's neck.
2 Healed: A western term meaning armed with a gun.

he would be no match for the Texan, even if had that jasper been alone, which he was not.

Finally, they stopped in front of this table and the new man of the trio reached over with his gun hand and lifted a chair that was across the table from Quigley and moved it aside. This gesture immediately told Quigley he was not the threat the other man was.

Finally, the boy with the bandage spoke, "You Quigley Hancock?"

By now he had his Colt in his right hand under the table and in his left hand he held the ceramic cup recently filled with hot Arbuckles[3] "I'm Hancock."

"Well, you killed our brother over in Wichita last month."

Quigley now realized what this was all about and why the rancor had formed on the man's face after hearing his name in the saloon. He also realized the chances of him surviving this morning were slim so he decided he would identify these men who were bent on killing him to the witnesses who now were clearing out of the line of fire, "Then that would make you the three that robbed *The National Bank* in Wichita a few weeks back. Where's that twenty thousand in gold?" he asked.

"Twenty thousand my ass," the new man said, but it was not him Quigley was looking at, in fact he was not looking into the faces of anyone of them, he had his own eyes locked on the right hand that rested so close to that cut down Colt. The second it moved, he flung the coffee into this man's face and stood, his legs turning the table over, which caught the youngest in the wrist as he was bring up the Kerr.

Quigley's first shot hit the new man, who was to his right, below the left breast, his next round went squarely into the center man's chest and then he shot the boy, who was now recovering from the table's fall. He then placed a second round into each of them without really thinking what he was doing. It

---

3 Arbuckles: The coffee of the plains.

was not an emotional reaction, rather a ground in reaction that had saved his life so many times he could not recall.

The power of a 45 caliber 255 grain soft lead bullet being driven by 40 grains of gunpowder was sufficient to kill any man when hit in the torso, but the round balls they carried in the percussion days of the war and many years after, were not so much the man stopper. Certainly, they would kill, but not always before an adversary could get off a round at you. So it had become his practice, whenever he could, he would place at least two slugs in each of his victims. Today his hand worked from instinct, not thought. All three men had died within a second of each other and none of them had fired a shot.

The dining room was filled with blue smoke and the smell of sulfur and the astonished faces of the others who had come there that morning to enjoy a quiet breakfast.

Marshal Masterson had been on his way there for his own breakfast when the sound of gunfire erupted from *The Dodge House* and he and his deputy burst through the door before Quigley had returned his Colt to his holster.

"Hold it. I'll take that," he ordered.

Quigley had no choice, he had just opened the cylinder door to eject his spent rounds when the lawmen came in and now, he stood there with an empty gun. Just as the man had done that night in the saloon, he allowed the weight of the revolver to spin it around to where his finger was holding it by the trigger guard and nothing more. Then he laid it on the table next to him and used both hands to open his frock showing no more firearms.

"You are under arrest," Masterson yelled out.

"What for?" Cried Bill Harris a co-owner in the *Long Branch Saloon* just down the street.

"He obviously has killed three men," replied Masterson.

"All three had their guns drawn and pointed at him before he even reached for his," Harris told the Marshal.

"That's pretty hard to believe," Masterson spat back.

"Well, it's the truth," Mrs. Chalk Beeson said, backing up Harris' description of the shootings.

Seeing he was outnumbered by the witnesses the Marshal replied, "Well, maybe, but he is a vagrant and was still carrying a gun north of the deadline, and he's going to jail."

"Well, I for one am sure glad he was," Mrs. Beeson said. "If he had not it's no telling who these ruffians might have singled out next. Go ahead and jail a man for defending himself on your dumb law, it just shows the decent people of Dodge what incompetent law we have here with Deger as mayor."

"He is not a vagrant," suddenly Paul Somerset said. "He works for me and he is a detective and has a right to carry a gun. He is my personal bodyguard authorized by the Governor himself and unless you want to defy the governor, you had best not arrest him."

Masterson, seeing he was in a losing battle and not wanting the mayor to find out he had defied the governor, he backed off.

"Well, he is forwarned. Any more trouble out of him and he'll have to leave town."

"That will not be a problem, sir, we are leaving your miserable village as soon as the train pulls out," Somerset said, and then motioning for Quigley to follow him, he turned and left the hotel.

Chapter Twenty Eight

The Coulson Packet Line

Buckshot had greatly pleased Captain Marsh with his unusual ability in mathematics and his willingness to learn. Their arrival at Saint Louis was as exciting an event as any the boy could remember and when told they would travel on to New Orleans, he was extremely enthusiastic about his new life. However, it was there that he was introduced to Sallie Coulson, the owner of *The Lady Denver* who had wintered in Saint Louis with his wife. Quite soon thereafter, Buckshot learned that Coulson, Montana was named after his boss.

"That's where I'm going," he said to Ramsey Cook on the main deck as they were taking on board 200-pound bales of cotton.

"I've been there, ain't much to it," Cook replied. He never had taken a shine to the boy after he showed him up several months before, so anytime he had an opportunity to present negative news to him he would do so.

"Why is that?"

"Just another port on the Missouri, in a God forsaken part of this land. Barren, treeless, brown prairie. Nutten' more."

"That's still where I'm going," Buckshot said, not discouraged by the tale.

Sallie who also was overseeing the loading of the cotton while standing on the second deck, overheard the conversation below and notched it in his memory bank. Captain Marsh had told him of the promise the lad showed and that he intended to make an apprentice out of him. Coulson had great respect for Marsh and agreed not to interfere with the Captain's decision.

Some months later when they headed back north on the mighty Mississippi, there was both thrilling happiness and a touch of sorrow. Whitey had heard a rumor that his father had shipped out of the port here bound for England and he would most likely also come here when his ship returned. Unfortunately, his father's return was anybody's guess, so Whitey stayed in New Orleans and waved to his friend as *The Lady Denver* moved out into the main channel.

The captain saw to it that Buckshot worked a few days at every position on the boat, but most of his time was spent either studying on the charts or in the pilot house, for it was there the boy enjoyed being the most and Marsh enjoyed having him nearby.

They were just twelve miles south of Saint Louis when one night while Cook was at the wheel, they struck a snag that tore a small hole in her bow and Coulson made a decision that would ultimately alter the life of the lad.

Captain Grant had brought *The Josephine*, another of Coulson Line steamers, into port the day before, but he was sick with what turned out to be pneumonia. *The Josephine* was a Sternwheeler, wooden hull packet boat 178' x 31' x 4' with two 15-foot boilers.

Her draft being much less than *The Lady Denver*, she was used exclusively on the Missouri. What made her special to many was she had been named in honor of the daughter of Gen. Davis S. Stanley. In 1873, she went up Yellowstone River carrying supplies for Custer's Seventh Cavalry. In 1875, Captain Grant took her up the Yellowstone farther than any steamer had ever gone since, all the way to *Hell Roaring Rapids* above Pompey's Pillar, 483 miles above the river's mouth.

Later the same year, she transported Canadian troops bound for Alberta and Saskatchewan. The following year, she became part of the Sioux Wars by transporting troops of Custer, Terry, Crook, and Gibbon. By 1880 she had made forty trips to Montana, most to Ft. Benton or Coulson, and she was the pride of the Coulson Line.

With Grant too sick to captain her back north, Sallie made a transfer. Captain Marsh would take over *The Josephine'* and hopefully by the time *The Lady Denver* was repaired Captain Grant would have recovered sufficiently to captain her on the Mississippi.

Marsh did not like the transfer. He had come to know *The Old Lady*[1] and knew where to suspect her shifting sandbars. He had not shipped on the Missouri for over five years, and never had liked her to begin with.

In a letter, Buckshot managed to scribble out to Sam Brooks, he explained he thought the transfer was a God sent blessing.

> *At last, I will get to Montana and perhaps*
> *find Reb Brown. After all that is why I left in the*
> *first place.*

He also told Mr. Sam that Ananias had died and was given a proper burial; however, he failed to explain how all of this came about or was accomplished.

---

[1] The Old Lady: An affectionate nickname for the Mississippi River.

I'm making a little money now that I work on the riverboat and if you will let me know the value of that mule, I will send the money to you. You know Mr. Reb Brown said I should always pay my debts. You can reach me by posting a letter to Second Mate Buckshot Gunter % of The Coulson Packet Line, Coulson Montana or to the same at Saint Louis.

Chapter Twenty Nine

Miles Abbey

Miles Abbey had been born on the ship enroute from England. His mother was a felon that had been convicted of killing a local tavern owner who she claimed was assaulting her at the time. Since she could not prove the assault had taken place, and since the magistrate could prove she had killed the man, she was sentenced to the gallows, or if she so chose, she could go to the new world where she would serve a sentence of seven years as an indentured servant to a royal family.

She chose not to go to the gallows and in the fall of 1831, she and her new-born son arrived at Road Town on the isle of Tortola. Although the emancipation act of the British Empire came along three years later, it did not apply to felons as they were not classified as slaves, rather servants and therefore Sir Chapman Abbey, the good friend of President William Rogers Isaacs, retained possession of the wench Fern and her child.

Sir Chapman was the owner of a huge beet plantation, but his passion was in the manufacture of 'The Abbey Schooner' a

Tortola Sloop constructed in his ship building plant using the fine white cedar found on the island. It would be there young Miles would earn his keep until the day he shipped out aboard one of Sir Chapman's larger Schooners bound for Cárdenas in the isle of Cuba.

A year later he was in Saint Augustine, Florida and still later in the port of Charleston in time to see the firing on Fort Sumter. He had never known his real name, either first or last; his mother had simply called him Miles until she died of malaria when he was six, but being the property of Sir Chapman, he took on the surname of Abbey.

In late May he offered his service to the pioneering Confederate Navy and soon shipped out on the *CSS Sumter* bound for raiding duties. During the next year, *The Sumter* would capture twelve ships flying the stars and stripes on the open sea, until she was interned at Gibraltar for repairs and subsequently sold in December of '62.

Soon thereafter she became the British cruiser *The Gibraltar* and continued her service to the Confederacy flying a Union Jack rather than a Confederate Jack.

In the spring of '63 after running the blockade around the mouth of the Mississippi, she unloaded her cargo of British small arms and powder before again taking to the high seas with a load of cotton, easily outrunning her pursuers. It was while she was in New Orleans that Miles Abbey, having a relapse of the disease that took his mother, departed ship's company. Six months later he was riding with Shelby near Shreveport.

Abbey had not joined the Confederacy because he owned slaves or even believed in the ownership of slaves, he was in Charleston at the time the first shots were fired and became swept up in the emotion of the event. There was also his natural dislike for the African and the very idea of making one a citizen galled him to the bone.

He took great pleasure in confronting colored troops in the field and was twice reprimanded by superior officers for his unnatural cruelty to such in a blue uniform.

Miles also spit a stream of tobacco between the boots of one of the officers who had just told him that over 80,000 coloreds had joined the Confederate Army and were serving well on the fields of battle, something he did not want to hear.

With the coming of the wars end, he happened to be at the same location Quigley Hancock was and participated in his first postwar raid on the stage carrying the Union payroll from Corpus Christy to Austin.

During the years he had ridden under the command of *The Arkansas Avenger,* he had not always been the ideal soldier. His hatred for the African, which seemed to have its birth in the island of his childhood where the darkies outnumbered the whites fifteen to one and this hatred soon transferred to anything Union and often resulted in a shoot first and talk later attitude. However, his uncanny devotion to proper discipline within the ranks and his seemingly ignorance of fear, made him a valuable man and one Quigley used often on his own raids of revenge.

It was also Miles Abbey who had been the one to shoot the second *WT* man who was roping fence posts. Billy Bowdrie fell to a single shot fired from Abbey's 45 Winchester less than a week after he began working for Somerset. Unofficially, there would be an extra fifty in the monthly payroll for every *WT* man they could account for, and when he received his pay at the end of the month, the others saw it was true. The war had indeed begun.

Chapter Thirty

Summer Snows

Ryan Rodriquez rode his horse along slowly following the walking Mendoza Haeckel and the herd of sheep across the Sweetwater River. They finally reached the land claimed by Karl Siebold during the first week of June 1880 and a sense of pride and accomplishment seemed to rain down on him. It was the first time in his life he had ever endured so long a journey or so long a task.

The high plains were still quite cool, and a two-inch snow fell on them just as they met Siebold. It was obvious the mountains to the north were getting a heavy coat of the wet snow. Siebold causally mentioned that it was a blessing to the land for this much moisture arriving so late in the season and promised of fine grazing grass for two months to come, which was appreciated by all who knew of such things. Ryan only thought of how wet he was and how much he had learned to hate snow.

The boy had never really been taught much about handguns. His father had them of course, but they were costly and the ammunition even more, so he had learned much more about the usage of a knife and had honed this knowledge into an art.

He could throw his knife with the precision most could a rock and for reasons known only to him, it always arrived at its intended target point first, little matter the distance. However, at the time he arrived at Fort Bowie he carried a rifle and would for the remainder of his life. A rifle meant security on the plains, but the use of a pistola' was as foreign to him as a bullwhip was to a storekeeper.

He would be tending some of Mr. Siebold's sheep who had roamed into the foothills near a small waterhole late one afternoon when the outline of a lone rider was seen approaching from the east. Ryan quickly lowered himself behind an unusually large bush of greasewood and waited for the man to come within a recognizable distance before he would make the decision to expose himself or not.

Once the rider was close enough that Ryan realized he was not a marauding Indian, he realized also he had never seen this man before and thought it best to hug the ground a while longer. He did not have to wait long to see the wisdom in his thinking for the cowboy rode straight into the small flock of sheep and began shooting them with his handgun.

After five rounds had been spent the shooter opened the loading gate and began ejecting his spent rounds. It was then Ryan rose and started for him.

The sound of his sandals striking the hard clay was heard by the rider and he whirled his bronc around to see what was approaching. Stacy Beck had no idea there was anyone nearby to witness his deed and upon seeing the young, dark skinned lad who was now running straight at him caused the transplanted Texan to feel the need not to leave anyone alive to report against him.

Kicking his spur into the side of the chestnut gelding he was mounted upon caused the horse to give a quick sidestep and then he started off. When he was far enough he felt sure the boy would not reach him, he reined up, turned back and began reloading his revolver. He had just finished and looked up from his task when the knife struck him in the solar plexus burying itself to the brass split-guard.

Stacy looked surprised at the crude wooden handle that now protruded from his chest never once feeling any pain. He unknowingly released his grip on the Remington and it fell away to the ground as he pulled with both hands at the mesquite handle, but for some strange reason his strength was failing him.

Soon after the intruder died, Ryan quickly drove the remainder of the small flock back towards the main herd carrying the Remington with him as evidence of what had happened.

Mendoza relayed his story to Señor Siebold who immediately gathered a few of his men and headed back to see just where this had taken place. Upon finding Beck several miles west of the Powder they decided to take his body back and bury him where the sheep could walk over the grave hiding his final resting place for a century.

The chestnut strolled into the *WT*'s western line camp just at sundown, riderless. Dakota was the first to notice him standing near the corral gate waiting for someone to open it so he could get to the feed trough. "Het, ain't that the mount Stacy took this morning?"

Curley quick-paced over and looked at the animal, "Yeah, and there is a considerable amount of dried blood on the saddle and fenders."

"Damn, Stacy must be in bad shape."

Curley shook his head slowly, "From the looks of this, he's dade."

There were only four men riding out of this shack, so Dave Dawson headed back to the main ranch with the news while Curley and Dakota took torches and tried to back track the horse.

They eventually found the bloody stain on the ground and the five dead sheep but nothing else and since they were over five miles west of the riverbed, they decided it best to not be found by whoever caught Stacy killing sheep, so they high tailed it back to *WT* land as fast as they could in the dark.

Chapter Thirty One

Poison Spider

There was not much in the little burg known as Poison Spider, a tall two-story hotel run by Joe Marquis, a general store and saloon, a livery with a corral, a blacksmith and wheelwright shop, placed there by the stage line so necessary repairs could be made when needed.

The store was owned by a brother-in-law of the Searight brothers who had the Goose Egg Ranch[1] some forty miles east. The saloon was owned by Sunny Tomson, but it was rumored that Paul Somerset was a silent partner.

The location of Poison Spider was on the stage road which ran between Bessemer and Lander with the stage stop being housed in the hotel along with the post office. It was also where Doctor Smyth roomed and plied his trade.

There was even some who said that Marquis ran the hotel for Somerset, but he never admitted this and had it been true, it is doubtful any of Siebold's hands would have been welcome in either of these establishments.

---

[1] The Goose Egg brand: used mostly on the remuda stock, with the Flying E being the brand used on the Searight brothers' beeves.

There was a girl named Marietta, who worked her own trade out of Tomson's place. Marietta was the queen of The Big Open in the 1880's. In fact she was the only single woman within 40 miles. She was in her twenties; and not the prettiest female who worked a saloon, but she looked fine on Saturday nights and many a puncher promised his month's wages for thirty minutes with her alone.

Etta, as she was known to the boys, also sold something else that made her more money than did her day job, so to speak, and that was information to Paul Somerset.

It was through her he learned about Siebold hiring his gun hawks and later about Miles Abbey being the killer of Sedgwick and Bowdrie. However, she never did find out what happened to Stacy Beck and this outraged Somerset.

One night at *The Poison Spider Hotel*, after she repeatedly told him she couldn't find out anything on Stacy, he became convinced she was holding out and was now also in the pay of Siebold. In a rage he beat her badly about the face scaring her for life.

Etta would have gone back to Cheyenne if she had the stage fare, but while she was unconscious Somerset had found her stash and took it with him, not as an act of thievery rather to keep her in her place. A few days later he realized he had made a big mistake for she was his best source of information, so he returned her money, but in the meantime, he made certain Marquis would inform him if she tried to take the stage out of town.

When Somerset returned to The Big Open from his journey to Kansas, he arrived with ten men, all wearing strapped down guns on their hips, some toting more than one. Included in the latter was Quigley Hancock. He, along with the others were told another outfit in the area had acquired the majority of his stock by means of a wide loop[2] and the lack of local law left it up to the ranchers to take care of the problem themselves.

---

[2] Throwing a Wide Loop: A western term meaning the rustling of cattle.

It made sense to Quigley, such was not uncommon on the range. In fact, he knew a large number of the big spreads had started the same way, and if the pedigree could be traced on most of the beeves along the border, the searcher would find they had Mexican ancestors, so Somerset's story was quite believable.

Quigley had at one time, back when he was living on the Scott farm, decided to no longer sell his gun, but after leaving her presence that idea had gradually slipped into the shadows of his mind, especially after the shootings in Kansas and the fact Paul Somerset had helped him out. He would ride for the brand[3] and that would be all there was to it.

On the third of July while several ranches in The Big Open were preparing for the Independence Day picnic and dance, scheduled to be held at Red Bluff Station, Quigley and Dakota were riding line along the east side of the dry riverbed when a shot rang out with the bullet cutting one of Dakota's reins just below his horse's neck.

They never saw the shooter and the wind was blowing so hard no smoke could be seen, but they both knew it had come from the west and that was *K—S* land.

Immediately both cleared the saddle, and after a while Quigley suggested Dakota mount up and hightail it back east, while he would wait there in the cut in case someone came to investigate their accuracy.

It seemed like a good plan to Dakota as he wanted to get clear of the gully anyway, but it was only a waste of time for Quigley. Eventually, after sundown, he moved over on the west side of the dry wash and began a wide circle looking for tracks. Finally he cut a trail that appeared to be fresh and he followed it straight as an arrow for several miles until he lost it on the stage road half a mile from Poison Spider.

---

3 Ride for the brand: An expression meaning a man would be loyal to the outfit he was accepting pay from.

Being bull headed, he heeled Apache and rode right up to the saloon where four horses, strange to him, were tied, one a tall sorrel, was still damp from a recent trot, but from which direction it had come was only a guess.

Quigley was wearing his long-barreled Colt on his hip; he preferred it when he was on horseback as anything he must shoot at would most likely be at a distance beyond his point shooting ability.

Before walking up to the doors he slipped the latigo tie-down from around the hammer, lifted the revolver, and let it drop back in the holster.

Then walking up to the swinging doors he stopped and looked inside. Two men were standing together at the long bar and two more were seated at one of the three tables. A slim girl in a short dress was walking their direction with a bottle and two glasses in her hand.

When he pushed the doors open the spring on one of the hinges squealed signaling its use, and everyone in the room turned and looked his direction, it was then he recognized Miles Abbey.

"Well I'll be damned," the man at the table said. "Look who the wind blew in."

This did little to turn the interest of the others from him and he wasn't sure if he liked the attention or not.

"My, you are a big one," Etta said as he slowly walked up to the table she was serving.

He just smiled and touched the brim of his hat before looking at his old confederate. "It do appear to be a small world at that," he finally said.

"Here sit and _______," Miles paused looking down and then turned to the girl who was still staring at the large man. "Etta, go get Quigley a glass, Honey, before he dries up and blows away."

'I doubt that,' she thought, but she did go back behind the crude bar and retrieve another shot glass.

It was then a big man came in through a backdoor and walked behind the bar. Quigley watched him for a few seconds analyzing him as a potential threat, but finally decided he was too overweight to be fast enough to be much of a bother, so he turned his conscious attention back to Miles and the other man sitting there.

Finally after a few minutes, during which Miles introduced Sidney McMullin, he got around to the question they all knew was coming sooner or later, "You working these parts?"

"Yeah, for the *WT*," Quigley said.

"Yeah, it figures," Miles said back.

"You?"

"The *K—S.*"

Quigley just nodded his head a couple of times as nothing more needed saying on the subject.

"What brings you to town tonight? I would think all you *WT* boys would be headed in for the dance tomorrow."

"Not all of us," Quigley replied as he looked up at the girl who had returned with his glass and then remained standing just to his left.

"You want to sit and have a drink?" he asked her.

"Sure," she said back pulling out the last chair.

"Hell, Etta you might as well cool off. Quigley is too old to pay your price."

"Not necessarily so," Quigley said back although he really was not interested in what she was selling. "I'm not as old as you, Miles."

"Yeah, you always said that, but I ain't sure."

It was obvious both men were testing the waters not unlike two dogs, which had been raised to fight their own kind to the death, would circle each other waiting for the upper hand before they made their lunge.

Finally Abbey said, "You never said what brought you in tonight."

"I trailed that sorrel tied up outside from Powder River and this is where he led me."

Quigley knew it was a live round and by him tossing it out, he waited for it to explode, which didn't take long.

"I ain't been no whar's near Powder River today," McMullan busted out, standing as he spoke and reaching his hand across to the butt of his Colt. When he stood his chair turned over and crashed to the floor again bringing everyone's attention in their direction.

"Easy Sidney," Miles said quickly. "You don't want to draw on Quigley. He'll beat you and then we will have to get someone else to replace you."

"You got a lot of faith in me, Miles."

"I've seen you both in action and believe, me you don't want to pursue this."

Slowly the younger man uncoiled and let his arm drop back to his side. "I still ain't been near Powder River."

"I guess I could have been mistaken," Quigley said letting the puncher keep his face in front of the woman. Then after downing his drink he added, "Well, I guess I have caused enough of a disturbance in here tonight, I'll be headin' on back east."

"Sorry to see you here working for the *WT*, Quigley."

"Yeah," he replied nodding his head, as he also was sorry to see Abbey on the opposite side, knowing it was likely sooner or later he would have to draw a bead on an old ally.

Chapter Thirty-Two

Montana at Last

Laramie Patay was in *McAndow's Saloon* when several men, obviously from the steamer that had docked earlier that day, came through the doors.

He never liked riverboat men; they were loud and always seemed to be looking down their noses at prairie folk. This bunch was no different especially the older man who they called Captain.

Finally, Perry walked up to the bar where the six men were standing and asked, "Alright Captain Marsh, what did you bring us this time?"

"A boat load of supplies for this God Forsaken frontier. But for you McAndow, I brung twenty barrels of Tennessee sour mash."

"Well, now we can sure use that," the owner of the saloon replied.

It was then Laramie heard it. At first, he was not sure he had heard it right, but as the conversation continued on the subject, he knew he was right.

"Do you know a Mr. Reb Brown from Georgia?" the new boy asked.

"I do. I surely do. Ain't seen him in quite a spell, but I do know him," replied the saloon owner.

Buckshot became very excited, "I come all the way from Florida to find him."

Laramie stood then and moved over closer listing more intensely.

"You don't know where he's gone do you?"

"Naw, can't rightly say I do, it's been a year or two."

The boy suddenly had mixed emotions. He had made it to Coulson Montana, it was where he started out to go with a squirrel rifle he had long since lost possession of, a mule that died on him, and thirty-eight dollars and four bits which had run out before he got north of Atlanta, but he had made it and fulfilled half his goal. Only it appeared Mr. Reb Brown was no longer there and that was depressing.

Laramie watched the lad as he lowered his head and moved away from the bar and start for the door.

"I know Reb Brown," Laramie said as Buckshot slowly walked past where he now sat.

The lad's head shot up and his whole face lit up. "You do?"

"Yep, he's my friend."

"Where can I find him?"

Laramie shook his head a couple of times before he answered, "He left here two year back."

"Do you know where he went?"

"No, I remember him saying he was headed south, but not back to Georgia."

"South, just south?"

"Well, I'm not sure, but maybe Wyoming."

"Wyoming?" Buckshot said, "Anywhere in Wyoming?"

"Pine something, Pine Bluff or something like that."

"You ever been on a riverboat?"

"Naw, I never had much use for boats."

"Would you mind coming with me, there are charts and maps on *The Josephine*, maybe we can locate where he went, on one of them."

The idea seemed exciting to Laramie. It was true he never had much use for boats, but he had never been on a big boat like the steamer docked down on the Yellowstone. Suddenly he wanted very much to go aboard her. "Sure, if I can help," he answered.

They looked over several charts and maps but found nothing in Wyoming that looked like Pine Bluff. Finally Buckshot located a new map on Captain Marsh's table that slowed a Big Piney Wyoming and there he pointed his finger, "Could that be it?"

"Yeah, maybe. I still seem to remember Pine Bluff."

"Well, there maybe be bluffs around this Big Piney that ain't on this map, it ain't all that detailed."

"Yeah, you're right, it ain't, but I see the Arapaho Reservation there, near Fort Washakie, that's where I'm headed."

"Really, why?"

"'Cause my mother may be there."

"Oh, is you mother a' Injun?"

"No. She is French, but she was captured by the Arapaho four years ago and I hear tell she might be there," he paused remembering what he had heard about the white woman who refused to be found by the army and he was embarrassed, he finished the sentence with, "being held as a prisoner."

"Oh, that's awful," Buckshot said then he added, "My mother is dead, she was murdered by nigger soldiers back in Georgia.[1]"

"Oh, that's awful, too."

"Yeah, but Mr. Reb Brown found them and hung them for what they did to her," Buckshot added as a final justification.

"I wish he had killed the ones what took my mother."

---

1 See the death of Tillie Gunter in *The Withlacoochee Renegades,* book two of *The Owl Hoot Trail.*

"I bet he would if we could find him. He's the best tracker I ever knew," Buckshot said.

Laramie thought of Black Band and remembered that even Reb Brown had said the old Crow was better at tracking than any man he ever saw, but decided he would not contradict Buckshot. Rather he asked, "Say, you want to go with me? Maybe we can find Reb and then he can help me find my mother."

The idea seemed really great for a moment, but then he thought of his responsibility to Captain Marsh and Sallie Coulson and his apprenticeship as a riverboat pilot. "Gee I'd like to, but I don't really think I can, I owe a lot of people."

"Oh, I understand," Laramie said back suddenly remembering Blackcat and Ginny back on Blackcat Creek and he, too, felt suddenly sad.

The events that took place in the next few hours were so unlikely that no one could have predicted them, or their outcome.

Bitterroot Whitehead, a trapper who took his name from the valley he loved so, got into it with one of the ship's crew in the saloon and when Captain Marsh tried to stop the fracas, Bitterroot sliced him across the middle with a Green River blade sending Buckshot's mentor to the floor bleeding badly.

Although he would survive the wound, he would not be able to sail for several weeks, thus Ramsey Cook was given the duty of taking *The Josephine* back down river, before the ice closed the Yellowstone until spring.

Buckshot, knowing he would not be able to withstand several months under the supervision of Ramsey asked to stay with Captain Marsh in Montana. *The Josephine* left on September the twelfth and made it almost thirty miles before Cook ran her up on a sandbar. Sallie, having no patience for incompetence, removed Cook and decided he would take the boat back to Saint Louis himself.

Buckshot took this all as, perhaps being one of God's mysterious moves his mother had often spoke about, and that in reality it had all taken place so he might have the time to go to Wyoming and find Reb Brown. Thus he decided he would, after all, travel with his new friend, Laramie, down to Wyoming. It would be May, perhaps June before Sallie returned with the steamer, so he had plenty of time to get back to Coulson.

Chapter Thirty Three

Old Loyalties

Marietta never forgot the beating she had taken by the hand of Paul Somerset and from that day forward, worked as secretive as she could to hurt him in return. She had little means to do this being stuck there so far from anywhere with no real avenue of escape, but the range war that had begun in The Big Open was the one topic on everyone's mind. In almost every conversation taking place in Poison Spider, no matter how big or how small, and it was through this she made up her mind to get back at Somerset.

The hands on both sides would find the little village of Poison Spider a desirable place to spend their month's wages, even though it was west of the dry riverbed, known year-round as Powder River, and therefore on land claimed by the *K—S*.

For one to say there were never any confrontations in Poison Spider would be a misleading thought, for surely anytime a bunch of hormone-filled boys, of the age most of the punchers were on those ranches, were thrown together and filled with bad whiskey, there would be trouble, but this small five-acre square seemed to be neutral ground for the war, for the most part.

There was something about Miles Abbey that a lot of women found magnifying and Marietta was no different. However, she realized what she had become and knew equally well she should not plan on being someone's loving wife, even though several of the cowboys had proposed to her when they were drunk and broke. Such promises had not come from the more mature, and certainly not from Abbey or Hancock.

Still since Abbey worked for the *K—S*, Somerset's main enemy, she began feeding him little bits of information she would collect in her nights at the saloon and hotel. Most of the small pieces meant little, but every once and a while one paid off and just such occurred on the night before *The Josephine* steamed out of Coulson where some two hundred and fifty miles to the south Miles Abbey was atop a little hill overlooking Powder River.

Marietta had told him she had overheard some of the *WT* boys laughing about stampeding as many of *K—S* beeves as they could east, onto their side of the dry wash, then cutting out all the unbranded calves, maverick or not, and burning the *WT* on them before running them back. This would create a hell of a problem for the *K—S*. Those calves still sucking would follow their mothers and soon be well planted deep on Siebold's land, only branded with the *WT,* and a claim of rustling could ensue, and Karl Siebold would have a hard time explaining so many of his herd bearing the *WT* brand.

Miles Abbey had to admit it was a good plan, one that could cause a lot of worry and perhaps more to his boss if they could pull it off, but he and a few of the boys decided they would put a burr in Somerset's plan if they could.

Word was the raid was suppose to take place Sunday night while Somerset was in Lander. Since the moon would be in its first quarter and rising shortly after sundown, they expected the raiders to come early and were there waiting for them.

If one could look at this country from afar, they might judge it to be mostly flat, but that would be a misconception. It is far more rolling than meets the eye, filled with small gulches and abyss here and there. Occasionally, one might see a few squatty trees struggling to survive, where the winds of winter drifted snow deep enough to allow the twigs to become saplings. None of these grew very tall and most never lasted beyond a season or two.

It was atop a short rise behind a few of these excuses for trees that Miles and four of the boys were keeping a vigil for the nightriders they expected to be heading for the low cut in the riverbanks.

For the most part the dry riverbed lay ten or more feet below the run of the plains along there, but years ago at the time of the year where it would destroy these banks, a large herd of buffalo had crossed this precise location and their thousands of strong hooves had rolled the banks down. Now when the early summer thaws occurred in the Big Horns, this area became a rather large lake, at least for this country. Of course, that had been several months past and now it only offered a nice gradual slope on which a rider could traverse Powder River at scarcely less than a trot.

Miles was sure if Marietta's information had been good, the night raiders would come through here, and it was here he watched and listened for the sound of men and horses. But his wait was long and disappointing for the moon was high and the night cold, without a sign of anything moving save a couple of small wolves working the riverbanks trying to flush a Jack.

This night had indeed been the time Paul Somerset had ordered this to occur, for he had accompanied the Widow Barns and her brother to church in Lander that day and would stay over at *The Wind River Hotel,* playing poker until well past midnight.

However, there had been a hitch at the main ranch over a hundred miles from Lander. Chuck Bitler, Somerset's foreman, picked out seven men to go on this raid but one of them was not there at the appointed time and this caused some delay in their getting off.

Quigley Hancock was riding the south line that morning when Apache had a shoe work loose and being so partial to the gelding, he refused to ride him on, for fear of laming the big animal. As a result, he was two hours late walking in, by this time Bitler had branded him a coward and selected Dingus as a replacement.

Miles Abbey had waited out in the cold night air just about as long as he intended to and had already replaced his Winchester in its scabbard when Andy turned his ear to the dull sound. "Listen," he said and turning to the east, everyman there stopped and did likewise.

They could hear little above the never laying wind of The Big Open as it swept its way along the prairie being interrupted by little more than the short sage and scattered greasewood or rabbit brush which seemed to cover this land as if it were planted. Finally, just as he himself began to give it up as a bad idea, Andy again heard something way off in the distance. "There I heard something again."

Once more they stopped and gave attention to the idea, but with short patience now Miles said, "I think you are hearing the bells of Marietta's ear bobs jingling," and both Chris Morgan and Dusty laughed, but Perry Taylor stopped them.

"No wait, he's right. I heard something too, way off yonder," he said, nodding in the moonlight towards where they expected the raiders to be coming from.

Finally, Miles heard it too. "Alright get your rifles and get behind cover and wait. No one fires a shot until I do. Understood?" he said without expecting a reply.

Gradually, as if they were ghost images, the seven riders began to materialize out of the night, coming at a steady trot and heading straight to the flattened banks of Powder River, just as Miles had predicted.

Dingus was a young kid, barely twenty years old from Colorado. He had moved there with his parents shortly after the war. His Pa had rode north working as a hand on a drive from the Brazos country of Texas and liked the looks of the land east of Cherry Creek. Then with his earnings, he returned and brought his family, where he homesteaded a little patch of ground on West Bijou Creek.

The Snow Ranch was begun in the early seventies near Rockland's land and he was soon to be the employer of Curtis Jackson, and later it was on *The Snow Ranch* Dingus learned his trade as a cowhand.

Dingus was exceptionally large for his age and most of the boys liked the Baby Huey of their outfit. This night he felt quite proud when Bitler chose him to replace Hancock, and his chest even swelled larger when, just before they reached the river, the foreman called him up to his side and told him, "As soon as we are across, I want you to take the point keeping a keen eye out for Siebold's beeves."

"Yes, Sur," Dingus replied.

Miles watched the two lead riders drop down into the wash and then back up; it was obvious a very large man was side riding the leader and he could think of but one man who fit that description.

"I'm sorry to do this Quigley, but you are getting rather careless in your old age," he said just under his breath.

"You say something?" Perry asked.

"The big one's mine," was the only comment he received for an answer.

Miles lifted his long barrel high and aimed at the moon, adjusting his sight alignment, before he slowly lowered it back to the big rider who was coming up the shallow bank. Holding his sight picture until each and every one of them was on the west side, before he began applying pressure to his trigger.

The sound of the big round exploding in the night air sounded like thunder, but Dingus never heard it. He simply threw both arms high in the air and arched forward before he fell from his now charging horse.

Every one of the bushwhackers had a sight picture on one of the riders before Abbey's rifle had sounded the alarm, some aiming at the same man, and in the next few seconds three more of the *WT* men fell near the body of Dingus Rockland. The others tried to whirl their now bucking broncs around and head for cover, back down the river some half a mile where the banks offered slight protection from the singing lead that seemed to fill the air.

The same bullet that passed through Dingus' neck, robbing him of future life, took Chuck Bitler's hat off. He realized from the number of shots fired, they had ridden into an ambush. Immediately, he spurred his mount and rolled of the left side of the saddle keeping one foot in the stirrup and clinging with a death grip using both hands on the horn, he rode away on what appeared to be a riderless horse charging from the sudden noise.

When Bitler was a couple hundred yards away he swung back up and laid low, making as dim a silhouette as possible for another hundred yards, and then by gently twisting his left wrist, he turned his bay in a sweeping turn to the south.

Paul Spalding had hired on with the *WT* when Somerset was recruiting pistoleros in Kansas and came north with Hancock. This night he was next to the last to ride out of the dry bed and up on the prairie before the first shot rang out.

In the following confusing moments, a 44 passed below his collarbone and lodged itself in the muscle of his left shoulder. He fell from his horse and crawled back down the slight bank and then north, away from where his friends were headed, there he lay and waited.

The whole affair had not taken a full minute from the time Abbey killed Rockland until the last round was shot, that being a futile attempt fired from one of the *WT* riders as he thundered away to the south.

Spalding had located the shooters from their muzzle flashes, and it was there he was staring when slowly the ambushers rose and walked forward to inspect their game. He could hear them talking, although he could not understand every word, he did hear one of them tell the others to look for any not dead and upon hearing this, he figured if located he would have to shoot it out with the four of them, odds that he did not like at all.

Finally, after each of the bodies were inspected the same voice again spoke, "Catch up their horses if you can, and let's take them deeper onto *K—S* land before we dump them. And look through those saddle bags for a running iron."

Spalding remembered Will Beach was carrying the branding iron and wondered if his was one of the bodies laying there staining the desert sand.

The last thing he heard for sure was one of the *K—S* men saying, "That sure was a good tip you got Miles."

Later when Bitler made his way back to the *WT* bunkhouse he saw Hancock there sleeping and he deliberately made enough noise to awaken the man. Looking over at the foreman, who was adding split wood to the potbelly, Quigley asked, "How did it go?"

"Well, you can be proud you weren't there, most of the boys won't be coming back."

"What happened?" the big man asked, swinging his legs off the side of his bunk and reaching for his makin's.

"Dry gulched, right there at Powder River, it was like they knew we wus coming," he said and then looking off at the far wall, he thought, *'Hell yes they sure as hell knew we wus coming, had to have.'*

"Where the hell wus you? You wus supposed to be here before sundown."

"Horse come up with a loose shoe," Quigley said back. "You was already gone some time, a'for I got in."

"Yeah, that might a saved your life. Better kiss that horse come morning."

Bitler did not want to get into a fight with Hancock. The man was much bigger than he was, and he sure as hell didn't want to get into gun slinging with him. He already heard about how Quigley had handled three brothers single-handedly when they jumped him in Dodge, so he just let it lay with what he had already said, but he wanted to call him a coward to his face as he had done to his back.

Around two in the morning, Christy King limped in on a horse that had a bullet high in its left hip, a bloody hole, but not one he could not recover from, if they could keep the blow flies off it until it healed.

Christy had been the one to fire the last shot as he rode away down the wash, but he had not been able to ride his mount very much because of the bullet wound and had walked more than half the way back.

The next morning Bitler took a dozen men and rode back to where the ambush took place, but only found the remains of one dead *K—S* horse and it was some distance from the scene. Even the blood stains had been covered over. It was on their way back that they came upon Paul Spalding walking east towards the ranch. Somehow, they had missed him on their journey out earlier that day.

Miles had been both surprised and a little relieved when they turned over the body and he saw it was not his old leader. He could not say he liked Quigley Hancock, but he did respect him. Hancock was the deadliest man he had ever ridden with and if Quigley knew fear, Miles had never seen it. Although he did know Quigley was a little soft at times, nevertheless he did not really wish to be the man who put him under and although, as he had shown, if the job called for that, he would do it. Still, he did not relish the chore.

The four victors headed straight for the saloon at Poison Spider after dumping the bodies in a dry gulch some eight miles on west of Powder River and there, as the whiskey flowed, so did the tale and Sunny Tomson had a full confession within an hour, should he be one to remember such things.

After they had been talking about the four dead men for a while, and laughing as if they had simply won a great sporting event, Marietta asked, "Was one of the dead Quigley Hancock?" Upon learning he was not, she seemed obviously relieved, an expression that did not go unnoticed by Abbey.

Chapter Thirty Four

The Sunken Cabin

Karl Seibold had divided his range land into roughly two areas, one for his cattle and the other for the sheep. He knew the sheep would require more grass than the beeves, but he looked at them as a two-crop investment. There were rumors of wool sheering pens, after the fashion done in Australia, being built near the Colorado border and he envisioned doing the same here on the *K—S*. His intentions were to sheer the grown sheep before slaughtering them for mutton and retaining the lambs for the next year's crop. Although mutton did not bring as much per pound as beef, it mattered not, all in all his sheep would bring him more profit than did his steers and profit was what it was all about.

Mendoza Haeckel did not like Wyoming very much. It looked not so different than Mexico, or Texas or Arizona, only colder, much colder. The wind here would bite savagely as early as October and he knew that as the winter came on, its bite would be much worse. But he did like working for Mr. Siebold. The man had paid him a fair price for his sheep, much more than he would have gotten selling them back in Mexico and had never failed to see they had the necessary provisions for his camps. He and the boy mostly ran the sheep west and farther north than where the punchers ran the cattle, thereby keeping several miles between them and *WT* riders.

Many years before, after striking a small amount of color along a creek that drained the thaw from the Big Horns, a few miners built a cabin along the stream where they could survive the winter and continue in their efforts in recovering the precious yellow rock. It was a good cabin for the times, dug seven foot deep and then covered mostly with lodge poles crisscrossed tightly then topped with rock. A short door was left to the creek side and at least one rifle port on each side between the roof and the level ground of the plains, just in case. From a distance of less than a hundred feet one could walk past it and never realize it was anything more than a short mound of rocks, unless smoke was seen escaping from below.

Mendoza chanced upon the cabin quite by accident one day when a lamb fell into its dark interior through an opening dug between the rocks on the roof, by a badger sometime in the past.

With more time on their hands than anything else, he and Ryan began working on the old dugout until they had it once again livable and a wonderful place to escape the never-ending icy winds that cut to the bone.

Once satisfied with their personal castle they packed to never share its location, or even its being, with another soul.

Although the wagon was their main abode, easing along with the sheep as they grazed off an area as they slowly moved on to new grass, their little secret was an ace in the hole, should the winter storms become too severe or should the Indians again begin their raiding on The Big Open.

Late December brought a storm thus far not seen that year. The wind picked up a little before full dark and soon thereafter, came the blinding snow. Within two hours the white powder covered the plains with a four-inch blanket and Mendoza decided it was time to utilize their ace in the hole and he along with Nombre Bola, their ever-faithful dog, steered the flock towards the creek near where their cabin lay.

The snow continued all that night and all the next day and only subsided sometime after midnight on the second night. The following dawn brought the brightest morning Ryan had ever seen. Unknowingly, they had hovered around the small fire, there in the cabin, throughout the eve of Christ's day.

Chapter Thirty Five

Christmas

Buckshot also thought Christmas morning was the brightest he had ever seen. The alcohol thermometer rested at twenty-five below, hanging there on the front porch of the sutlers store at Cantonment Reno.

It was hard for him to believe it. Being raised in Florida, where it was severely cold when the temperature dropped below twenty degrees, and here he stood with it twenty-five degrees below zero, the worst he had ever experienced, and he really didn't feel all that cold.

He had bought a long coat from the sutler that had been made from the hide of a buffalo and although it was a little long on him, he was quite satisfied to stand there and breathe in the icy air and view the white blanket that covered everything he could see in every direction, save the mountains ahead. Hearing a lot of banging going on behind the store, he stepped off the porch to investigate. The sound of his boots crunching the ice-covered powder was also something new to him and he smiled at the thought as he walked around the log building to where he could see three men in blue, one was swinging a double bitted axe trying to break through the ice that covered Clear Creek, while his two buddies made jokes at his effort.

Buckshot also smiled as he thought, *'These are Yankee Soldiers, not so different than the ones we had to kill when they invaded Estherbrook.'*

Suddenly he remembered how he himself had hid in the fork of a large magnolia tree while the Yankees walked single file under him enroute to attack his home and how he had shot the last in line with his 22 Remington squirrel rifle. The vision of Mr. Reb Brown patting him on the shoulder and telling him what a good shot he was, brought a warm feeling to his insides. The fact he had fallen asleep that morning while on scout duty had long since been clouded over and tucked away in the back of his mind[1].

"You better get back inside 'less you get frostbit," Laramie warned.

Turning, he saw his friend leaning over the rail of the front porch and reprimanding the easterner.

"Frostbit, what's that?"

"That's when your fingers and toes fall off and sometimes your nose."

"Augh hell, it ain't that cold," Buckshot said back.

Laramie leaned back a few seconds and then reappeared, "This here thermometer says it's twenty below."

"Twenty-five," Buckshot corrected.

"Alright, twenty-five. Now come on back inside you ain't even got on no gauntlets."

He did have to admit his hands were beginning to sting, so he decided not to argue anymore and do as Laramie suggested.

Carey Johnson, the sutler at Reno, said he, too, had heard of a white woman living with an Arapahoe buck, but shook his head when asked if he had ever seen her. "Naw, if it is true

---

[1] See: *The Withlacoochee Renegades* book two of the *Owl Hoot Trail* trilogy.

and mind you, I doubt it in this age, she would not be allowed around those what might tell the army on her. A injun could get himself hung fur such these days."

"I was told they stayed on the reservation at Fort Washake."

"There be Shoshone there, they hate the Arap as much as they do the Cheyenne. Don't seem likely."

"No, Sur, you are wrong there," a soldier interrupted. "We put 'em both there together come last spring," he nodded his head as if he approved with his statement. "I reckon the government figures they will fight it out and kill each other off so we won't have to feed 'em no more."

"So, there are Arapahoe on the reservation?" Laramie asked, pleased with this new knowledge.

"You bet there is, plenty a 'em," the man said and then he gave his head a quick twist as if some bad memory suddenly shot forward in his mind, "Don't like 'em Arap myself. Hope 'em Shoshon' kill 'em all."

"Which direction should we take to find it?" he asked Johnson.

The soldier butted in and began, "Well, if'n you follow 'The Trail[2]' south 'til you come to the North Platte and west past Louis Guinard's bridge, and then on past Red Bluff Station 'til you come to Independence Rock. There you pick up the Sweetwater and follow it south to the big fork and then west again along the Little Wind, you'll come to it 'ventually."

"Taint no such, Ft. Washake ain't on the Little Wind."

"Well, maybe not the fort itself, but the reservation is," the man in blue replied, nodding his head. "And besides, you never told 'im about Poison Spider." Then turning to the two youngsters he continued, "They's got a fine hotel there and a saloon and a little black haired saloon girl what will make ya forget about the bite of the wind. Why I wus__________."

---

2 'The Trail' in eastern Wyoming usually meant The Bozeman Trail that ran from Platte River Bridge north along the eastern slope of the Big Horns and then turning west past the mountains to Bozeman, Montana.

"Oh hell, Buist you could talk the ears off a' elephant," Johnson said, and then as he finished folding the trade blanket and adding it to the stack already on one of his counters, he added, "He's right about Poison Spider. It's between Red Bluff and Independence Rock. Might want to ask there fur better directions to the fort."

"How far is it?" Laramie asked,

"Oh, I would reckon not morn' 50 or 60-mile cross country but you would miss it fur sure, 'specially with this stuff on the ground. It's probably nearer a hundred by road and that's the surest route if'n you plan on makin' it."

Chapter Thirty-Six

The Truce

At that very moment Quigley Hancock was entering *The Poison Spider Saloon*. He had spent the night in one of Joe Marquis' warm rooms and now, after the bed had caused his back to ache almost to the point of bending him as he walked, he was just glad to be up and moving about.

The punchers of both the *K—S* and the *WT* had called a truce on account of it being Christmas and he planned on spending his off time in town sharing some of his gray backs with the local establishments and their employees.

Neither Karl Seibold nor Paul Somerset were in on the truce and neither knew of it, and the cowboys planned to keep it that way if they could.

Sunny Tomson had closed the wooden doors in an effort to keep out the cold and Quigley had a hard time getting them open. Finally the doorknob latch gave in and the big door slowly opened. "Damn, Sunny, I thought you wus closed," he said, heading over to the potbelly to warm his hands and feet. "You aught a' get that door fixed."

"Haint nothin' wrong with my door. I want it tight. If'n you were as strong as you claim, you wouldn't had no trouble wit' it."

Quigley looked over at Charlie Sims, who had his chair pulled up close to the stove, and raised his eyebrows as if to say, what's wrong with him?

"Augh, Sonny you got a burr this morning?" Charlie asked, looking over at the skinny man who was sweeping up near the bar.

The man didn't give him the courtesy of even an answer; rather keeping on with his chore.

"I reckon that Chinnie girl he claims is a cook done cut old Sonny off and he's on the warpath this morning."

Still the barkeep did not answer or even recognize the boys were there.

"Speakin' a' cooks, Sonny can a fellow get something to eat this time a day?" Quigley asked.

"You got six bits you can."

"Six bits, hell that's highway robbery," Simms said. "Whar's your Christmas spirit?"

"In the cash drawer, you blame cowpokes come in here a' hollering and screaming and shoot off your blame six-guns all night and then expect Christmas spirit come morning. Well, you got some gall, that's all I got to say," he answered without even looking over at Simms.

"You know what I got to say Sonny?" Quigley spoke quite seriously and suddenly the man stopped with his broom. He did not look up because he suddenly realized he might have riled the big gunman and that was never something he wanted to do.

"I say, I want my steak bloody and my four eggs runny and here's a Yankee dollar to prove it," Quigley said and flipped the silver coin over on the bar where it bounced a couple of times before stopping flat with Lady Liberty facing up.

A sudden sense of relief blanketed Tomson as he looked at the 1878 minted coin. "I'll tell Friggie to cut you one out right away," he finally said as he swept the silver dollar off the backside of the counter.

Quigley was just finishing his breakfast when the sound of someone else having trouble with the front door interrupted the silence of the open room and they all looked over to see who it might be. Finally the figure of Chris Morgan came in to view. Looking around and seeing the two *WT* riders sitting there caused his strong hand to drop down where it could hover over the stock of his Smith & Wesson 44.

Seeing this, Charlie did likewise, but Quigley simply laid his fork on the table and then raised both hands slightly above the table showing he did not intend to start trouble. "Easy Charlie, it's Christmas, remember. Come on and let's all put our sixguns on the bar and have Sonny keep them until we leave."

A small amount of the stress relaxed, but still, the air was filled with tension and everyone there knew any spark could set off a blaze of gunfire.

At that moment coming in behind Spalding walked three more *K—S* hands the last being Miles Abbey.

Immediately the older man sensed the situation and called out, "Well, if it ain't my old friend. Merry Christmas to you, Quigley. Let's us get rip-roaring drunk together and piss on the names of Karl Seibold and Paul Somerset."

Miles' statement cut the tension and Dusty laughed, but Perry Taylor wasn't so sure about the cease-fire. He wanted it to be true, but he remembered the shellacking they had given those *WT* boys back on Powder River. *'Are they willing to let bygones be bygone for a whole day and night,'* he wondered.

Sonny Tomson also wondered and hoped it was true. "Come on boys, unbuckle and lay 'em here."

Quigley was the first, next came Miles, and then the others followed.

Miles pulled out a chair across from Quigley and raised his palm as if he was asking for permission to sit. Quigley moved his, palm up, hand over the table and then the two old allies smiled at each other across a table of dirty dishes.

"What you been eating there you ole Arkansas _______?"

Quigley raised back up in an obvious protest to being called by his former alias and Miles smiled and then finished, "Razorback?"

"Old Sonny's got him a Chinnie woman fur a cook and she knows just when to get the critter off the fire 'afore makin' it tuff as a cross tie," Quigley replied, nodding to his plate on which a clean gnawed bone lay.

"Well, Sonny, come on with a few steaks."

"He gets six bits," Charlie said speaking for the first time since the *K—S* hands came in.

"Six bits?" Miles yelled as in protest.

Eight bits to you Miles Abbey," the barkeep yelled back just as loud.

"Well," again Miles yelled, then in a much lower and calmer tone he continued, "bring on some eight-bit steaks, hellfire Sonny, it is Christmas after all."

Marietta had been busy the night before and did not get to sleep until the sun was rising in the eastern sky, so she did not make her appearance until nearly five that afternoon.

The sun had driven the temperature up to five below, but by the time she opened the backdoor of Sonny's saloon, it was dropping once again. She had put on a pair of long-johns, which some cowboy had left in her room back in the summer, and a long prairie dress she owned, under the heavy buckskin coat she had a trapper bring back in the early spring.

The sound of the wind rushing in when she opened the door brought on a host of groans and other less polite complaints but the sight of her entering so dressed caused an uproar of laughter.

"Damn Etta, I thought it wus the Parson's wife coming in here to bring down sho' 'nuff condemnation on us," Paul Spalding said and then they again laughed.

"Hell boys, if the Parson's wife showed herself in here, you all would be trying to talk her into a free poke before she got the first paragraph of her sermon out," Etta shouted back and flung off her coat.

"That's right a' God, we would," Perry agreed.

The Christmas celebration continued well into the night while Sonny kept his tab on the drinks that flowed, and Etta kept a trail of stomped down snow between the saloon and the hotel. Sometime a little after eleven, while Quigley was involved in a serious game of draw poker, Etta came to him and asked, "Ain't you gon'a come with me just once?"

It was obvious she had already drank too much, for her speech was slurred and she was quite unsteady on her feet and she rested her not so large breasts on his shoulder as she spoke.

"Not now, honey. I got a good game going here and I plan to take all these punchers' money. That is, what you and Sonny have not already took," he said not looking up from the cards he held in his left hand.

Miles Abbey, also by this time, was in an equally inebriated condition to Etta and he spoke up, "Come on Etta, I'll give you a whirl."

"No," she said back, which brought attention to the whole place. Never before had any of them heard her say no.

"Aww come on, I'm primed and ready."

"No. You ain't no gentleman. I want to go with Quigley."

"Not now, Etta, I'm hot here in this game."

"Yeah, and I'm hot here," Miles said grabbing at the cut in his chaps.

"No. I don't like you. You ambushed little Dingus Rockland and then you come in here and laughed about it," she spat out at Abbey.

Suddenly the whole atmosphere in the saloon changed, the air was once again charged and ready to explode.

Abbey remembered that they, in fact, had done that very thing. But at the time there were no *WT* riders in the place, now there was six and one of them was Quigley Hancock, the one man in life he feared, and knowing that fact, had become an obsession with him.

From as far back as he could remember, he had feared no man. Even as a boy his boldness and courage had shown bright and above all others.

During the war, he was always the first to board a captured ship and later when they were raiding from horseback he rode alongside Quigley at every opportunity and none of this changed after the war. But not once had he rode in front of *The Arkansas Avenger.*

Miles realized killing was a pleasure to him, especially the Africans and the blue-clad invaders, but he had never seen anyone kill so easily as Hancock.

Quigley killed without thought, without pleasure, without remorse. Miles had long since come to the conclusion Quigley Hancock killed because some dark memory burned deep within him and he killed without quarter, and this frightened him, for he knew Quigley would kill him just as surely as he would 'a Abe Lincoln, had he considered it necessary.

All of this was there somewhere in his conscience mind, but the effects of the alcohol had allowed a cloud to cover it and at the moment, he forgot about his fear for Quigley and simply remembered he had some reason to dislike him and this almost got him killed the night of Christmas in the year 1880 when he spurted out at Etta, "Yeah, you think I'm a murderer? What do you think of *The Arkansas Avenger?*"

The moment he heard the words spill from his mouth suddenly he once again feared Quigley Hancock, but now it was too late.

The saloon was suddenly so silent all could hear the crackling of the pine as it burned in the potbelly across the room. Quigley looked up from his poker hand into the blurry eyes of his old compadre, who likewise was staring back. Every other eye in the place was also locked on the tight drawn face of the big man at the table.

Suddenly Miles' hand swept like lighting down for his Colt but only found the roughness of his dungarees, and he realized he had shown his hand and been found wanting. His hideout was in his boot, a far distance from his gun hand and he knew full well Quigley would not ever be giving up all his weapons, and he knew without question his opponent was much nearer his than he was, and for the first time in his life he looked death in the eye, and it scared the hell out of him.

No one there that night could later recall how long the time span between Abbey's move and Quigley's response. Some say a full minute. Perry even said it was a full two minutes no less, but most finally agreed it was only a few seconds. Nevertheless, no one there had ever lived through a few seconds that seemed to take so long.

"I suppose, she would have the same mind about him as she does you, Miles, if he was here."

Abbey knew he would live now, at least for a little while. For some reason Hancock had chosen not to kill him. What that reason was he did not know nor understand, but whatever it was, he was thankful for it and he turned and walked over to the end of the bar and said, "I'll be taking my gun now, Sonny."

No one had yet moved other than the defeated man and even Sonny Tomson was not sure what he should do. Finally, he looked over at the table and saw Quigley give him a nod and he slowly went down to where the gun belts were laying and looked at the pile, but he couldn't remember which one belonged to Abbey, so he just began picking up one and setting it aside until he got to the last two. As he reached for the black rig with two short barrel Colts, Miles said, "That's the one."

Abbey took the belt and turned so his back was to the others in the room and there he buckled on the rig and adjusted the holsters so they rode correctly on his hips. Then without looking back he left through the front door.

Finally, Christy King laid his hand of cards on the table as he said, "I wonder what he meant by that?"

Buford Gillyard was the first to reply, "I think he was indicating *The Arkansas Avenger* is here on The Big Open."

Quigley, still in his chair holding his cards in his left hand, and once again every eye in the place turned to him save one, "Well, who the hell is *The Arkansas Avenger*?" Christy asked.

Quietness once more swept the saloon until finally, Quigley spoke, "He was an ole outlaw that worked Kansas after the war. They say he killed a lot of folks avenging some wrongs he witnessed during the conflict."

"Well, what's that got to do with us? He ain't around here is he?"

"No, I don't believe so. I heard he died and is buried on a little farm down by the border to the Nations," Quigley added. Then turning to Sapp and Thorbs he asked, "You calling or folding?"

Sapp looked at his hand and then back at Quigley and said, "I'm folding."

"Me, too," Thorbs added.

"Well, from what you laid down Christy, I reckon the pot is mine," Quigley said. And then he raked the coins from the table into his Stetson and pushed his chair back. It was only after he stood that the others saw his right pant leg hung up above his boot exposing the stock of a short barrel Colt.

"Looks like Christmas is over. Reckon I'll head on back to the bunkhouse," Quigley said, and then he walked over to the bar where Sonny handed him his gun and belt. After cinching it up tight, he went out into the cold clear night.

"You reckon it's him?" Dusty Salser asked.

"Doe'no," Sean Hennessey replied. I never seed' *The Avenger* but I heared tell he was a big man like that."

"What's the big deal if he is?" Christy asked.

"I heard tell he killed more than a hundred men," Sapp added, ignoring the boy's question. "And to think he bunks next to me."

"They say once when Jesse James heard *The Arkansas Avenger* was coming after him, he hid and cried," Shelly McCrery added to the conversation.

"Augh, that's pure bullshit. Jesse never cried in his life," Perry replied.

"Well, I don't know about Jesse James, but I sure as hell would hide and cry if I heard he was coming after me," Paul Spalding said.

"I wonder if Miles is hiding out there som'mers and crying right now," Hennessey suggested.

Quick in the defense of his foreman, Effird Nelson replied, "Miles never hid from no man."

"Mee'be, mee'be not, but I thought he was gon'a piss his pants there for a minute," Hennessey said back.

Christy turned and looked at the woman who had not spoken a word since the whole affair exploded, "I don't know, he seems so nice."

"Yeah, *The Arkansas Avenger* would have killed Miles in a spit, if he had exposed him. Quigley never even attempted a move."

"Does seem strange, don't it?" Sapp agreed.

Looking towards Lost Cabin Wyoming

Chapter Thirty Seven

The Platte River Bridge

The two riders arrived a little past sundown at the small trading post beside Louis Guinard's bridge that crossed the North Platte River. They were almost too cold to dismount and their horses looked too tuckered out to walk to the barn, but after these chores were finally accomplished, they entered the store.

Hours before, Buckshot had lost all thoughts that this weather was not too cold after all. He was sure that whatever that affliction Laramie had talked about was upon him and he would not be surprised if his feet and nose did fall off before morning. In fact, he had decided that even if they didn't, he was not going to ride away from the next warm place he found, no matter what.

"You two must be running from the law or a passel of wild savages to be out on a night like this," Mrs. Shelby said when she saw the young men enter her brother's store.

"Ain't no wild savages no more, the army done killed them all," Louis said.

Neither boy said anything for a long time—they just huddled around the stove and tried to warm themselves. Finally, the ice that had formed on Buckshot's eyebrows began to thaw and the result was water now filling his eyes and burning them to the point he could not see. No matter how much he rubbed them the more they burned.

"Here, Child," Mrs. Shelby said, "stop rubbing your eyes like that. You only make 'em worse. I got some water here that you can use to wash 'em in. That'll help."

He didn't like being referred to as Child, but at the moment, he was in no condition to argue the point, so he just nodded his head and followed her over to the ceramic basin into which she was pouring some water.

When she was satisfied with her work, she turned to her brother and said, "Put that pot back on the stove and we'll bile up some more coffee for these two, they need something hot to their insides, and soon."

Judge Carey's wife invited the Searight brothers and their families to have Christmas goose on the CY, but in order not to have bad feelings in Red Bluff, John thought it best to also invite Paul Somerset and his wife Gayle.

Somerset's grandfather arrived on the shores of East Jersey aboard a three-mast ship out of England in 1770. He had little money but a burning desire to succeed in the new world with a keen interest in politics, especially that of the Tories.

However, King George III had said concerning the American Colonies, "We must either master them totally or leave them to themselves and treat them as allies." When it became obvious to the king the best outcome for everyone concerned would be to leave them alone, Cory Somerset quietly submerged into forestland of West Jersey to become successful in the lumber business and leave politics to the less industrial minded.

Paul's father also was in the lumber business but never to the extent of Cory Somerset's. He had a real feeling for the land and a deep satisfaction in seeing the products of his labor rising from the ground. As a result, he left Jersey and moved to Maryland to become a farmer. Little Paul was caught up in the conflicting guidance of two extremely powerful and stern minded Somersets, one gratified by growing and the other who excelled in harvesting what nature grew without his assistance.

By the time war came Paul Somerset was forty-two years old, he owned both the largest farm in Washington County, Maryland, and the number one lumber company in New Jersey. His lumber business furnished wood to the Navy and his farm food to the Army. All seemed well until September of '62 when Lee's men occupied that farm, and Burnside doing everything within his power to remove the men in gray.

By the September 18, Somerset's farm was in ruins and his ground so disturbed and polluted with burned powder and iron shell it would not produce again for three years. The following month *The Troy Lumber Works* burned to the ground, some saying it was started by an incendiary, and apparently was an act of Southern saboteurs.

Paul sold his farmland below value, and the government rebuilt the sawmill, but the idea of losing both his inherited fortunes to the turns of war cut a deep gulley within him, where often in later life when things were not going well, he found refuge from reality.

He invested in several enterprises during the post-war days but none of them ever amounted to a great deal until finally, fifteen years after the battle near Sharpsburg, he arrived in Wyoming with just enough cash and hard backing to begin the *WT* and he was determined to make a success of it, even if it killed him.

Paul's wife Gayle was fifteen years his junior and their only surviving child, Cory hated everything most men held dear, and most of all he hated Wyoming. Therefore, he was allowed to return to the east to paint.

When the rider brought the invitation to the *WT*'s main ranch house Paul was elated. To him, it meant the Judge and the Searight brothers were finally ready to join with him in eliminating Siebold, his barbwire and his sheep. Gayle was just grateful they had not been excluded from the others in Red Bluff.

The dinner was prepared by the Mexican help the Judge had employed as cooks long ago on a drive from Texas. Although they were not socially accepted by his eastern background neighbors, he liked each of them and had kept them on these many years.

Soon after they had begun the meal Paul started in his campaign against Seibold, but the Judge cut him off quickly by saying, "I appreciate your concern on these matters Paul, but we hold dear to our southern tradition of not discussing business in front of our womenfolk. So, if you will indulge me and hold such talk until later, I would be most appreciative."

It was a reprimand, no doubt about it, and both Gayle and Paul felt its sting, but they were guests in another's home and would not take offense at their host's request, however, the wait seemed to distress Paul, more so than did the chili peppers in the stuffing.

Finally, when Francisco served cigars to each of the men, Mrs. Carey rose and said, "Well ladies, I see it's time we surrender to the fact it is a man's world and leave them to their own vices."

Every man rose while the women were leaving the room and quickly began milling around the decanters of bourbon the servants had brought in and placed on a table especially for them.

Paul Somerset having been kept quiet for so long could no longer stand it and almost immediately stated, "Well, I am sure you all have heard how my men were murdered on Powder River a few weeks back."

"Yes, that was an unfortunate occurrence," Greg Searight said. "Do you have any proof who did it?"

"Who did it? Why there is no question who did it, it was Seibold and his band of bushwhackers. Who else could it have been?"

"I do believe you are right, but what evidence do you have? We are a long way from the county seat and any real law enforcement, and to ask for their help without proof would make us look rather sheepish," Greg said and then immediately regretted the expression.

"That's another point, sheep. Everybody knows no steer will graze where sheep have been and he now has a herd of over a thousand ruining our land, to say nothing of the barbed wire."

This kind of exchange went on for several more minutes until finally, the Judge spoke, "There is no question about barbwire being bad for our open range policy, but there may just be a profit in sheep, at least someday," he paused and took several puffs from his cigar before continuing, "and Greg is right; until you have proof *K—S* men were the ones who killed your hands, there is little that can be done, Paul."

It suddenly was plain that he had not been invited to this gathering to discuss the problem plaguing The Big Open, and that in itself infuriated him more than anything else. "Well, if you won't help me on this, I will take care of that bastard myself," he said just short of a shout and slammed his glass down so hard it broke and cut his palm. Looking down at the red blood that suddenly came rushing forth he added. "This is not the last of this, you will see." Then he turned and left the room

Late the next afternoon while he was riding line a bullet whistled past Dusty Salser's head and he realized Christmas was over.

Chapter Thirty Eight

False Spring

The first week of February suddenly found warm chinook winds blowing out of the southwest and everything began to thaw. The frozen grass began to look better, and the shallow creeks lost their icy covering.

On the fourth, the temperature got all the way up to thirty-eight, which was an increase of sixty degrees from what it had been a couple of weeks before.

It was during this time Buckshot and Laramie returned from Fort Washakie. They had not found the Arapahoe or his woman, but they had found others who also knew of such a woman or at least the belief such a woman was there in the Wind River Basin. The reason for their return was they needed supplies and also a Shoshone had told them there was a man who worked on a ranch on Powder River who was called Reb.

In *The Poison Spider Saloon* Buckshot asked the woman working there, "Do you know a Reb Brown?"

She slowly shook her head, "No, I don't think so. What does he look like?"

"He's big and has black hair; he is very fast with his gun and is from the south."

She still shook her head, "I know a man who is a Reb alright, but he goes by the name of Quigley."

Immediately they both took interest, "Is he a very tall man?"

"Yes."

"And very broad in the shoulders?"

"Yes."

"Usually wears buckskin?"

"Yes," she said as every question had indeed been true.

"Does he ride a big horse with white spots?"

"No, he rides a paint horse."

"Oh," Buckshot said a little less enthusiastic.

"He could have a new horse," Laramie suggested.

"Sure, he could," Buckshot agreed.

"Do you know where he is?"

"No, but he was here yesterday. He works for the *WT* outfit."

"Where are they?"

"East of here, the other side of Powder River," she said, and then added, "But I think he is riding line north of here."

"Can you give us directions? I've come all the way from Florida to find him."

"Florida, oh my, that is a long way."

After loading their pack mule with fresh supplies, the pair headed out looking for Reb Brown.

That night, for the first time since November, Paul Somerset came in the saloon. Chuck Bitler, Sean Hennessey, and Zeb Sapp were with him and Etta could sense something was up.

Somerset not once even looked in her direction, but Sapp could not resist moving over close to where she was leaning against the bar and saying, "Hey Etta, I gon'a have me some bonus money this month, how 'bout a poke on credit?"

"Where the hell would you get bonus money?"

"Shu," he said and lifted his finger to his lips, "Not so loud."

"What's going on Zeb?"

"I can't tell ya, but I'll have some bonus money coming after this, maybe tonight."

She now was certain something was in the works and for Somerset to pay extra, it had to have to do with the *K—S.* "When do you want a poke?"

"Tonight, when we get back, maybe tomorrow night."

"Where are you going?"

"Up north. We're going hunting."

"Hunting, in the Big Horns? Hell, this little heatwave ain't thawed out them mountains."

"Maybe we ain't going to the mountains, maybe we know where there is some game right down here not so far away."

"You're crazy."

"No, I ain't," he said and then looked over at Somerset who was talking seriously with Sonny Tomson and then back at the others and then back at her. Finally he said, "Can you keep a secret?"

"Sure, you know you can trust Etta."

"We're going sheep hunting. You want some wool?"

"Naw, Somerset wouldn't dare."

"Sure as shooting, and he's paying us a dollar a head for every dead sheep we kill. I got me three boxes a' ca'tridges, that's 150 dollars in dead sheep."

"I'll believe it when I see it," she said and then she turned and walked over behind the bar and got out a bottle and poured herself a glass of rye. From where she now stood, she could hear some of what was being said between Sonny and Paul, at least until Sonny saw her there and said in a downgrading voice, "Ain't you got something to do? Go yonder and wash them shot glasses."

"I'll do better than that. I'll just go back to the hotel," she yelled at him before downing her drink and charging out the side door.

Etta did go to the hotel, but only to change into her riding clothes and then she headed down to the livery and rented a buggy from Oscar Wells.

"Whar you wantin' ta' go Miss Etta?"

"Just want to get out of town on this lovely warm night."

"Well, I put ole Thunder on fur you, if you get lost just give him his head and he'll bring you back home."

"Thank you, Oscar, and if nobody finds out about my ride, I'll see you get something extra when I get back."

The hostler removed his hat when he heard that and smiled widely exposing the loss of a canine tooth, "Gee, Miss Etta, I shor will say nothing, to nobody."

"Thank you, Oscar," she said, and then gave him a wink before she dropped the long lead along the horses back.

Buckshot and Laramie had searched all along the cut that had been pointed out as Powder River but found nothing. "You think we'll find him before another storm blows in?"

"I doe'no, but I ain't come this far not to keep on looking."

"Yeah, and he might know something. Hell, he might be here looking for my mother himself. If'n he heard about the white woman being held captive by the Arapahoe. I'll bet that's just what he would do."

"Come on let's drift farther north, that's where that woman said he had gone."

It was well after dark when they came upon some higher ground and there off in the distance was the faint flicker of a small fire.

"Look, a campfire," Buckshot said. "I'll bet it's his."

"Maybe, maybe not. Could be Indians, or bandits, or just a bunch a' cowpokes, none of which I want to come upon in the night. Anyone a' them likely to shoot first and talk later if'n someone comes upon them out a' the dark."

"Yeah, I guess you are right. What do you think we should do?"

"Well, we could make a dry camp here and wait 'til morning when we can see them, and they can see us."

"Yeah, that may be better," Buckshot agreed.

"Come on, looks like there's a little arroyo yonder, where we can get the horses off the skyline."

"Good thinking," Buckshot agreed.

They watched the little fire for a while, but the draw of sleep was too great and soon both boys were fast asleep.

Mendoza and Ryan had made their camp just across the creek from where their hidden cabin was located. They had not brought the sheep on the west side of the creek before and it seemed a good time to do so while the ice was not so thick, and the sheep could get plenty of water.

Ryan had gone over to the dugout and retrieved a can of peaches they had stored in their little cache and had just passed the can to Mendoza when the sound of riders approaching was heard.

Neither had much for guns, neither were gun people. They had kept the revolver the man who shot the sheep had dropped after Ryan killed him, but it was in the dugout and of course, they still had Ryan's single-shot rifle he had brought from Arizona, but it was just for when the wolves got so thick that Nombre couldn't keep them away. It was not a gun for protection, not really, not when all the riders in these parts had repeaters and were good at shooting them.

Their best source of safety would always be to be as inconspicuous as possible and when trouble appeared on the horizon to make themselves scarce. This night when Nombre, who no longer was a pup, gave the first indication something not normal was out in the blackness, Ryan sat up from his bedroll and softly called out, "Mendoza."

"I am here I have been listening. I think he hears horses coming, three, four me' bee."

The big white dog growled even more forcefully now. He often did so at night when something was prowling around the flock, but on those occasions as soon as he was certain the men were awake, he had always took off on a run to earn his keep, this night he made no effort of leave.

"We better move over next to the wagon," Mendoza said and seeing the boy getting up he did the same.

"Your rifle is in the bed, no?"

"Si', near the back."

"You get it, and then lay under the wagon and stay out of sight."

"Si."

"And Ryan," he paused before he finished,

"Si?"

"You stay there, don't show yourself unless you have to."

"Si, I will."

Time always seems to drag when one is waiting, especially when the outcome of the wait is in question, and such was the experiences of the two sheepherders who waited near the old army ambulance they had converted into their home, there on a cool night in Wyoming's Red Desert.

Finally, a high cloud moved on towards the east and the quarter moon revealed the men approaching. Mendoza counted five and he reprimanded himself for missing the count simply from listening, however, he was also relieved to see the leading horse to be white, and he figured it to be the big stallion Mr. Siebold usually rode.

"Hello, the camp," came the voice from fifty yards out where the riders had halted.

"Hello and welcome," Mendoza replied and then turning his head he added just above a whisper, "Ryan remember, stay out of sight."

He didn't hear an answer, but it was alright, the wind was beginning to sing in the bare limbs of the cottonwood trees that lined the little creek.

At that moment he heard the voice of Karl Seibold say, "Mendoza, good to see you are alert. I don't trust that *WT* bunch."

"Yes, I am alert, but you didn't come all the way out here to tell me that."

"No, I came to bring Mr. Murray, he is interested in buying my sheep on the hoof."

"You would sell the whole herd?" Mendoza questioned, wondering what a sheepherder could do in Wyoming without any sheep.

"Yes, he has made me a good offer, he wants to move them over to his ranch near the Nebraska line. He will take you on as well."

"That would be good for me," Mendoza replied, not sure if it would be or not.

Miles Abbey turned to Sidney and said just above a whisper, "Like I said, Murray can't see much on a night like this, I don't understand his wanting to come out here, tomorrow would have made a lot more sense."

"I know, but he wants to make the morning stage for Red Bluffs so__________."

"Plum stupid if you ask me," Martin Henry said not quite as low as the others had.

"That will be enough of that," Siebold scolded.

Suddenly everyone froze when the obvious sound of a wagon approaching from the south was heard.

"Get over behind them trees and take cover. No one should be out here tonight," Seibold said and then he added without even looking at the man, "Haeckel make yourself scarce."

Mendoza did not need telling, he moved over behind his wagon and then lowered himself down to where he was just squatting Indian style. "If things go wrong here you and me will head for our cabin," he said to Ryan.

"Si," the boy replied.

They did not have to wait long before the silhouette of the buggy appeared on the rise some seventy yards off and there it stopped.

"Abbey, get a bead on that teamster," Siebold said.

"Can do," came the reply as Miles removed his Centennial Winchester from its scabbard and slid back the dustcover. A quick look down, while the lever was partially lowered, revealed a reflection of the moon on the brass case of the long cartridge and being satisfied his chamber was loaded, he brought up the lever and reached with his thumb to cock the hammer.

Miles had a good sight picture on the single person who was now descending the hill at a fast speed. However, before he fired, they heard the voice of a woman and he lowered the long-barreled gun and slowly dropped the hammer down, then without even thinking about it, pulled it back to where the click of the first sear assured him it was on the safety. "Etta, what are you doing out here?"

"Oh, thank God I've got here in time," she said being so relieved she suddenly felt faint.

"What's that whore doing out here in a sheep camp," demanded Karl Siebold.

Catching her breath, she used her gloved hand to push back several strands of hair that had fallen over her right eye as she bounced down the roadless hill. "This whore came to warn you."

"Warn us of what?"

"The *WT*. They plan to jump this herd and kill them all and the sheep-man who brought them here. They are offering a bonus for every dead sheep."

"Now look here, Siebold," Murray began. "You didn't tell me about any trouble with your sheep."

"Shut up Murray. You ought to know when you bring sheep into cow country there will be trouble, surely you aren't that much of a greenhorn."

Chapter Thirty Nine

Massacre Meadow

The sound of the riders approaching had not awakened the boys, but no one could have slept through her running that buggy, hell-bent for leather, down the hill. Now both Laramie and Buckshot lay there on the crest of the little cut in the slope of the hill and watched the goings-on in the camp below.

They could not hear what was being said but it was obvious a woman was now down there.

Suddenly, their attention at the camp was dramatically jerked away when a boot was planted not a foot from where Laramie's left hand lay on the edge of the arroyo. Both boys immediately turned their faces up and saw the five men cautiously moving down the hill towards the small fire and the gathering below. Each man had a long gun in hand, it was quite obvious they had come for business.

Buckshot knew an ambush was in the making and he felt obligated to do something, but when he started to raise himself from the ground, his friend placed a hand on his shoulder and stopped him. "No, we don't know which side is right here. These men may be a sheriff's posse and them that came into camp a few minutes ago rustlers."

Buckshot had not thought of that so he lowered himself back and agreed to wait and see what the events below would reveal.

"I don't see why we should take her word for all this. She could be telling us this to get us away, Mr. Seibold."

"I don't think so, Etta here is the one who has been slipping me the information on the *WT*. It was her tip that lead us to Powder River that night so we could jump them before they could rustle our stock. She also has given me other tips that always panned out," Miles said.

"I see," Siebold said.

"I see, too," came a voice from the darkness, which caused them all to whirl around.

"I wouldn't be reaching fur no iron if you know what's good fur you, there is a gun trained on each and every one of you bunch a' bushwhackers."

"Who are you?" Ryan heard Karl Siebold ask.

"The devil come to pay you a visit."

"It's Chuck Bitler, Mr. Seibold. I would know his twisted voice anywhere."

"How right you are Abbey. Now you bastards drop your hardware, yonder next to the fire, so I can see 'em fall. All except you Abbey, you just hold that fancy rifle you got there up high, I want to compare a spent round I have been carrying with me with one in that Winchester, one I found where Blaine Sedgwick was murdered."

Miles did not like this one bit, he realized there were more of them out in the darkness but just how many he couldn't be sure of. *I will have to give up my rifle and most likely the Colt but the little S&W in my boot might just be our saving grace.*

I must maneuver around so I could get to it in a flash, but not until they all showed their sneaking faces.'

Suddenly he felt a hard poke to his back and he knew the barrel of a sixgun was tight against his body, almost at the same time the Winchester was jerked from his hand and then he was pushed forward closer to the fire.

The Dude suddenly began to talk so rapidly no one could really understand half of what he was saying, but the general idea was he had nothing to do with any of this and he wanted to be let leave before he witnessed something.

Not once since the *WT* riders appeared had Etta spoken a word or made any other emissions. She seemed scared into silence and this was not like her at all.

It was Chuck Bitler who turned and engaged her, "So you are the squealer, and all this time I thought it was Hancock. Too bad, I liked you and I simply hate him. I had much rather kill him than you."

Mendoza was surprised at her reaction to the statement. Her whole demeanor suddenly changed and she cut into him fearless and with a fury not seen here before, "You cock-less, whiney bastard, you might be able to murder a defenseless woman. Beating women seems to be a trait of the higher echelon at the *WT,* but don't you ever think you could get the best of Quigley Hancock, he would have you for breakfast and then order a bloody steak to settle his stomach."

Bitler holstered his handgun and then moved Miles' rifle to his left hand before he reached up and took her by the upper arm and flung Etta from the buggy. The gesture spooked ole Thunder and the horse took off into the night before anyone could stop him, almost running down Murray in the process.

Etta hit the ground hard on her face and upper body, the suede skirt she was wearing flew up high on her back, exposing the pair of white long-johns she had on underneath. This caused Ryan to turn his head and when he did Mendoza motioned for him to follow. They slipped backward from under the wagon and down into the icy water and lying on their stomachs crawled across the creek as slowly and noiselessly as possible.

Just as they reached the east side a shot rang out and they recognized her cry, this was soon followed by another lighter gun going off and then the unmistakable report of a heavy rifle.

"Come on," Mendoza said as he pushed Ryan up the other bank, "Get to the cabin quickly."

The last words they heard, that were recognizable, was Karl Siebold saying, "You'll hang for this Bitler."

Buckshot and Laramie witnessed from the top of the rise the flashes from the muzzles and then the long silence, before the seeming unending discharge of weapons that went on and on. The sounds of squealing and dying sheep were obvious, until finally the ground began to shake and they realized what was left of the herd was charging off into the blackness.

It was some fifteen minutes after the last shot sounded that the firing of the wagon took place, and then shortly after that, the raiders came back up the hill, this time riding horses. They once more passed quite close to where the boys hid, and in the moonlight, Buckshot looked straight into the face of one of the killers, but the man did not recognize his viewer as anything other than a dark spot on the prairie.

Both boys stayed as still as they could for a long time listening to the men behind them change to their own mounts and go through the saddlebags of those they had rode from the scene.

Then after a long period of quietness Laramie said, "I think they have gone."

The two slowly rose, staring off into the eastern sky but neither saw anything moving.

"What do you think?"

"I think we should stay hid until full light. If anyone is still alive down there they might take us for a couple of them."

"Yeah," Buckshot agreed.

At first, the *WT* crew intended to go into Poison Spider to let Doc Smyth look at the wound Abbey had put in Thorbs' upper shoulder, but decided to bypass the town and cut a trail directly back to the ranch.

No one said anything as they rode, everyman was wrapped up in his own feelings about what had happened that night and it wasn't until they were three miles out before Dakota spurred his cayuse and moved up beside his foreman. "Mr. Bitler, I never did see that sheep-man."

Immediately Bitler reined to a stop and turning and looking at the others asked, "Anyone a' you shoot the sheep-man?"

No one answered.

"Anyone a' you see the sheep-man?"

Again, he received no answer.

After taking a deep breath he turned to Hennessey and said, "Take Sapp and go back and see if you can find him. We can't have no witnesses walking around."

"Yas Sur," Sapp said pulling hard on his left rein. Hennessey was not so quick to respond, it was getting light ahead and would be, long before they got back to that creek. He remembered the buggy running off and wondered if the horse would make its way back to town. Going back to the scene of their night's work was not one bit to his liking, but he just didn't know what to do about not going.

Buckshot had laid there the rest of the night and try as he may, he simply could not go back to sleep, finally just as the sun was slipping over the rise and lighting the valley below, he began to see the dead animals laying everywhere. "God, there must be a hundred or more dead down there."

"Maybe twice that many," Laramie suggested, but what he was staring at was not dead sheep. "Look," was all he said as he pointed towards the trees.

Buckshot tried to follow his point but there were so many white balls down there he was not sure which he was supposed to notice finally he asked, "What are you looking at?"

"The men. Those hanging there from the trees."

Now alerted as to what to look for he, too, saw the bodies slowly turning in the breeze.

"Holy smoke, they hung 'em."

"Come on, let's go down and see if anyone needs our help."

Slowly his friend stood and followed the blonde boy down the hill. They were less than fifty yards from the creek when Buckshot saw movement to his right and he threw out his arm stopping his friend and nodding.

It was then Mendoza appeared from the earth and suddenly the older man and the two boys looked into each other's faces and they all saw fear.

Laramie was the first to move and he brought his Colt out of its holster and pointed it at the man. "Who are you? Where did you come from?"

Laramie had given his old 1872 model to Buckshot to use until he bought one of his own and the lad immediately pulled his own Colt and aimed at the man.

"I am no boo'dy. A simple shepherd that is all, no more."

"These your sheep?" Laramie asked waving his pistol barrel around at the dead animals."

"They are mine."

"Then where were you last night?"

"I was here, hid from the bad men who do this," Mendoza replied and then a little ashamed when he saw the expression on the boy's face, he added, "I have no gun, no way to fight back."

Buckshot saw the very smallest amount of round barrel pointing out of the dugout at Laramie and figuring the man holding the gun did not yet realize there were two of them, he slowly eased back a few steps and pointed his own weapon at the dark opening from which the muzzle appeared.

Mendoza was not one to miss things himself and seeing the other boy moving back he finally called out. "Ryan, verbo intransitive decir español que se habla en México."

"Si," came the answer from behind the rifle.

"Tell him to put down the gun," Laramie instructed.

"Degar fusil largo."

"Si," again came the reply and slowly they saw the barrel point up and then out of sight before the tall lad came forth from the hole in the ground.

"Hee's name Ryan," Mendoza said, pointing at the skinny lad dressed in striped pants and a white shirt, both of which were so dirty neither appeared to have been washed in months.

"Any more down there?"

"No, this ess all," Mendoza replied.

"Who are these people?"

"Oh, sweet mother of Jesus," Mendoza said looking over at the two men swinging from the limbs before he crossed himself, and then without any other thoughts, he walked down the bank and into the icy water towards the dead men.

Following him, the three boys also seemed unable to take their eyes from the distorted faces of the men. Karl Seibold's tongue was swollen and bulging from his mouth, his head was tilted straight back, and his eyes looked as if they might pop from their sockets with the slightest jar. The other man, in the business suit, showed none of these signs. His head was simply cocked off to one side and the area of the neck that could be seen above his collar was deep blue, almost black.

Then Buckshot heard a whimper and whirling around he saw movement and finally focused on the rear leg of the large dog that jerked from time to time. It was there in the morning shade that the other bodies lay. Three men dressed in the duds of cowpunchers and the woman. Large pools of blood were evidence that none had died instantly.

Buckshot looked closely at each's face and although he felt a weakness stir in his stomach at the gory scene, he was relieved to know none of the dead was Reb Brown.

"Who are they?" again Laramie asked.

"This man, he ess Mr. Karl Seibold. He 'es the owner of the *K—S* ranch," he said, moving his arm around the area indicating everywhere one could see, "Dis man, he came to buy de sheep. I don't know 'es name."

"There, 'es Mr. Miles Abbey. He 'es de foreman," Mendoza said and they each suddenly realized this man had been shot in both arms and booth knees, as well as in the chest, but from the huge stain of blood, they surmised the slug to the chest had not come early in his dying, perhaps even after he had bled to death from the other wounds.

"Oh, Mama Mee'a. They had killed Miss Etta too," the shepherd said when he realized the body over next to the burned-out wagon was that of a woman.

"We need to tell someone. Where is the law around here?"

"I do not know," Mendoza said back. "There is a village, Poison Spider, there ten miles, perhaps more," he said pointing to the southeast.

"Buckshot, if you want to wait here, I'll go and get help, but I wouldn't move nothing until others see what has been done here."

The boy nodded his head and then turned to watch the tall Mexican boy walk over and drop to his knees before lifting the dog's head on to his lap.

Laramie had not gone more than three miles when he saw a wagon and three men headed north generally in his direction. He stood as tall as he could on the stirrups, and waved his hat in the air, attracting their attention. Quickly the three mounted riders started in his direction.

When they arrived the large man on the paint horse asked, "Son, we are looking for a woman who might have been thrown from a buggy last night, have you seen anything of her?"

"I think so," he replied using the sleeve of his shirt to wipe his brow before returning the wide-brimmed hat to his head and then he told them of where he was headed and why.

"The nearest law is down to Rawlins, the county seat and that's a 20-hour ride for a man who knows the way," Quigley said back. "Best you show us where this took place. We'll get word to the law later."

Laramie was not so sure about this suggestion, but he really didn't know what else to do. He had no idea where this Rawlins was and only vaguely where Poison Spider lay, at least from where he now was, so after thinking a short period on it, he nodded his head and turned his horseback in the direction he had just come.

Mendoza did not know Quigley Hancock, but he had heard the *K—S* men talking about the giant who rode the big paint gelding and that some thought he was *The Arkansas Avenger*, so there was a bit of panic sweeping over him when he saw Laramie leading the others down the slope towards Massacre Meadow, as the little cove in the cottonwoods would forever after be known.

When he rode in under the shade of the trees absorbing the scene about him, and before dismounting Quigley asked, "Anybody know what happened here?"

Mendoza said nothing. He now wished he had never come out of the sunken cabin. Here, before him, was the deadliest man in the Big Open, and a member of the same outfit that had done all these killings, somebody was sure to tell him that he had witnessed the whole thing.

Finally, Buckshot said, "These people were here last night, and some ambushers came from yonder," pointing up the east hill, "and they killed them all."

"You know who did it?"

"No, I was too far off, but they do," he said pointing to the two Shepherds.

"Who?"

Mendoza shook his head quickly back and forth, but Ryan, still holding his now dead Nombre, said quite forcibly in perfect English, "*WT* men."

This surprised both Laramie and Buckshot, they had no idea, until that moment, the boy could understand or spoke their language, and Buckshot immediately began thinking back of all the things he had said in front of the tall boy, assuming he could not understand him.

The language might have been a surprise to them, but the news was not to Quigley.

"Can any of you identify the men other than them being *WT* riders?"

Mendoza quickly replied, "No, we were far off and the night was black."

"I can," Buckshot said. "At least one of them, he almost stepped on my hand when they were leaving."

Mendoza felt a pain sting him when he heard the statement, *'This young man just signed his death warrant,'* he thought.

It was then Quigley noticed the small boots protruding from under the blanket that covered one of the bodies, and recognizing them to be woman's button-up shoes. He walked over and lifted the gray wool covering and stared into the cold blue eyes of Marietta Williams, although he did not know her surname at the time.

Slowly he reached down and gently closed her eyes and then lowered the blanket. Without consciously realizing it, he drew hard within his mouth and filled it with saliva and then swallowed it as if to wash away the nasty taste he suddenly held within him. Then he rose again and turning to the boy he asked, "Will you ride with me to the ranch and point this man out to me?"

"No!" Mendoza suddenly exclaimed, "He should stay here."

Buckshot looked over at the man and then he said to him clarifying any doubt as to his courage, "I most certainly will go and identify him."

Again, Mendoza crossed himself and lowered his head.

"Come on boy, let's get on with this, while the others get busy with the grave diggin'."

When Buckshot mounted and rode up beside him, he looked over and asked, "You ain't got no rifle?"

"No, Sur."

Looking back, he saw a yellow Winchester that lay near the burned-out campfire and called to one of the others, "Hand me that carbine yonder."

Oscar Wells looked over to where he indicated and then picked up the short rifle and reached it to Quigley, who nodded his head then turned and handed it to Buckshot, "Here, you got one now."

"Thank you, Sur," Buckshot said as he took the rifle and looked proudly at it. *'Gee, this is just like the one Miss Nadine[1] had.'* "Thank you very much."

"Well, I reckon whoever it belonged to yesterdee won't mind you having it none."

"I'll take good care of it."

Quigley smiled a little before he answered, "I'll bet you do."

They had not made two miles when the two riders were seen approaching.

"Don't say nothing about knowing anything about that back thar."

"Yes, Sur."

When Sapp and Hennessey arrived Quigley nodded his head, "You boys are kinda off your range aren't you?"

---

[1] Miss Nadine: Reb Brown's wife.

"On a________." Hennessey started and then stopped. "Bitler ordered us to do some checking fur him."

"Well, I 'spect it would have something to do with the killin's back there at the crick."

"You know about that, huh?"

"Just came from there."

"How you find out so quick?" Sapp asked,

"A runaway buggy came into town this morning and Wells asked me to ride out and try and see what happened to its driver. That's when I come on it back there."

"Oh, I knew that buggy was trouble."

"Shut up, Sapp," Hennessey said.

"It don't matter none. I know you two were in on it."

"That damn Mex, he did see it all, didn't he?"

"No, he wasn't there. Off after some runaways when the shooting started and just got back as you were leaving," Quigley lied to them. "You headed back to finish him off?"

"Yeah."

"Shut up, Sapp."

"I just want to know one thing."

"What's that?" Hennessey asked.

"Why did you shoot Miss Etta?"

"Oh, she was the one what has been telling Abbey all our plans, caught her red-handed last night blabbing about our raid."

"Sapp, I told you to shut up," Hennessey said almost in a scream.

"It don't matter none, he's a gon'a find out sooner or later. Bitler can't keep his mouth shut about something like that."

"Was Somerset there too?"

"Naw. I don't know if he even knows about it or not," Sapp again answered.

Buckshot had heard of such things happening, but he never really realized they were true, but before he could blink his eye the short barrel Colt, which had been mostly hidden by the man's vest, was in his hand and barked twice.

Sean Hennessey suddenly arched upright with the strangest expression on his face and then sort 'a eased off his saddle backwards. What hit the ground was no longer alive.

"What the ________?" Sapp yelled.

"Just can't abide with killing a woman," Quigley said and then he turned the muzzle at the shorter man.

"No, no don't. I never killed her."

"Who did?"

"Bitler shot her, he also shot Abbey, shot him in the legs and the arms and laughed as he bled down and then he shot him again just for good measure."

"Who else was with you?" Quigley asked.

Sapp looked at the cocked revolver and stammered as he spoke, "You ain't gon'a shoot me are you Quigley? We ride for the same brand."

"Who else?"

"Well, there was Bitler and Hennessey and Eddie, Abbey put a slug in him before he went down."

"I know Bitler, and that worm would not have led no raid with just you bunch, who else?"

"Curley, and Dakota, he stayed back and held the horses."

"That's all? I don't believe you."

"I swear to you Quigley, that's all! Now you ain't gon'a shot me, are you?"

"Just can't abide shooting a woman or a man who would stand by and let it happen," and with that, he squeezed his trigger and a hundredth of a second later, the front of Sapp's coat burst open as the 45 slug took the button in with it.

Sapp looked up and slowly spoke before he too fell from his saddle, "You are him."

Buckshot was not new to killing, he had shot a man with his squirrel rifle when he was barely six years old[2] and had seen almost a full company of soldiers shot in the big pasture in front of where he lived, but this was the first time he had been so close when a man was gunned down, and the sight of it was quite sobering. Still, he was not frightened and in a small way felt justice had been dealt to some of those who had murdered back at the creek.

Quigley dismounted and went through the pockets of the dead men and then removed their weapons and dropped the saddles and bridles to the ground before slapping Sapp's horse on the rump. Hennessey's horse took off in a fast trot after the other.

Remounting, he turned Apache and spoke as he did, "Come on, I know who did this now. Ain't no need fur you to ride into that lion's den. When those two horses get back without their tack, everyone will be alerted back there."

Buckshot followed the big man and wondered. After they were halfway back to the creek he asked, "If you knew it would alert them why did you do it then?"

"I want them to know what's coming," was all that was said.

Mendoza sure was surprised when the two rode together down the long slope.

That night Quigley, the two new boys to the Big Open, and Oscar Wells rode out to the **K bar S** bringing the body of Karl Seibold with them and told Callie what had happened to her husband.

She was a stout woman, standing taller than either Buckshot or Wells and as tall as Laramie. Her German accent was much stronger than any of them had ever heard from her husband and her words cold and without emotion. "I say to Karl this very week, these sheeps will get you killed."

---

[2] Buckshot shot a man: See *The Owl Hoot Trail Book Two, The Withlacoochee Renegades.*

"Well, there was a note pinned to his shirt, it mentioned the barbwire, not the sheep," Oscar said.

"The same," she said. "These men, dey have so much, dey want more. Dey want it all. When dey kill us all, dey will kill each other to get more. It is the way of all Kings. Just like the old country. Here is no different. Karl thought so, but he vas wrong."

"What are your plans now Mrs. Seibold?"

"I know not, maybe I sell. Maybe go back east. I stay for a while."

"Well, Mrs. Seibold, if you will have me, I will ramrod your ranch until you sell," Quigley said. "Your foreman was killed along with your husband."

She looked at him in the dim light of the coal oil lantern and then said, "Ya, that would be good. You are the foreman now, these men come with you?" she asked looking at the two boys.

"Yes, if they want," Quigley replied.

"Ya, that is good," she said and then without uttering another word she turned and walked from the room leaving them to find their own way out.

Wells climbed into his buckboard and lifted the long leather leads, "Well, I best be getting back to town."

"Will you send word to the sheriff about all this?" Quigley asked.

"Yes, I will do that," he agreed nodding his head. "Send out a note on the westbound tomorrow."

The nodding of Quigley's head served as an answer and after the man and wagon moved away, he turned and said to the boys, "Come on let's see who's here." Then they walked down to the bunkhouse where he told the men about what had happened and introduced the two new hands to them.

"I don't understand why she made you foreman, you ride for the *WT*."

"No more," was all Quigley gave for an answer.

A long time before Oscar Wells placed the letter on the stage for the sheriff down in Rawlins, word of Quigley Hancock moving over to the enemy's camp reached the *WT* and it angered Somerset and frightened Bitler.

Somerset had indeed ordered his foreman to stir up trouble with Siebold's men and to kill as many of the sheep as he could, but he had not ordered him to kill any man. However, now that it was a done deal, he could do very little about it except ride the wave and prepare for an all-out battle. He still had more men than the *K—S* and he doubted that Callie Siebold had the capital to last very long against him. All he had to do was continue on as they had and what the winter winds did not do away with, time would, and time was on his side.

The only thing he had not considered, or even knew of for that matter, was *The Arkansas Avenger.*

Quigley drew out the youngest riders he had and made them into a special squad. For the first three weeks, weather permitting, he had Laramie, Buckshot, Dusty and Chris relieved of all ranch duties and instead, given orders to ride and shoot until their revolvers would shoot no more and then boil them in water wipe them dry and begin shooting again. They first learned to hit a hen egg at ten paces, then twenty. Next, they were instructed to shoot simply by pointing their arm at a rock roughly the size of a man and after mastering this, they were instructed to shoot from horseback until they were proficient at it. Then it was shooting at the rock as they rode past it first one way and then the other.

Quigley bought all the 44 Henry and 44 Winchester center-fire ammunition in Poison Spider, then gave Ole Dave, the Jehu[3], two double eagles to bring back more from Rawlins. It arrived on the same coach as did Deputy Bass.

---

3 Jehu: The Stage Driver, derived from the Old Testament Jehu who drove his chariot furiously.

Wiley Bass had worked as a lawman for about ten years, mostly in Missouri and Kansas. Later, he worked a little while in Pueblo, Colorado, right after the railroad made it that far, but he had to kill a man who was connected to some of the town officials. So he drifted north, finally into Wyoming.

Cheyenne first, and then Rawlins in '79, where he took the job as number two in the office of Sheriff Dixon. Wiley was not a big man as most lawmen go. He stood some five foot eight and weighed little more than a hundred and eighty pounds, but he was quick and could be nasty when provoked.

Few knew it but he had been a member of Col Kitchen's regiment of the Seventh Missouri Cavalry who was feared by many a Red Leg and Jayhawker that happened to be unfortunate enough to be near Crowley's Ridge in '64.

Unfortunately, he had taken a nasty leg wound from a twelve-pound Napoleon shell that killed his horse. Luckily, he was picked up by another Gray Coat before the enemy reached him. However, he would not again serve his country on the battlefield.

That kind of fighting had honed his skills well and the job as a lawman often needed just such skills. Twice over the years, he had been assigned to track down *The Arkansas Avenger,* but one thing or another came up and the bandit had eluded him on both occasions. Now he was talking face to face with him and didn't even know it. "You were the first to get there after the killings?"

"No, two of my men were the first. I came along a' hour or so later."

"But you seed all the bodies."

"I did," Quigley agreed as he rolled a smoke and then put his makin's back in his vest pocket.

"Which ones were hung?"

"Seibold and a dude. I don't know his name."

"What's this about a note pined to one of them?"

"Yeah, I have it in my saddlebags. Here I'll get it fur you," Quigley said, and then he turned and walked over to where he had drop-reined Apache in front of the saloon. Taking out the folder paper, he handed it to Bass.

"After reading it he asked, "Which one?"

"Siebold."

Bass nodded his head as this had been his suspicion.

"Anyone actually see the shooting?"

"Not that I can say," Quigley replied almost telling the truth about it.

"How long you been working for Siebold?"

"I started after he was killed."

"Where wus you before?"

"The running *WT*."

"What caused you to change over?"

"Mrs. Seibold needed the help and Somerset don't."

All these questions Bass had already asked others, but he wanted to see how truthful Hancock would be with him, thereby knowing how much he could trust him in the future.

"One last thing."

"Yeah?"

"Was you sweet on the woman?"

"She was a good woman," Quigley replied and then took a deep draw from his smoke, holding it for a few seconds before he blew it out.

"The sheriff authorized me to deputize someone up here if I felt the need. You interested?"

"Nope."

"I think you would do a good job," Bass said looking hard at the big man.

"I'm already doing a good job, working for Mrs. Seibold."

Bass nodded his head a couple of times and then turned and walked away.

Quigley picked up his cartridges from Dave and slipped him a bottle of rye as a tip for not letting anyone know about them. The old-timer just smiled and winked back at him.

On his way back to the *K—S*, twice he saw someone following him, but the snow was blowing so hard he decided not to wait on the rider.

Finally, just as he was removing his saddle the skinny boy rode the mule up to the corral fence.

"Mr. Quigley, I want to help you."

"How can you help me?"

"I am good at tracking, and I am good with this, he said as he lifted the long knife from its scabbard under his coat.

"You're that sheep boy, aren't you?"

"Si. I am who you think."

"Why do you want to leave your sheep?"

"They killed my nombre bola," he said back.

"What?"

"My dog."

Quigley nodded his head and then said, "Well, bring your mount on in the barn out of this wind and we'll get some supper an' coffee in us anyway."

Ryan followed a few steps behind him into the big barn. The temperature inside was as low as outside, but the wind was not so strong and very little snow made it through the cracks between the vertical wallboards.

Quigley had no use for the boy but knew he was likely to get lost if he sent him back during this ground blizzard, so he would allow him to stay at least overnight.

Buckshot was the first of the outfit to see him and he was a little unsure about the taller boy who didn't even wear a gun. He conveniently forgot, a year before he himself had only a single-shot rifle. Nonetheless, he did as instructed and handed the boy a tin cup of hot coffee and then said, "Supper is over, but I 'spect Mr. Beville will be rustling up something for

Mr. Hancock. I'll see about getting you a plate, and there is a spare bunk next to mine if you want it."

"Gracious," Ryan replied and then he suddenly remembered Mendoza's teaching, *'I must think American if I am to speak American.'*

The wind kept it up all that night and most of the next day, but around three in the afternoon it suddenly laid and all became very quite on the plains.

"Alright boys, I hate to say it, but we got cattle to find before they freeze to death in these drifts and Ryan, I think you would serve Mrs. Siebold much better helping with the sheep, you know them better than any of us and you sure don't know beeves."

"I will do as you say, but when I see these men who killed my dog, I weel kill them."

Quigley understood his feelings, *'That dog and old Mendoza were about the only things the boy had in this here world, and now half of them had been taken away from him.'*

Ryan had not just left the sheep by vanishing in the night. Mendoza had allowed him to go into Poison Spider to get a few supplies they needed at the camp. He had brought the wagon but left it at Mr. Marquis' store so the supplies could be loaded and, on an unplanned emotion, followed the big man when he left town. Now that he was back, he hitched Generosa to the wagon and went inside through the backdoor.

Ryan paid no attention to the two men who were talking to the Storekeep. Instead his eyes were focused on the three jars of stripped candy there on the shelf.

Eddie Thorbs and Shelly McCrery had also been sent to town for supplies, but Thorbs just couldn't come and go without the opportunity to tell a tale or two while they were there, not that Joe Marquis was interested in the least. It was during one of his long and uninteresting spills that he glanced over at the boy who was waiting patiently nearby.

Suddenly Thorbs dropped all thought of what he had been so engrossed in and exclaimed, "Hey Shelly! Look, it's that Mex kid from the sheep wagon."

Ryan immediately turned his attention on the two cowboys who began walking his way.

Speaking low so Marquis could not hear him, he whispered, "Bitler said if we caught either one of them sheepers we wus to eliminate 'em. They might a' seed everything that night."

Ryan did not know what the word 'eliminate' meant but he had seen hate before and he understood it very well and began backing up away from the advancing men.

"Leave the boy alone," Ed said.

"You stay out of this Marquis. This are *WT* business," Thorbs answered.

Suddenly Ryan felt his back against the wooden counter and realized he had nowhere to run without climbing over it and he doubted he could do so without the cowboys being on him first.

"Auh Eddie, leave 'im be. He can't even speak English. He can't hurt nothing, he's just a scared kid," Shelly said and backed off a pace.

"No. Bitler said we wus to get 'em," and he slowly began lifting his sixgun from its holster.

Ryan watched as the long barrel was eased up and then turned directly at him and he knew if the man cocked it, it would lead to his death whether here or some other place along the trail they would take him. So before the man's thumb was able to reach the curved hammer, he shot straight at him and with the swiftness no one could have believed, cut Thorbs from ribcage to ribcage and then dashed past them both and out the front door of the store.

Eddie Thorbs dropped his Colt on the hardwood floor and turned to look at his friend, "He cut me Shelly. That blamed Mexican kid cut me."

McCrery looked astonished at Thorbs who was now trying to hold his stomach in such a way to keep his intestines from spilling out, but the flow of blood was such that his hands were becoming slippery and his friend knew it was a losing battle.

Ryan already had Generosa hitched to the buckboard that Quigley had sent them to replace their burned-out sheep wagon, so he jumped on the spring seat and slapped the leather to the mule's back and yelled loudly, "Get up," as he remembered the cowboys doing.

Word of Thorbs' killing spread rapidly across the Big Open, and the story went from mouth to mouth quite differently depending on who told it. Both Ed Marquis and Shelly McCrery said Thorbs had pulled his gun on the boy before he was knifed, but that part seemed to be absent from the way most of the punchers heard it, especially at the *WT*.

Paul Somerset immediately offered a reward for the boy in the amount of $100 dead or alive. When word of this reached the *K—S*, Quigley regretted sending the boy back that morning and decided to bring him in after all. *'He will be safer here at the ranch than out there on the prairie with just Mendoza,'* he thought. Then turning he said, "Buckshot, you and Laramie cut out a good mount from the remuda[4] and head up to the north country and find the Mex boy, bring him back here."

"Yas, Sur," Buckshot replied feeling pride in being given the assignment, and for reasons unknown to him, he let his old deep southern accent burst forth in his answer.

Just as the two were leaving Quigley stopped them. "On your way back cut west and steer well clear of Poison Spider. I don't want you a running into any *WT* hands, or other bounty hunters for that matter."

"Yes sir," Laramie replied and when the two headed out, Quigley stood in the cold wind and watched them for a long time before turning and heading towards the barn.

---

4 Remuda: Spanish term meaning the horse herd.

Chapter Forty

The Arapahoe

Black Horn Nose had offered four good ponies for the girl with the sun hair, but the old warrior demanded six, an unheard-of amount for a girl not yet fully grown and he refused. Still, the sight of the pretty little face and the long yellow hair captivated him and finally on the very day the Comanche were breaking winter camp in their preparation to move south before the coming snows, he led the six ponies over and tied them in front of Pacing Bear's tepee and waited.

After looking over the horses with a long and keen eye, the old man sent for Sun Child and traded her to the Arapahoe brave.

Sun Child had been only four years old when she came to live with the Comanche and had no remembrance of her life before, including the fact she had the Christian name of Cynthia Loren, or that her father had been killed and his scalp was the blonde one that hung from Pacing Bear's lance. Neither did she remember her mother being sold to the rich Mexican. She only remembered being well treated by Pacing Bear and his wives and she was not at all happy when she learned she was being traded to an Arapahoe she had never before seen.

However Black Horn Nose was infatuated by the girl and soon she was the queen of his world and when she came of age, Sun Child became his bride. That had been in the year the white men found the yellow rocks on the Arapahoe reservation in Colorado and moved in by the hundreds. Often conflicts would ensue between the two cultures and soon Black Horn Nose became a feared warrior, and most respected by his fellow Arapahoe, as well as their friends the Northern Cheyenne.

By the time their second child came, his lance sported seven additional scalps. He was as good a hunter as he was a fierce warrior and their teepee was never without food. All of this started to come to an end by the time of the treaty at Medicine Lodge Creek in October, 1867, when the Cheyenne and Arapahoe were restricted to the land from the Kansas border south to the Red Fork of the Arkansas River.

A good piece of land when the buffalo were there, but when they moved north or south, there was very little left for the Indians to hunt and by 1875, the buffalo were becoming less plentiful.

Five years later Black Horn Nose led a party of thirty-five families north into Canada seeking a place to live in peace, but the Assinaboine and Crees did not want to share their land with these people from the south and the small band of Sun People turned back south, stopping at the agency in Fort Belknap on the Milk River for supplies. Afterward, they agreed to go to the Shoshone Reservation in the Wind River Range.

Sun Child was thirty-six years old when Laramie Patay heard of her existence and the two passed within three miles of one another as he went north in his search for his mother, and she and her family traveled south towards Wyoming.

Twice before, her husband had been threatened that she would be taken if found, for it was unlawful for any Indian to have a white captive. But their love was far greater than white man's threats and she continued to elude all searchers for her. Sun Child did not like being on the land of their old enemies the Shoshone. She had wanted to return to the Cimarron Country, but she knew they should not go there, not after the trouble with the black-white men, which had been the reason of their journey to the land of the Old Woman[1] in the first place.

By late December 1879, times were becoming hard on the Indians in the Nations. The Buffalo had not come south in herds like always before and food was scarce. Although she never would do so in front of Black Horn Nose, Sun Child wept silently late at night after her starving children finally were asleep.

Still, he knew of her tears and felt a great weight upon his shoulders for not properly feeding his family. Finally, in desperation, he approached a family of black white men who farmed at the northern boundaries of the Nations in an attempt to trade for food, but the woman who first saw them was frightened and ran home screaming.

"What is it, Bonnet?" Seth shouted as he stopped her run by grabbing her shoulders and shaking her.

"Indians!" was all she could say.

He turned just as the party of four rode into the field from the riverbank.

"Lord Jesus," he said and then releasing her, he too began to run for the log house only a hundred yards away. "Josh, Josh," he yelled as he ran.

"What is it?" shouted his brother as he came from the little house.

"Hostiles."

Immediately Josh turned back inside and just as his brother and sister-in-law entered through the doorway he stepped out and fired his shotgun.

---

[1] The Old Woman: What the plains Indians called The Queen of England.

The Indians were too far away for a scattergun to be effective but by chance, and bad luck for all concerned, a single ball of birdshot hit Sky Eyes in one of his blue eyes, blinding him on that side for the remainder of his life.

When Black Horn Nose saw his oldest son fall from his pony, he became enraged and charged the cabin. When close enough, he sent his iron tomahawk on a flight true as if shot from a rifle into the skull of Josh Tookes, just as the man again raised the old single barrel muzzleloader.

Returning to the others, he saw his son would live but his rage was still not quenched, and he ordered the cabin fired. They waited at rifle range for the occupants to come out while the roof blazed brightly.

Mariah Scott saw the black smoke rising thickly in the morning sky and giving no thought as to what could be the cause, she quickly loaded a small barrel in the back of her buckboard and headed for the river to fill it. Once having accomplished this task, she charged towards the source of the smoke.

Her arrival had been unexpected by the Indians and upon seeing her, Carved Stone let out a war hoop and heeled his spotted pony toward the wagon.

Mariah heard the yelps of the charging boy and dropping her reins, jumped from the buckboard and grabbed her own rifle, quickly sending a 32 round into his young chest, toppling him backward from his horse.

Black Horn Nose seeing this, allowed his fury to once more accelerate, but when his son began trying to rise from where he had fallen, his father suddenly began to find a war between emotions raging within his own heart. Finally, love won, and he slowly rode ahead holding his lance high over his head with both hands.

Mariah had quickly reloaded her rifle and had a fine bead drawn on the approaching savage, but she sensed he no longer was a threat and when he stopped beside the man, she had shot, she lowered her rifle to her waist.

She watched as the older man slid from his pony and with loving care lifted the wounded man in his arms and then turned and carried him back to where the other rider still sat upon his horse.

They never saw these Indians again. However, the tomahawk that had killed Josh and the lance that the other Indian had left there beside the bloody stain on the cold ground both proved without any doubt that these had been Arapahoe.

Chapter Forty One

The First Reward

Mendoza had not heard about the reward, but when he did, he was not surprised. *'The men who killed my sheep and hung my boss will not be punished, but when a WT man gets cut by a boy defending himself, there 'ees a reward.'*

Turning he looked at Ryan, "Si you most go with them, Señor Quigley is right. It 'ess no longer safe for you to be here. Many men will come searching for you because of d'ess dinero."

The news was welcomed by Ryan. He had become suddenly more than the Mexican boy who tended the sheep, he was worth one hundred American pesos dead or alive. *'Few can boast of more.'*

Mendoza had secreted a government carbine[1] he found in one of the scabbards left by the dead men that night, and he decided to give it and the ten cartridges he had to Ryan. "This

---

[1] Government Carbine: Short barrel version of the 1873 Springfield. It was issued to US Cavalry Troops and fired a 45-70 copper cartridge known as the Government 45 round.

weel protect you muchos better than your old rifle, trade with me, it is all I need here to chase off the wolves."

"But what of the mal hombres?[2]" Ryan questioned.

"I alone could not stop them if I had a hundred rifles. So, what need do I have with that one, it 'ess best for you to have it," he said, nodding his head.

They could see the logic in what he said. Alone with a single shot rifle that he usually left in the sunken cabin, he would be no match if riders came intent on doing him harm. So, Ryan took the Springfield and the rounds before hugging his ole friend, then he mounted the horse they had brought for him. It was bigger and younger than his own, which he left for Mendoza, just in case.

Less than an hour after the three rode off to the southwest, two horsemen topped the rise to the east of his camp.

Curly watched the old man for a while and then turning to his pard he said, "Buford I only see the one."

"Me, too."

"What do you think?" Curly asked.

"I reckon the boy's down thar som'ers, if we can't find him, we sho' as hell can get that old Mex to tell us whar he be," Gillyard replied.

Without any more conversation, Curley spurred his horse and they started moving down the slope.

The sheep had grazed off most of the grass near the sunken cabin and slowly drifted further north some three-quarters of a mile. When Mendoza saw the two coming, he knew their game immediately, but really had no place to hide, and nothing to fight them with, except his brain and courage.

"Whar's that Mex kid?"

"No hablar Englash," he replied and lifted his shoulders.

"The boy? Ah, how do you say, ah, chico, little chico?"

"Ah, chico. He 'ess cierto que."

Gillyard shook his head, "What the hell did he say?"

"I think he is saying he is gone."

---

[2] Mal hombres: Mexican for evil men.

"Gone whar?" Gillyard shouted at the older man and drawing his new Remington he pointed it at the shepherd.

Mendoza opened his eyes as wide as he could and then threw both of his arms as high as he could and started whimpering.

"Shooting him ain't gon'a find the boy."

"I ain't gon'a shoot him. I just want him to think so," Buford said back as if Curley should have known this.

Hearing the man's words gave Mendoza an idea and he immediately dropped to his knees and bowed his head and began praying unceasingly.

"Hey stop that," Gillyard ordered. "You. I said stop that." When that didn't get the results he wanted, he fired a round at the man's feet causing dirt to fly up stinging Mendoza's legs, but he only increased the volume of his chanting.

"Hell, Buford, you got him so scared he ain't gon'a tell us nothing," Curley said, and then turning his horse's neck he added, "Come on let's see if we can track 'im."

"Oh, you dumb son-a'-bitch, I ought to shoot you," Gillyard said, and then as if he just had to do something to show his power, he shot his last four rounds at the sheep killing one and wounding another.

When they rode away Mendoza stood and watched them disappear over the western horizon, *'It 'ess not I who 'ess the dumb son-of-a-bitch, Señor.'*

It was well past dark when the two rode into the *WT* spread. "Where the hell you two been?" Dakota asked.

"Looking fur the Mex kid," Curley said back as he dismounted.

"Didn't find them?"

"We found the sheep alright, and that old Mexican, but the boy was gone. I 'spect he high tailed it back to Mexico when he heard of the reward on his head," Curley said. Then as an afterthought he added with a snicker, "Buford did bushwhack a few lambs though, that ought to be good for a dollar or two."

"Shut up, Driggers," Gillyard shot back.

However, this only caused both of the others to smile at each other.

A heavy snow began falling the following day and lasted most of the night. This was followed by a day of total calmness before the winds returned the next day and blew most of the white blanket off towards Nebraska.

Quigley had expected this, it was the pattern of the weather on the northern plains and he had worked over a plan in his mind.

Just at sundown he called together his squad of young riders and told them to get their gear and mount up. "We're going on a midnight ride."

When Ryan saw what was happening, he came to the foreman. Quigley saw him coming and knew what was on his mind. *'The boy has not been trained. He can't hit a damn thing with a handgun and a rifle is practically useless from the back of a galloping horse, but how the hell am I gon'a tell him no again?'*

"Señor Quigley, _______," Ryan began, but he was cut off.

"Get your carbine and get mounted with the others. I might need someone to hold the horses," Quigley said, knowing full well that was very unlikely.

Ryan smiled broadly and then ran towards the barn. Buckshot nodded to him when he saw Ryan saddling up the horse they had brought to him that day.

The two had become quite good friends in the few weeks since Ryan had come to work at the main ranch. Mrs. Seibold had also come to like the lad. He was extremely quiet, very respectful and never complained about anything she asked of him.

Late one afternoon after sowing some feed to the chickens, she spotted Buckshot staring at the old guitar her husband used to strum and having no need for it, she gave it to the boy. She would have also given him lessons, only she had not the slightest knowledge of how to play a string instrument.

It was alright, Buckshot began teaching himself, much to the discomfort of his friends who shared the bunkhouse with him.

However, this night there would be no time for guitar playing. This night, the moon would be bright when it came up, in a couple of hours, and it was during this time of mostly darkness Quigley rode deep onto *WT* land.

He was not really worried about being spotted, during the long months he had worked there he got to know the routine of Bitler's thoughts, and he doubted anything had changed very much. Besides, the *WT* outnumbered the smaller spread more than two to one, even after losing a few hands early in the war. Quigley felt confident Bitler would not be expecting anything out of the ordinary on a cold night like this.

When they were a mile shy of Somerset's home, the moon was just beginning to appear on the horizon, illuminating the ranch yard and buildings. There he stopped his men and explained for the first time what his plan was.

"Look yonder at that herd of beeves they have been brought in close to keep them from getting down in some draw and freezing to death. Mostly there will be only two riders out on a night like this, and with the wind up, they will be huddled down inside their coats, trying to keep from freezing themselves.

We'll ease up on them and take 'em by surprise. I don't want a shot fired if it can be helped."

He stopped and let this sink in before he continued, "Once we get them out of the way, we'll stampede the herd towards the house and then high tail it back here to this very spot. Everybody clear on that?"

Receiving no comments, he nodded his head satisfied they were all in tune and slowly moved towards the three hundred longhorns bunched ahead.

On the ride over, Buckshot had thought his feet were frozen for sure, and remembering the earlier warnings, was certain they would soon fall off. However, now as they rode down that sloping grade, he suddenly felt warm, even hot and was afraid he would soon begin to sweat.

He wondered if a man could sweat when it was below freezing, but couldn't find a satisfactory answer within himself, and dared not ask others for fear they would think him ignorant.

Paul Spalding was, just as Quigley predicted, moving as slowly as he could and not be totally stopped. His head could not be seen and it looked like his hat simply sat atop his turned-up collar. Both hands were deep in the pockets of the coat and his reins loosely tied together and dropped over the horn.

The whine of the wind hid any sound of them approaching, and even the whooshing of the lariat Quigley swung in a big circle before dropping it over the rider came silently to his victim.

Paul jerked when the rope hit him, but he was too cold and deep in thought to react quickly and was sliding off the back of his horse's rump before he really knew what was happening.

Quigley had never had any trouble with Spalding, and only drug him a short way before he stopped and looped several more rings around the puncher where he sat.

"What the hell?"

"Just set easy Paul, and you won't be hurt."

The cowboy shook his head a couple of times and then looking up at the huge man, recognized who was there. "Damn Quigley, what 'gew doing?"

Remembering Spalding walked with a strong limp, caused from being thrown some years back and breaking his thigh bone, he knew he could not get very far, very fast on foot.

His plan had been to either tie the riders up, or at least take their boots and horses, but because of the temperature being so low and with this man's limp, he just dropped the rope and said, "Paul, best you stay out of the way until this is over."

"What's over?"

"Ryan, get his handgun," he ordered still looking at the *WT* rider.

When the boy got up close to Spalding, he looked at him and said, "Hey, ain't you that Mex kid what has the reward on his head?"

Ryan didn't reply as he lifted the Colt from the man's holster.

"Better get his whole rig," Quigley added, so the boy unbuckled the gun belt and jerked hard on it causing the man to spin around on the frozen ground.

"Hey."

"Go easy, Paul. I could leave you the same way Bitler left Seibold and the boys," Quigley said, and immediately Spalding's mouth clamped shut.

Quigley nodded his approval at the way Ryan had handled himself and then said, "Keep the sixgun. We'll teach you to use it later. Take his hat and ride his horse and lead yours."

Ryan nodded his head and taking the reins of the *WT* mount he returned to his own horse. There he mounted the strange animal, then reached for his own reins and began leading him away.

When they located the other outrider, Quigley stopped. "Ryan, you are about the same size as Spalding, ease up close to him and get his attention if you can. If you have to get the drop on him with that, don't shot unless you have to. I want to keep this as quiet as possible."

Ryan, now feeling the pride of being so chosen, moved out towards the other *WT* man. The others fell in a few yards behind and moved off to the side where they could flank them.

Buford Gillyard would not be so easy. He too was huddled down in his coat, but not so oblivious to his surroundings and he saw the rider approaching, "You ought 'a be on the other side a' the herd," he said.

Ryan knew better than reply, which Gillyard took as unusual, but considering the cold and the wind he was not yet alarmed. Finally, when Ryan was only a few yards away he asked. "You got any makin's? I done used all a' mine."

Again, he received no answer and this time he was curious, suddenly he realized the striped coat the rider was wearing was not the fur-lined buckskin one Spalding had on and he went for his gun, "Hold it right there."

Quigley heard the command and hoped the boy had done as he had instructed, and was holding the Colt on the older man, but no report came and he decided not to wait any longer. He spurred his horse forward towards the dim outlines ahead and the others followed.

When they got there, they saw Gillyard lying on the ground staring up at the stars through lifeless eyes.

The sight of his throat having been cut from ear to ear almost upset Buckshot's stomach. Suddenly he gained great respect for a man who knew how to use a knife.

"I thought I told you to get the drop on him?"

"You said no shoot," Ryan said back strongly. Then a little less defensive he added looking down at the dead cowboy, "He ess one of de caballero's who come that night."

"Alright. Let's get on with this," Quigley said then he removed from one of his saddlebags a white sheet Mrs. Seibold had given him just for this project. Passed one end over to Dusty and said, "Hook your stirrup in one end and hold the other high and let's make a sail."

Almost immediately the wind grabbed at the cotton and it blossomed out and began bulging brightly in the moonlight. "Yee Haw," Quigley yelled, and the others followed suit.

The cattle seeing the strange white sail coming at them immediately panicked and began to run.

As instructed, the others moved out to the sides, keeping the stampede headed straight for the buildings just over the rise.

Chuck Bitler felt the vibration before he heard the roar. Unsure of what was making his bunk move he sat up and swung his legs over the side.

It took a few seconds before he realized just what was happening. When it hit him, he jumped up and grabbed his hat and then located his pants. Running for the door that separated the foreman's private quarters from the rest of the bunkhouse, he threw the door open and yelled, "Stampeeeed!"

However, he could see most of the men were doing as he, trying to get their duds on.

When sure the beeves would not change their course, Quigley nodded for Dusty to drop his side and then he began rolling the sheet around his left arm, before turning and heading back to their prearranged rendezvous point.

Laramie was the last to return, and as he rode up, he saw the big man watching intently through a long telescoping glass at the happenings below.

Quigley was silently counting the horsemen that were taking off after the racing herd. Once satisfied, he motioned for the others with a short wave of his uplifted arm to follow and then eased down the slope with the moon on their backs.

Just as they approached the outer rim of the ranch yard, he stopped and reaching back into his saddlebags, he removed a small round oil can. Pitching it to Buckshot he began tearing the sheet into strips. "Pour that coal oil on these and let's make some torches." Then turning he added, "Ryan, break away some of the smaller pieces of the corral to tie these too."

"What are we going to do?" Buckshot asked.

"We are going to fire all the buildings."

Suddenly, remembering back to what the Union Troops were planning to do to his home back in Florida, Buckshot was not so sure he wanted to be a part of this. "But what about Mrs. Somerset?"

"She's in Red Bluff tonight," Quigley said, and then he thumb-nailed a Lucifer and lit his torch. The others did the same and so Buckshot also followed the example.

The Bunkhouse was the first to go up, followed by the barn. When it came to the larger house Quigley stopped them. "This one I'll do myself." As he dismounted and walked up the steps entering through the front door.

They waited for a few minutes and Laramie was beginning to get nervous. "They are bound to have seen this and headed back by now," he said nervously.

"Yeah," Buckshot agreed, looking towards the west, the direction *WT* riders were last seen charging over the hill.

Finally, they saw the brightness appear through several windows and they knew he had set the fire in many rooms throughout the two-story house. Still, they waited until he finally appeared back on the front porch.

They all saw he was looking straight at something, and turning their heads following his gaze, they too saw the man approaching. His obvious limp identified him as Paul Spalding.

Quigley mounted and rode up beside the exhausted man who was shaking his head, "Boy, oh boy, Quigley, you sure done gone and stirred up a hornet's nest."

"The stirring was when *WT* hands killed Etta. I'm just paying back what they did to the home of those Sheepherders back there on the Crick."

Then he looked over his work, before turning back to the man standing there below. "And you tell Somerset, if he wants to continue this, I'll be waiting and I'm better at this kind of thing than he is, or that two-bit foreman of his."

"I'll say that, but I don't know what Gillyard will say."

"Don't you worry none about what Gillyard is goin' to say, I sure as hell ain't." Then he touched the front brim of his hat and led his bunch away to the south.

Paul looked around and finally saw his horse standing off a couple of hundred yards down reined, and he slowly, on sore feet, headed off hoping he could catch the cayuse.

He had just mounted when he saw the others coming back on a dead run. Pulling up beside him, Somerset yelled, "Who done this?"

"Can't rightly say, Mr. Somerset. They wus wearing hoods when they jumped me."

"Where's Gillyard?" Bitler asked."

"The last time I see'd him, he was on the east side of the herd," Spalding said, truthfully this time.

"Hell, it were that Quigley Hancock and the *K—S* outfit, and you know it."

"Mee'be. Like I said, they all were wearing white hoods."

"Why didn't you warn us?" Somerset screamed at him.

"They jumped me. Took my gun and put me a foot. I just now caught up my horse."

Turning to Christy King and Dakota, Bitler said angrily, "Go find Gillyard, he's probably afoot too."

On the long ride home, Buckshot leaned over to Laramie and asked, "How did he know Mrs. Somerset was going to be in Red Bluff tonight?"

"I don't rightly know, but it's his job to know such I reckon."

This made sense to Buckshot and he nodded his head in approval.

Two weeks later Deputy Bass showed up at the *K—S* wanting to talk to Quigley.

"You don't know nothing about it? You think I'm plum dumb?"

"What did their riders say? They're bound to have had some out looking for the culprits?"

"One was found with his neck slit, and the other claims hooded men jumped him and set 'im afoot."

"Hume," Quigley replied, smiling inside at Paul Spalding.

"Well, I reckon you had better question him some more."

"Can't. He lit out of the territory last week."

"Well, since you are here, I got a complaint on the *WT* outfit. A couple of their hands came upon our land and roughed up our sheepman and killed a few of our stock a couple weeks back." He then stopped and took a deep breath before continuing. "But unlike those who sent you here, we can identify them what done this." Then he began rolling a cigarette. "Said they wus after the little boy who helps him watch the lambs."

"Little boy and his lambs, that the same little boy that spilled a *WT* man's guts all over the store in Poison Spider?"

"The way I hear it from the store-keep who witnessed it, was that man had his gun out and was threaten' the boy before a knife was seen."

"I heard that too. That's why I ain't after him."

"Tell me, something Deputy, how come rich men can place bounties on the heads of folks that didn't do no wrong, but when their men do wrong, nothing is done about it?"

"I'm working on it, Hancock," Bass said, as he kicked the cold ground with the toe of his boot. "If you had taken that badge when I offered it, you could a' cleaned up this mess and I wouldn't had to make this two-day ride."

"I got a job already, don't need yours."

Quigley knew he was one up on Bass at the moment, but he also knew Bass was no fool and he would have to play his cards carefully. He also knew Somerset was sure not going to take the burning of his home sitting down, so he had better be ready. *'Much better to work so the law is always on our side or Somerset's money and influence with the Cattleman's Association would be enough to get warrants issued if we screwed up, and then Bass would be back.'*

He had been lucky with Spalding high-tailing it out of the country. He realized it had been a mistake letting him see who they were. Years ago, he would have just killed any witnesses, but after the shooting of Stanly Scott something had come over him and he never again wanted to be a part of the killing of innocent folk.

"I'll tell you what, Wiley Bass. If you convict the ones who were responsible for the lynching of Mrs. Siebold's husband, I'll help you find the ones what fired Somerset's house."

"I'll bet you would," Bass said and then turned and taking his reins in hand, mounted his zebra dun. "Time will come when you'll need help, Hancock."

"Have a safe trip back to Rawlins, Deputy Bass," he said fighting with all his might the smile that was trying to erupt across his face.

Bass heeled his gelding and took off to the south without looking back.

Quigley had not known about Etta feeding Abbey information, but he wished he had a scalawag in the **WT** camp right now. *'They will be coming, and soon, I'm just not sure when and where.'*

Finally, he decided that with the few men he still had, his best bet was to tighten up what had to be protected and place his men out as far as he dared, hoping someone would spot trouble before it arrived.

Something else suddenly hit him. *'Bitler won't give a continental damn about Mrs. Siebold being in the home or not when they come to even the score, so I need to get her out of here and fast.'*

"Dusty," he yelled.

The tall boy of about 20 years came out of the barn with a pitchfork in his hand, "Yeah?"

"Saddle up that Smutty Morgan and head out to the south after Deputy Bass. Tell him I have a deal for him if he will come back."

"Right now?"

"Right now. He's got a ten-minute head start, but that Morgan is good for the run. Now hurry."

"Yes sir," Dusty said, and turned quickly and disappeared back in the barn.

Now he had two problems, one convincing his stubborn boss-lady to leave and what to offer Bass in trade.

"I know Mrs. Siebold, but we are down a couple of hands as you know, and now Bass says Somerset is blaming us for his house catching on fire."

"House catching on fire. Quigley, I can see how a man's house can catch on fire, but when his barn and bunkhouse burn at the same time ________." She let the statement fall as it would.

"Yes Ma'am. I suppose there were a lot of cinders falling that night."

"I suspect there were," she said back. "That don't mean I aim to leave my home. When I come back it might be cinders too."

"Not if I'm alive."

"It's out of the question. Where would I go anyway?"

"I've already sent a runner to bring back Deputy Bass. He can escort you to Rawlins and from there you can take the train either direction. I'll send for you just as soon as it's safe."

She suddenly gave in to a deep frown and shook her head. "I-I just can't."

"Ma'am, I don't know why you want to fight me. With you here, I'll have to assign at least three men to watch over you and I need every man I have to watch for the approach of **WT** riders when they come. And you know they ain't going to send me a letter advising me when to be ready."

"Oh, alright, but to Rawlins, no further," she said, and this seemed it was as far as she was budging.

He really didn't like it. Rawlins was the county seat of Carbon County and Somerset was sure to have business there on occasion. If not him, some of the other big ranchers in the area who might know her on sight, but he figured he might as well take what he was able to get while it was on the table. It may not be there for long.

"What kind of deal?" the deputy asked.

"I'll tell you what the motive was in the Etta Williams murder."

"She was killed because she was there," Bass replied, as if that was simple.

"Perhaps, but why was she there?"

"Plying her trade, I reckon."

"Wrong. She was there to give Miles Abbey information on the *WT* spread. She would not have been killed that night if Bitler had not discovered she was a spy."

"How do you know this?"

"There was a witness."

"Yeah, I know. Those two boys, but they were up on the hill, they already told me they couldn't hear any of the conversations."

"There was another, closer. We have never revealed this for his own safety," Quigley said but decided not to tell him there actually were two witnesses.

"I need to talk to him."

"He's not here. I got him hid out where Bitler can't get to him," Quigley said back.

"Well, before I go arresting Bitler fur this, I will need to hear it for myself."

"Fair enough. Now will you take Mrs. Siebold to Rawlins?"

"Do I have a choice?"

"One other thing Bass."

The deputy looked hard at the big man as if to say, this had better be good.

"I think it would be better if no one in Rawlins knows who she is."

Bass gritted his teeth, but he knew this was also probably for the best, so as a reply he nodded his head.

An hour later Quigley called Ryan and Buckshot, "Boys head up north and get Mendoza and his sheep back near the ranch. I know that bunch hate them sheep almost as much as they do us and I can't protect him up there and the ranch down here at the same time."

Seeing they understood, he added, "And then hightail it back here. I'll need you more than he does."

He began placing a rider at five locations, some two to three miles out around the main buildings. "You will be relieved every twelve hours but stay alert. If they see you first there is a good chance you will never see the next sunrise."

He then called in Dusty, Chris and Laramie. "Boys be ready to ride at a moment's notice. I want you out of here when the attack comes, that way you can hit them from behind. So as soon as we find out from where they are coming, you head out the opposite direction and cut around behind them."

The boys shared the pride in being the chosen few at the *K—S*, and after his little talk, their chests seemed to swell two inches.

That night they waited, and the same the following night with no signs of any trouble. However, on the third night Effird Nelson, who was due south in a little draw that cut from the rise, spotted several mounted riders moving from the east to the southwest and he immediately cut a truck for home to report.

Quigley sent Dusty out on the Morgan to bring the others in, but it was a futile move as no raiders showed that night at all.

The next day two hours after sunup Quigley rode out with Effird to see if he could track them. Hopefully to a camp where they could strike from. But when the two came upon the trail left by the horsemen, Quigley was astonished to see the tracks were made by unshod horses.

"What does it mean?" Nelson asked. "I ain't heared of injuns in these parts in nigh on five year."

"I'm not sure. They are generally headed for the reservation over on the Wind, but I don't know where they would be coming from."

"You reckon Somerset is planning on using injuns to jump us?"

"I don't rule out the possibilities of anything, but where would he have contacted them? There just ain't none east a here 'cept up in Montana."

"Can you tell what kind they are?" Nelson asked showing real concern.

"Naw, not from what I see here," Quigley said back, but he was curious. If he had not been so desperately needed back at the ranch, he would have followed them and seen just what they were up to.

"But I don't think they are a war party. See those drags? They're made by lodge poles. This little bunch has their women and children with them."

Quigley then mounted and pulling on his reins, turned Apache's head. "Let's head back, and Nelson, don't say anything to the others. I don't want Laramie going charging after them looking for his mother."

"Yes, sir."

Of course, this was true, but he really was more concerned about his men getting nervous over fighting Indians. He had trained them to fight gorilla style, with cowboys as their opponents, and they were confident they were better at it than the *WT* men. But that feeling might not be so strong against hostile Indians.

Chapter Forty Two

Raiding Indians and Indian Raiders

From a far hill, Black Horn Nose studied the barn, bunkhouse, corral, tack shack, and the Seibold house that made up the *K—S*'s plaza. Then he took his twelve men and their families in a wide detour around the cluster of buildings.

He wanted no trouble with the white men who worked there.

He had taken his people to Fort Laramie in an attempt to get permission to go north to live with their friends the Cheyenne instead of their old enemies the Shoshone, but all they received from the agent there was the same as it had been at Fort Washakie. "Word will be sent to Washington about the request and we will have to wait for a reply."

He wondered many times who this great Chief Washington was, and how he could have so much control over the white men everywhere. *'His medicine must be very powerful.'*

Somerset wanted his foreman to do the very same thing to the *K—S* outfit as had been done to him, but Chuck Bitler knew Hancock would be watching for such.

He wanted to come up with something different, something unexpected. He also realized they did not have enough good hands to retaliate at that time. That is not to say they didn't have enough men working there, but most of those were common cowhands. They were hard and tough, they had to be to ride the range in such a harsh climate, but they were not gunslingers and could not be counted on for a real down and dirty fight. Neither was he sure if they could be counted on to keep their mouths shut afterward.

Somerset had once again sent south for more gun hawks and Bitler wanted to wait until they arrived before he made a strike, but the boss didn't like the delay and was applying pressure for some action.

Exactly one week after they lost the ranch buildings, he and three men went to clean out the sheep herd, but it was nowhere to be found, obviously having been moved back nearer the K—S's main spread, so he returned empty-handed.

The following morning before sun-up he sent Curley Driggers and Isaac Hardy to find the sheep and to generally keep an eye on the K—S. It was these two who reported the Indian camp southwest of the K—S spread, around a little buffalo wallow, which still held moisture from the previous storm that had laid so much wet snow on the plains.

Suddenly Bitler thought, *'Perhaps these Indians have been provided just for our use.'*

Less than an hour after Quigley and Nelson turned back from the Indian trail, Bitler had every able-bodied *WT* man who could ride a horse, armed with a long gun and headed for the Indian camp. Arriving a little before dawn on April Fool's Day in the year 1881, they dismounted and loosened the cinches of their saddles giving a slight respite to their mounts awaiting the change in the eastern sky.

From where they waited atop a slight rise far off to the south, Independence Rock could be seen, appearing to be no more than a tiny anthill in the vast openness of the Red Desert.

Below in the depression as soon as it was full light, the women began taking down the tepees and making ready for travel. While this was happening, Bitler ordered his men to encircle the camp, and once satisfied this had been accomplished, he, with Curley Driggers on his left, and Dakota on his right, rode over the hill directly towards the band of Arapahoe.

Black Horn Nose saw them coming and quickly assembled his warriors, with orders for the women and children to stay out of sight as much as possible. Then he walked out to meet the three riders who had stopped some eighty yards out from the little band.

"You speak English?" Bitler asked.

"I speak the white man's tongue."

"You are on our land, that's trespassing, it's against the law."

"All of this is the land of my forefathers, you are on it," Black Horn Nose replied swinging his arm widely about him.

"Yeah, maybe back then, but now this here is *K—S* land and you are trespassing and we aim to collect a toll fur you trespassing over our ranch."

"Toll?" the Indian questioned, "What is this toll?"

"Means you have to pay. We want one of your women or your blood."

"You would take one of our wives?"

"We'll give her back when we are through with her. It's the law of the *K—S*, give us one or die," Bitler said, letting his voice rise just a little at the end.

"Bitler," Dakota said in a most disheartened voice.

"Shut up Dakota. I know what I'm doing."

The old Indian looked around at the riders, they were all out of range for the bow, some of his men carried rifles but not all and they had a very limited amount of bullets for them. Nevertheless, he saw no way out and when he turned back, he had his tomahawk in hand, and before any of the *WT* men realized what was happening, the iron headed hatchet was twirling over and over. It caught Dakota high in his right breast burying itself three inches. The boy screamed and fell backward off his horse.

Almost immediately thereafter, a burst of gunfire erupted from the others behind Black Horn Nose and one Henry round struck Bitler in the left wrist. Driggers was hit twice, once in the leg and once in the right side of his head, taking off most of that ear, but he managed to stay mounted and he and Bitler lit a shuck back as fast as they could, leaving Dakota screaming on the ground.

The smoke had not cleared before the volley of rifles and shotguns began pouring fire into the little camp from the men surrounding them, but Bitler had had enough, and when he reached his men he did not stop, rather kept riding northeast as fast as his horse would carry him. This surprised everyone, so without someone giving orders to the contrary, they all followed him.

Sun Child was the first to see her youngest son fall to the hail of lead that rained upon them. A heavy buffalo round hit the twelve-year-old boy squarely in the back of his head and exited through his right eye taking most of his face with it.

Several others had also been hit, mostly women and children who were closest to the men on the hill behind the village, and a few of these wounds would be fatal. But the only person who lay dead at the moment was Wea Kae ha', known to the soldiers at Fort Washakie as Little Hawk Eyes.

Bitler, even though in great pain, rode as straight as he could towards the *K—S* spread. When Driggers fell from his horse due to loss of blood, Bitler had him strapped over his saddle and continued on until they were close to the *K—S*, there they dropped his body, then turned to the northeast and soon disappeared into the white blanket of wet snow that still covered much of the land as far as he could see.

Lucius Reed watched them pass from his point of concealment but since they no longer seem headed in the direction of the ranch, he did not investigate their passing further and did not report it to Quigley until after he was relieved at noon.

As soon as they passed the *K—S*, Bitler had his men scatter, riding in pairs in different directions so they no longer would leave the obvious trail they had since the raid on the little Indian camp, and he and Christy King cut a trail for Poison Spider.

It was this wide trail they had left that would bring Black Horn Nose straight as an arrow to the *K—S* buildings. The old chief stopped only long enough to remove the scalp from the dying Driggers and then on they charged towards to ranch.

At another time, or under different circumstances, he would have taken his band and continued on to Fort Washakie and let the army punish those responsible. But the wailing of his wife and the rent in his heart fed the desire for revenge with such force he had no place in his conscious mind for doing things the white man's way. Not this time. This time he would return to the old ways, to the days when an Arapahoe was a man, not a slave, or a whimpering dog begging for others to feed him, to right a wrong was what he must do. This day his scalping knife once more ran red with the blood of those who would murder women and children.

Terry Ellick was who had relieved Reed, and in his haste to get back to the warmth of a wood stove and a hot cup of Arbuckle's, Reed was over a mile away when he realized he had failed to tell Ellick about the riders he had seen passing from the southwest to the northeast an hour before. *'Hell, they were sure high tailing it on by. I don't see no reason to go all the way back just to tell him about it. I'll tell Quigley and he can make that decision.'*

How did this happen?" Doc Smyth asked him as he tended to the shattered wrist.

"I wus riding out towards our south line shack when a sharpshooter blasted me," Bitler replied.

"You see who it was?"

"He was big, as big a man as I ever seen, can't say fur sure but there ain't but one man around these parts that big, and he was riding a paint horse, too."

"If you are referring to Quigley Hancock, I hate to disappoint you. I seen him posting a letter over at the hotel about an hour ago, and from the amount of blood you have been losing, this couldn't have been much longer than that or you would a' been dead by now."

"It still could have been him," Bitler said disappointed his plan was busted.

"Nope, ain't no way he could a made it to or from that line camp in time to shoot you, and still get back here when I seen him. You must be mistaken, Bitler."

Doc Smyth had always been friends with Paul and Gayle Somerset, but he had to admit this range war was well out of hand and he could see a big part of the cause lay at the door of his friend, and friends or not, with the owners. He never had any use for Somerset's foreman, and especially so after he had heard the rumors that it was Bitler who had shot Etta Williams.

Doc had been a regular customer of the young girl and he was quite fond of her and tried more than once to get her to stay out of the way of the trouble that was brewing around Poison Spider. For that reason, he had no sympathy for the obvious pain he was putting Bitler through while he probed the wound.

Quigley had indeed posted a letter that morning, to one Miss Camilla Gustav at the Elk Horn Hotel in Rawlins Wyoming. He also had left a small, tied handkerchief in which was a silver dollar with a note to give it to Ole Dave when he came in. Quigley was confident, upon seeing the coin, the Jehu would understand its meaning and hand-deliver the letter to Mrs. Seibold, for the man who bought Dave a drink, had bought Dave's loyalty.

It was well past noon when Quigley dismounted Apache and placed his saddle over the corral's top rung, and it was almost that very moment Black Horn Nose was bloodying his knife by removing the lock and scalp from the not quite dead Terry Ellick.

The cowboy had been sitting quietly behind one of the big rocks that had been formed thousands of years before when pressures from deep in the earth expanded and caused several limestone boulders to form into a massive pile on either side of this little rise.

From his position, he could see anything moving to the south or the east; he didn't worry much about anything to the west, it was unlikely *WT* hands would come from that direction. Besides this was where Reed had been, and he could see nothing wrong with its location.

The approaching Arapahoe had watched Reed being relieved and chose to allow him to depart unmolested, securing the lookout that remained behind would be alone and unsuspecting.

Terry heard the sound made by the bowstring being released and for a moment he thought, *'I've heard that sound before, where was it?'* He did not have time to dwell long on the subject before the tin point sliced into his back and protruded out four inches after passing through his left lung. He did have time for one last thought before they were on him though, *'Oh, yes, that is what makes that sound.'*

Quigley had moved into the house after Mrs. Seibold left, not so much for the luxury, rather so he could be there to protect it should the need arise, and he was in the room Karl had used as an office sitting behind the desk when Reed came in to report sighting the line of riders moving past that morning.

"How many were they?"

"Well, I counted eighteen but there might have been more. They came straight at me for a long while and I was just about to high tail it back here when they suddenly stopped for a minute or so and the turned sort 'a east and rode out of sight."

"Well, I don't know what to make of it, but I don't like it. Why would anyone head straight for this ranch and then when they were not three miles away, turn off? Unless they knew we were expecting them and that could only mean *WT* hands?"

Quigley reached for his big hat, and stood after properly setting it upon his head, he strapped on his Colt rig and cinched it down tight before starting for the door.

"I hope Terry stays alert," Reed said thinking about his friend.

"I'm sure he will especially after you told him about 'em, if he's got good sense he will."

Reed almost told his boss about failing to tell Ellick of the line of riders, but just couldn't bring up the courage at the time.

Black Horn Nose never liked taking women with him on a raid. He especially did not like having Sun Child anywhere near the whites when her hair was not stained with the die of the Huckleberry that grows in the high meadows in the spring and summer, but those places are deeply covered in snow in early April. By now all the stain she had applied months before, was gone and her hair once more flowed as bright and silky as it did the first day he saw her, so many years before.

He realized she was truly a skilled fighter herself and had before killed Utes at his side when they were attacked along the Cache la Poudre, even when she was heavy with their first child. *'Now they were out to revenge the killing of her last child,'* he thought and he knew he could not stop her from once more riding at his side in such a time of danger.

Quigley had just picked up his Winchester and started through the front door when the first war-hoops were heard. Immediately looking over to his left, he saw the line of Indians coming at a fast gallop headed straight for the three men who had come out of the bunkhouse and started for the barn.

Perry Taylor, Jacob Wells, and Nandres Hall were caught out on the open with only one handgun and no rifles between them. Taylor fired a wild round at the lead horseman but immediately knew his shot would go high and before he could recock the hammer, a long lance was hurled through the cold air to pierce his heart.

Quigley watched with admiration at the horsemanship of these new enemies. They came at a full gallop hanging off the side of their cayuse with one hand grasping the mane and their legs tightly clamped around the horse's body showing only a portion of the leg above his back and an equally small amount below the belly and firing a rifle from under the animals' neck as they passed. One such fellow placed a bullet in the face of Jacob Wells as he passed.

Quigley had gotten off two quickly aimed rounds as they passed. Then when they were out of the yard some eighty yards, he watched them sliding once again atop their cayuses' backs and bound off for the rise to the north. He quickly lifted the windage slide on his rear sight and took a fine bead before squeezing off a shot. The second rider in the line suddenly threw both arms high and to his sides, indicating a hard hit. Then just before he passed over the rise, he fell from his mount and lay still.

"Come on," Quigley shouted to Laramie and Buckshot, who just now were riding up to the house. "They won't be expecting us to attack so soon and I want a piece of them before they can make another run at us and possibly fire the buildings."

Apache was in the corral unsaddled, but Quigley Hancock was no novice to bareback riding himself and within seconds, he was on the great geldings back with a Colt in each hand. Years before he had trained Apache to respond to knee pressure and the tall horse was as responsive to this as he was to reins. Buckshot and Laramie, unsure what all had happened, charged off after their leader.

They saw three Indians returning over the hill just before they reached the downed rider and Quigley blasted two of them before they could rein up their ponies.

The surprise on their faces was plain to see a split second before their expressions changed to those of pain as the heavy 45 slugs tore into their chests.

The third Indian was quicker than the others and he immediately dropped off to the side of his pinto upon seeing the charging whitemen and thus was protected from the rain of lead that belched from the revolvers of the cowboys. But his beautiful black and white tobiano[1] was not so lucky and three of the heavy slugs entered his powerful body and he stumbled, throwing the rider.

Quigley, seeing the predicament of the downed man and wanting a prisoner to question, charged straight at him before the man could stand or reach his fallen rifle.

With the white man's horse between him and his yellow rifle, Black Horn Nose twisted his body with full intention of dragging the man from his horse, but when he looked up, he was looking straight into the big opening at the end of Quigley's pistol, and he knew such a move would bring his immediate death. Instead of lunging he took a deep breath and then turned his attention to the bodies that lay nearby, then he dropped to his knees and began to wail a strange chant.

Laramie who had continued over the hill expecting more to be following those three was surprised to see the other Indians had continued on towards the north. *'I wonder why these three came back alone,'* he thought, pulling up his horse, he watched for a while then slowly turned back towards where he had last seen his friends.

Quigley somehow seemed to sense that the warrior was now in great pain, as he clung to the body of one of the fallen. Then he crawled to the other and again his cries came from deep within his heart, finally his eyes focused on the body of the one Quigley had shot from the porch. This one lay twisted, somewhat grotesquely, after falling from the fast-moving horse and the man's howl suddenly reminded him of the sound Mariah Scott had made the night he had helped in the murder of her husband, and his wail shook him.

Black Horn Nose rose to his feet and staggered the fifty yards to the body of his one true love in this world and lifted her with his arms and held her close to his chest and once more

____
[1] Tobiano: Piebald pattern when black and white.

began a sorrowful chant that touched those who were close enough to hear it.

Quigley eased his heel to Apache's side and the big animal moved forward walking slowly up to the man and there he stopped without being given a command to do so.

It was then Quigley saw the color of the woman's braided hair and he suddenly felt weak, *'Have I just killed the mother of Laramie?'* he wondered.

"She is your woman?" he asked, and the Indian looked up and replied. "She is my woman, the mother of my three sons who were all alive yesterday and who now lay cold at the hands of white men."

Suddenly Quigley realized why the affection had been displayed for the other two who they had just killed.

"Why did you attack us?"

"Because you attacked us," the older man said back with growing hate in his eyes and quick motions of his hands.

"We have not attacked anyone. We were expecting an attack, but not from Indians, from other white-men."

Black Horn Nose heard the words, but they did not make sense to him, so he just stared hatred at the big man on the spotted horse and held tightly to Sun Child.

Quigley saw from the corner of his eye his other men had returned from their pursuit. He dared not take his eyes off the man below him for he fully realized this man would think nothing of his own death to strike one last revenging blow at those who had just taken so much from him, but he also needed to do something that mustered all the courage he had left, "Laramie."

The boy had stopped his horse beside Buckshot and the two were talking quietly between themselves over this firefight until Quigley's voice interrupted them, "Yes, Sur."

"Come here."

The lad rode up beside him and looked at his boss, "Yes, Sur?"

"Is that your mother?" Quigley asked.

Suddenly he felt as though a javelin had pierced his heart at the very thought and his eyes began to swell and he slowly turned his head to the two bodies on the ground. *"Qui, that is a woman. Qui she does have blonde hair like mine. Qui she is the same size as Mee'ma,'* All these thoughts shot like bolts of lightning through his young mind, but he couldn't see her face, he couldn't be sure, so he slowly dismounted and walked up to the man who held her and he asked, "May I see her face?"

The Indian didn't understand what he wanted at first and then seeing the tears building in the white boy's eyes, he slowly lowered her body from his tight grip until her head fell away exposing her face and Laramie fell to his knees and began to cry openly.

Quigley now was sure he had truly killed the boy's mother and his own stomach began to tighten and he wanted to spit, but there was no saliva there to form it, so he just tried to swallow.

Finally, Buckshot saw the yellow braids on the dead woman, and he asked tenderly, "Is that your mother, Laramie?"

The buckskin-clad boy stood then and returned his latigo hat to his head and wiped his nose with the sleeve of his coat then turning he shook his head as he reached for the reins of his horse, "No, it is not Mee'ma, but I feel it is who we have been searching for. I should have known Reb Brown would have told me the truth, but I just had to try."

"Buckshot, ride back and get the buckboard, we need to help this man bury his family."

That night he sent Nandres Hall, with an extra horse, to make the seventy-mile gallop to Fort Washakie to report to the army what had happened there. He knew nothing other to do with Black Horn Nose than lock him in the tack room with the bodies of his wife and two sons.

Four days later Nandres and a lieutenant with a detachment of seven troopers arrived at the *K—S*.

It was then after long conversations with Black Horn Nose that the facts began to come out and both adversaries realized the sorrow of the mistakes that had been thrust upon them.

"Do you know who was responsible for the attack on their camp?" Lieutenant Brown asked Quigley.

"Well Lieutenant, there has already been enough suffering over people thinking who was responsible for that, and even though I would bet a year's wages, I shan't say without proof."

For a long time, the three boys, Laramie, Ryan and Buckshot, had stood back and listened while the old warrior talked and answered questions. Much of what he said didn't make a lot of sense to them, but when he told of coming to the Powder River country soon after the big fight in the Valley of the Greasy Grass, where Yellow Hair was killed, they all took notice. Everyone by this time had some knowledge of General Custer and his last fight at the Little Big Horn River in southern Montana and to hear any account of it, no matter how small, was of great interest.

"We first went to the Elk Mountains and stayed three moons there, and then a scout saw many buffalo here, so we came down and hunted. There was a few Arapahoe, but many of our Lakota friends were led by the great war chief Crazy Horse, and we camped north of here where we found men who look for the yellow rocks and we fought with them and killed, two but they had a lodge that was built over a hole in the earth and we could not kill them all so we tired of this small fight and moved on south to the river that crosses the prairie."

He stopped and looked at the hill to the east and then his eyes turned to the south and again he spoke. "It was here we camped, and Sun Child cooked the liver of a calf and we were happy. That night we made a son, but his spirit did not like the white-man being on our land and it departed soon after it came here."

Ryan leaned over to Buckshot and whispered, "I think he is talking about our sunken cabin."

His friend nodded his head, but gave no other reply, not wanting to disturb the questioning of the Indian.

The next morning the Army took the old warrior and left, and even though he had been responsible for the deaths of several of his friends, somehow Laramie felt sorry for the man who was bound and bent and looked very much as if his spirit did not want to live in a land where there were so many white men.

Quigley walked up beside him as he watched the column leave. "I see your heart goes out to him."

"Oui, he was much a man, a great fighter once, and now he is nothing, has nothing."

"I think the lesson here is, he was once a great man, something to be proud of, and from what I can tell, he only fought for what he believed in. It's mighty hard to condemn a man for that."

"We killed his wife, his sons, now he has nothing, nothing to live for."

"Well, he has his memories, and they are worth a great deal to a man who has no regrets for what he has done in his life. In a few months, after time has healed some of the wounds in his heart, he will remember those good times and be proud. It's those of us who have done things that haunt us who will someday be miserable remembering our deeds. A condition you should strive never to find yourself in," Quigley said and then, just before he turned and walked back to the house, he added, "I'm glad that was not your mother."

"Oui," Laramie replied, but he was not so sure. Now his hopes of finding her were once again shattered and just a small part of him wished it had been her who they had just buried in Mrs. Siebold's cemetery behind the house up on the little rise. *'At least I would know she had a Christian burial,'* he thought.

Quigley gathered his little group of well-trained men, boys would be a better description, but to them they were men and to him they were men. In fact they were as old as many of the men he had rode with during the war. Dusty Salser, Chris Morgan, Laramie Patay, Buckshot Gunter, he even took Ryan Rodriguez and they headed out to find the trail left by the twelve riders seen by Lucius Ree.

Tobiano Piebald Pinto

Chapter Forty Three

White Raiders and Raiding Whites

It was Laramie who first cut the trail and soon Quigley could see it was a direct line from where the Indian had said they were camped toward the ranch and he nodded his head, understanding a little more how the Arapahoe would have thought they were following men from the *K—S*. "Come on let's see where they split off and headed towards the *WT*," he offered.

They had not traveled far when Buckshot pointed out the circling of the birds.

"Yes, I see them," Quigley said, and just over the next rise, they came upon the body of Driggers. He was lying on his back with a frightening expression on his drawn face. The scavengers had already feasted upon his eyes and only dark hollow holes were left. The dark crimson oval where his hair had been removed was near his forehead and the sight caused Ryan's stomach to quiver and he was afraid he might become sick, something he did not want to happen in front of his friends.

Unknown to him, all the young men were experiencing the same fear at the sight of what had been a man not all that long ago.

"Well, there is no longer any doubt whose trail we are following, that's Curley Driggers and he is a *WT* hand. Has been for nigh on a year now."

"That's Curley?" Dusty uttered, more as a question than a statement. Until this moment he had not recognized the dead man and suddenly he thought of playing cards with Curley in Marquis' Saloon back before all this had begun.

"Let's go."

"Ain't we going to bury him?" Dusty asked, horrified at the thought of leaving his ole poker opponent for the buzzards, magpies, and coyotes.

"I'll send a lesser man than we have here to do that. We have others to find," Quigley said, and suddenly Dusty felt a little ashamed for his statement.

Soon they came upon the place where Bitler had scattered his riders and he did likewise, only not quite the same. "Laramie, you take Dusty and Chris and follow one of the trails, but don't get too close, and don't get in a hurry. I don't want you seen and I sure don't want you riding into no ambush. As soon as you confirm where they are headed, hightail it back to the spread and wait for me."

Then turning he added, "Buckshot, you and Ryan come with me. We'll follow the one who was leaking."

Buckshot frowned at the statement and then looked back at the disturbed sand below but saw no sign of blood.

"Which trail do you want me to follow?" Laramie asked.

"It don't matter. They all will lead to the same place eventually," Quigley said, confident in his answer.

Even though the trail was light and somewhat old by that time, Quigley soon deducted it was leading to Poison Spider and he suspected it led straight to Doc Smyth's door. So, despite the fact it was very dim at times, onward he rode at a steady pace which amazed the boys.

"Afternoon Doc."

"Hello, Mr. Hancock," the man who opened the door replied.

Doctor Smythe came to Powder River country via The Overland Trail Mail stage back in '78. Not long after Marquis had opened the hotel and was immediately needed when a cowboy was brought into town with a severely swollen arm caused by the bite of a prairie rattler. Doc stayed to treat him, and the stage rolled on.

Before the next westbound arrived, he had treated two gunshot wounds and was asked to attend to Gayle Somerset, who had just miscarried a child. After that, he decided to sojourn a while seeing that even in this little burg his services were needed.

Not long thereafter Etta Williams arrived, and even though she was almost twenty years younger than Doc Smythe, he took a fancy to her and she sealed Poison Spider as the end of his westward journey.

"I been trailing a man who lost considerable blood. His tracks lead right here."

"There's no one here."

"There has been," Quigley said very sternly.

"I treat men who bleed every day," Archie Smythe offered.

"I ain't interested in them. I only want to know about the *WT* man who came here yesterdee, shot up."

Doc Smythe always had respect for Quigley Hancock, and even though there were some who murmured quietly, and behind his back that he was the murderer known as *The Arkansas Avenger,* personally Doc had seen only actions of a gentleman and a straight shooter out of the foreman, and he didn't want any trouble between them.

However, he also had respect for the fury which most surely would rush from Paul Somerset should he find out that he had revealed he had treated one of the *WT* outfit, who perhaps had received his injury in a less than respectable manner, so he simply replied. "As to whom it was, you'll find that out yourself easily enough. I will tell you only he had a gunshot wound to his wrist."

Quigley nodded his head and lowered his eyes to the gold chain that swung easily from one pocket of the Doctor's black wool vest to the other and then he asked, "How bad was he hurt?"

"He'll never use that hand again."

Quigley ever so slightly nodded his head a couple of times then he slowly raised his eyes until they were locked with the brown eyes of the shorter man in front of him and there they stopped. "Which hand?"

"Not his gun hand. If that is what you are wanting to know."

Again, he nodded his head so slightly that anyone who was looking at him and not paying close attention would have missed the gesture. "Obliged," was his only comment.

Turning, he walked back across the dark planked floor to the front door of the hotel and then out to where the boys sat, still mounted just beyond the single hitching post.

"What gew' find out?"

"Come on, let's get us a drink 'afore we head back home," was Quigley's answer. So, they rode beside him as he walked, leading Apache, across the slushy street to *The Poison Spider Saloon*.

Marquis had imported a new working girl from Cheyenne who they soon found out was named Zerelda. She was several years older than Etta had been, and her years as a saloon girl showed in the lines on her face and bags under her eyes. Nevertheless, she was the only Belle in town or within forty miles for that matter and she was getting all the attention the lovesick cowboys could afford.

They stayed only half an hour before Quigley motioned for his boys to follow, and reluctantly they did.

"That girl Zelda, she ain't hard to look at."

"Her name is not Zelda, it's, Zerelda," Buckshot corrected.

"Zelda, Zerelda, it matters not. She ain't hard to look at," Ryan said, remembering the smile she had given him and the feel of her palm as she had slowly rubbed his chin and right cheek once as she walked past the bar where the three had stood while drinking their whiskey.

Quigley heard the boys talking, but what they were saying did not enter his conscience mind.

Christy King and Shelly McCrery had been in there as well, and before Sunny Tomson could get to them and shut up their conversation, Quigley had learned five new men had come west on the same stage that brought the new girl. He also heard McCrery say that Bitler's arm was in bad shape, and he was down with a fever.

It was more than he had expected to find out and now it was time to get back to the outfit as soon as he could and get them prepared.

Riding into the Siebold spread Quigley was surprised and not all that pleased to see the zebra dun Wiley Bass rode, tied to the top pole at the corral. "Boys, see to Apache for me, will ya?"

"Sure, Mr. Quigley," Buckshot replied, taking the reins from his boss' hand.

When they led the horses into the barn Ryan spoke somewhat in a critical manner, "Why do you not speak his name? I call him Quigley like all the others. What ess 'dis Miser Quigley?"

Buckshot removed the saddle from the big stallion and swung it over a stall rail before he answered, "I don't expect you to understand, but where I come from you call those who you respect Mister until they tell you to do otherwise. Mr. Quigley is also from the south and for me to do otherwise would be discourteous."

"I 'tink you loco sometimes."

"I 'tink," Buckshot replied mocking his friend, "you are a skinny half breed sometimes."

"At least I am tall, not the size of a woman."

"When you are as tall as Mr. Quigley, you can brag about it. Until then, you are too skinny to brag much," the shorted boy replied and shoved Ryan against his own horse playfully.

Bass was sitting in the room Quigley had taken as an office, drinking from a Birdseye cup, when he came in. "Make yourself to home," he said.

Quigley saw the smoke rising from the cup, and felt the warmth coming from the potbelly where he had left the coffee pot the day before, and realized someone, and probably Bass, had started a fire in it.

The idea of hot coffee after the cold ride from town seemed to be a good idea, so he too reached for a cup before he asked, "What brings you out into the real world?"

"I was following up on a lead and heard about your Indian trouble. Want ta' tell me about it?"

"You just said you already heard about it," Quigley answered. He already figured Bass would not be any help to him and most likely a pain, considering what he had to do with the *WT* outfit, and really didn't like him being anywhere around.

"Not from the horse's mouth."

"The horse responsible for the Indian trouble is not stabled on *K—S* land."

"Oh, and I suppose you are going to blame your Indian problems on the *WT,* too."

"Seems like I heard a long time ago the expression, 'Thou sayest,' used by a man much bigger than anyone around these parts. Although I sometimes wonder if Paul Somerset believes that."

"What are you talking about?"

"It's beyond your upbringing, I'm afraid," Quigley said, enjoying the opportunity to get in a dig at the deputy.

"Being a smart ass won't get you anywhere; now tell me about the Indian trouble."

Quigley told him what had happened as he had learned it and ended with, "If you send a telegraph to Fort Washakie to a Lieutenant Brown, he will verify what I have told you. Also, should you have the inkling to take a ride, cut a shuck into town and talk to Doc Smyth.

"Or you can ride over to the *WT* and talk to Bitler if you want. Although I'm sure he will try and blame his shot-up wrist on a *K—S* hand, but even the law will surely see, sooner or later, all this ties up like a thirteen loop knot[1] and we both know what they are used for."

"Yeah, only I ain't sure whose neck it will fit, just yet," Bass said back harshly.

"Oh, given enough time I think even you will figure that out," Quigley replied before he took a draw from his cup.

This conversation did not improve any during the next few minutes and finally, Quigley asked, more to change the subject than in seeking information, "You get Mrs. Siebold situated alright?"

Bass saw through the switch in the subject right off, but also knew they would be beating a dead horse to continue with what they had been talking about, so he nodded his head and replied, "Yeah, she is at *The Elk Mountain* registered as Miss Camilla Gustav, whoever the hell that is."

"It's her name before she was married," Quigley said, and immediately regretted saying it. Even though he did not think Bass was a *WT* man, he always felt like a fool when he gave away information that was not necessary, and who she was or had been was none of Bass' business.

"Well, she is there. I ain't sure how long she will stay, you know that's one strong-willed woman."

------

[1] Thirteen loop knot: A hangman's knot.

"Yes, I've noticed that," Quigley agreed. "I would appreciate it were you to watch out fur her."

"I'll do my job here, and there," Bass replied, and sat his empty cup down on Quigley's desk.

"That would be a nice change."

"I see I'm getting nowhere here," the deputy said and stood.

"Supper should be about ready. I'll tell Hank to fetch you a plate before you leave."

"No, thanks. I got some jerky, 'asides I don't cotton to mutton," Bass replied, getting in his own dig.

"Well, tonight we are going to forgo the lamb and have some dog; we found it boiling in the Indian camp and saved it for uninvited visitors," Quigley shot back.

A few minutes later, he watched as the deputy walk over to the corral and talked to one of the hands for a few minutes before he mounted and rode out to the north.

Quigley didn't concern himself with questioning Wells about what Bass had asked him. He knew the man would tell the same story as he had, at least as far as he knew it. Besides he had something else on his mind and it was not a pleasant subject.

Chapter Forty Four

Ole Dave

The stage road, after it passed through Poison Spider, turned south for a few miles to the southernmost point of Powder River before cutting west again towards the junction of the Wind and The Little Wind rivers, then southwest into Lander. From there one could go either to South Pass City, which by then was almost a memory of days gone by, or back southeast to Rawlins. It was there at the point of Powder River where Quigley was waiting for the westbound.

"Howdy, Dave."

"Howdy back. I see'd gew here a fur piece back and took gew as a road agent 'til I see'd that there big Paint you're a sit 'en, and then I knew it were you."

"I'm obliged you didn't cut down on me, Dave," Quigley said back, giving the old man a compliment.

"Almost did, but 'haint no 'nother animal in these parts what shines like your mount do, so I held off a plugging 'ya."

"Again, I'm obliged."

"Now, what in tarnation are you doing way out here?" the teamster asked, wrapping his leads around the brake-handle before reaching for the canteen he kept in the boot.

"You carrying passengers?"

"Naw, not this trip."

Quigley nodded his head and then he lifted one leg and crossed it over the horn and leaned back resting against his high back saddle, "You the driver what brought the new woman to Poison Spider a few days back?"

"You know of another what makes this westbound run?"

"Yeah, there's Charlie Wilder."

"Oh him. Well, it were me," the old man said after taking a draw from the canteen and washing his mouth before spitting most of it out.

"That day, you brung some men, too."

"Yep, five a' 'em."

"Where they from?"

"Can't say, but they be gunhawks fur shor. Everyone a mean-looking critter, especially that one with the scar on his face and the marled eye," Dave said. Then squinting his own he added, "Goes by the name Gila Drifter, carries a' Arkansas toothpick in his left boot and one a' them Merwin[1] self-cockin' fast shootin' revolvers in a cross-draw rig under his fancy coat."

"Thanks. I'll be watching for him. Do you know who the others are?"

"Do I know? I drive this here coach, don't I? I know everything what happens to 'er."

"I should have guessed that," Quigley replied smiling at the driver. But he got no more response other than Dave nodding quite obviously at the idea.

"Well, who are they?"

"Oh, yeah, well let me see, there is that little fellow called Donny Wadsworth and aside him was Francis Wheeler, they

---

[1] Merwin & Herbert: A double action Revolver often in 44 WCF.

called him Francis and also Frank, I don't reckon they even know him all that well 'emselves," Dave said. Then looking down at his feet he seemed to suddenly drop off into deep thought. Finally, his head jerked back up and a smile crossed his face, "Thar were that one what carried a short barrel seeder gun they called Art Linton and the 'udder one wus ________," once more he stopped and thought but this time it came to him much quicker, Jim Catron," he said again smiling broadly. "He's from I-a'-way. I heard 'im say so."

Quigley flipped him a five-dollar gold piece wrapped in a sheet of paper and nodded his head. "I'd be obliged if you would see Mrs. Siebold gets this."

The driver looked at the paper, but Quigley could see he was looking at it upside down and realized Dave couldn't read, "I'll do it fur you, carry it ma'self and hand it to 'er."

"Thanks, Dave. You're a true friend."

"I try a' be. Now if'n you need help wid' 'em you just call on ole Dave and I'll plug one fur ya."

"Naw. You will do me more good with your iron cased and your ears unholstered."

The old man gave him a big wink and then reached for the long latigo ribbons by his right boot.

Quigley backed Apache up a few feet off the road and there he sat watching the stage disappear over the rise to the west in a cloud of dust and a clamor of squeaks, moans, and groans as she rocked to and fro on the thick leather straps that held the coach to the frame beneath.

He thought a long time on what he should do next. *'When I started this, it was all to avenge the murder of the girl.'*

Had he not been on the *WT* payroll at the time, it might not have bothered him as much. But it did bother him, and he just couldn't abide having his name associated with men who murdered innocent women. Now, everyone anywhere around knew that fact, but he was still there fighting another man's war, a dead man at that, for the good of a woman he didn't really like all that much.

'None of it makes much sense, but not to finish it would be unthinkable. I just have to figure out how to do it and save as many of the lives of my men as I can and stay away from the hangman's noose at the same time. No big deal.'

Long ago Quigley learned to figure out what he most likely should do and then doing something else, for he knew his adversaries could think too, and they most likely would expect him to do the logical thing.

He also had learned well during the war, when it looked like you're outnumbered, the best tactic was to attack and with these new gunmen in from the east, he felt outnumbered.

Not that his boys weren't good, they were honed to a sharp edge. But they were green to killing and the men they would most likely be meeting would be old hands at it.

On the high plains, it could snow any month of the year, although it was not common in July and almost never in August. However, this was April and before he made the six miles back to the *K—S* a wet shower of freezing flakes was dropping rather rapidly.

'If it keeps this up some heavy drifts could result when the wind returns.'

After putting Apache in the barn and giving him extra feed, he walked over to the bunkhouse and called to Nandres Hall.

"Yes, sir," the older man replied.

Actually, Nandres wasn't as old as all thought, in reality, he was only ten years older than the boys yet he seemed old somehow. He also moved with a limp and that kept him slower than the others and this just added to the idea of age.

"Make a sweep around the place and send all the men in from the outposts. I need to talk to them."

The idea of riding out for over an hour in this wet shower was not one of joy, but the puncher never once showed his displeasure with the assignment.

After he was out of sight, Quigley explained his intentions to those left behind, and when the others gradually began to drift in, he sent out fresh replacements to cover their posts.

Finally, when Hall and Taylor came back, he told them to get some chuck and then take turns as lookouts for the remainder of the night.

Later, he and his boys headed out, each leading a spare horse. He had instructed them to feed the ones they led, but not the ones they rode.

As the midnight hour of April 14 approached, Quigley and his little band of guerrillas sat atop of the same rise they had not all that long before, overlooking the *WT* outfit below.

The storm had ceased and with the aid of a full moon, which bathed the eleven-inch blank of wet snow, the scene before them was as bright as if it had been daylight.

Only two nights before he had made a surveillance of the *WT* and saw that a barn had been built and a new bunkhouse mostly finished, but no construction had been done on rebuilding Somerset's home, so he surmised the rich man and his wife were staying over in Red Bluffs with one of the other big outfits, which made this raid sit much better with him.

There were three tents down there, two that looked the size of a Sibley[2] but the other was a much larger wall tent, probably two wall tents put end to end and it carried a brace of chimneys indicating two stoves. But on this night, there was no smoke rising from any of them and Quigley concluded no one was awake to stoke them.

----

2 Sibley Tent: Named after General Henry Sibley, it roughly resembled the teepee, being roughly eighteen feet in diameter and twelve feet high. There was a hole at the top where a Sibley stovepipe extended. About a dozen men usually occupied one during Mr. Lincoln's war.

Looking over at his men he said, "It's time to change horses and let these go. They will find their way back to the feed trough. Now get ready to do battle once more."

While they were changing saddles from one horse to the other, he continued explaining his plan. "I figure the majority of the hands will be in that big tent yonder. One of the smaller ones will be a cook tent and I suspect it is the one with the most smoke stain on the top, as you can see. The other will be where Chuck Bitler is sleeping and maybe his new gun hawks. It is this one we want to hit the hardest. Nevertheless, don't let your guard down. Bitler is a proud sort a' fellow and it might just be he is keeping that one all to himself, in which case our real danger will come from the big tent."

"Laramie, take Dusty and Chris and get to that far rise yonder and wait until you see us start down the hill, then you do the same. Buckshot and Ryan will stay with me. The closer we get before they find out we are here the better off we will be," he said. Then looking at the boys he asked, "Does everyone understand?"

They all nodded their heads and being satisfied with his explanation, he finished, "Alright Laramie, head on out."

After they had gone, he turned to Ryan, "I want you to ride in with us but if, and only if, we are able to make it all the way down without detection, your job will be to fire the tents and then get back to higher ground where you can cover us with your rifle. I don't want you in the firefight down there with that long gun. You'll be much more help up here."

The Mexican boy nodded his head and then turned to his friend and said, "Good luck amigo."

Buckshot smiled and held out his hand, "Good luck to you, you skinny half breed."

Quigley, now atop Apache, knew he was well mounted and could outrun anything the *WT* outfit had, but he was not so sure about the others, so at the last minute he turned to Ryan and said, "As soon as you fire the last tent, open the corral gate and try and run off their mounts. Then hightail it back up the hill."

"Si. Can do," the tall boy replied confidently, but Quigley was not so sure; Ryan did not have the benefit of the training the others had, and he worried some about the oversized kid.

It took almost forty minutes before the other three appeared on the far hill, but there was no problem identifying them through his long glass. As soon as he saw Laramie wave he said, "Okay boys, check your guns and make sure you are fully loaded."

Then he started down the slope towards the camp below.

Quigley had been incorrect in one of his calculations, that being the first building rebuilt after the fire was not the barn, rather one far more important. It was to this Shelly McCrery found the need to go that snowy evening in April.

He had a bad case of the flux[3] brought on by eating a piece of beef that he had thawed in the sun too long. His stomach was in an uproar and he spent most of the day and night there. In fact, he had been so troubled that sleep escaped him for a day and a night. That is, until this very hour. After finishing off a bottle of calomel while sitting on the throne, he had fallen off fast asleep.

He didn't know what had awakened him. Perhaps it was the cold or the wind as it suddenly once more began to stir. What the culprit happened to be was immaterial to him. He was once more awake and that was all he cared about at the moment.

Slowly he stood and brought up one of his suspenders over his shoulder before he opened the door to begin the fifty-foot march back to the tent. He was surprised, realizing the snow had stopped falling and he looked upward at the bright silver ball that hung so proudly high in the eastern sky. *'It is such a pretty night,'* he thought and then as his gaze returned to earth, he saw the black spots on the hill. At first, he thought

---

3 Flux: Extreme diarrhea.

they were beeves, but as his eyes focused, he realized there were men riding them.

Shelly reached for his Colt only to find nothing belted to his middle. He then started to scream but knew the depth the men in the bunkhouse slept, out of pure personal protection, in order to defeat the snoring of the others. So he turned and espied the only surviving vertical piece of the original *WT* spread and he ran for it and began jerking the rope attached to Wesley Bobo's dinner bell.

The sudden clanking rang like thunder in the little valley and Quigley knew they had been discovered. Turning to Ryan he shouted, "Open the corral gate first."

Then he spurred his horse and the great gelding charged down the remaining one hundred yards of the slope and he met Jim Catron just as the man came out of the tall tent.

Quigley dropped him there with two quick pistol blasts to the chest. The gunman screamed and fell backward through the flap that served as a door.

'*So, they are in the Sibley after all,*' he thought. Then he emptied his right revolver into the walls placing each shot about four feet off the ground. Immediately shouts and screams burst from within the white canvas, so he assumed some of his rounds had found a mark.

Quigley quickly returned the empty horse-pistol[4] to his right pommel[5] holster and reached for the one on his hip.

He had long before learned to appreciate the fact that the longer the barrel the less the measure of error on the part of the

---

4 Horse-pistol: Colt made revolvers in three frame sizes, The Horse-Pistol, which was carried in a pommel holster, a belt-pistol which was carried in a holster usually belted around the waist, and a small pocket-pistol which was carried concealed on or about one's person.

5 Pommel Holster: Guerrilla fighting from horseback required a well-armed rider who often carried several revolvers. One of the best places for this was in a small saddle bag arrangement that rode in front of the horn and holstered a single revolver on each side of the horse's neck. This bag was called a pommel holster.

pistolero and for this reason, he always carried Colts with 7-½ inch barrels, save when he was gambling, for which he relied on the little 3-½ inch silver jewel, with the finely checkered ivory stocks.

On this night, as always when on a raid, he carried all of his revolvers.

Shelly, seeing what was happening, and knowing he was unarmed and defenseless, turned and started back for his little house. Once inside he quickly shut the door.

Buckshot had become a superb shot with both rifle and revolver and he placed carefully aimed rounds at anything that moved, dropping two men as they ran from the wall tent. He was just about to fire on a third when the sound of many hooves pounding caught his attention. He turned to see it was only the remuda that had been in the corral, frightened and charging through the little tent city.

Laramie, Dusty, and Chris were now approaching from the east at full gallop and the sight caused one of the hands to turn and run back away from the open flap of the tent.

Ryan had done his job well at the corral, but now he was unsure, *'Should I attempt to fire the tents, or go back and cover them from the hill with my rifle?'*

Finally, he lit one of the torches he had brought and spurring his mount, headed straight for the big wall tent, upon whose top he tossed the burning staff.

Then turning his pony, he targeted the tepee he had watched Quigley fire into first. But before he could strike his next Lucifer, he spied a man taking deliberate aim at Buckshot's back and without thought he flung the unlit torch at him.

The short willow branch hit the man's elbow a split second before the gun's hammer fell, which interrupted his aim, causing the bullet to fly off target just enough that it struck the boy at the very outer flesh of his left shoulder. Buckshot dropped the gun he held with that hand and looked back in time to see that man once more cocking his revolver.

Ryan also saw this and being without a pistol he reverted to the weapon he had found so useful all his life, and in less that the blink of an eye the sharply pointed blade found its mark driving deeply in Francis Wheeler's neck, slightly below and behind his left ear.

The man dropped his gun and reached to his neck with that hand, but he failed to find the strength to pull the knife free, and as his life's blood spurted in great gushes upon the white snow, he saw the boy who had killed him and thought, *'My God, he ain't even got a gun.'* Slowly he dropped first to his knees and then to his face.

Buckshot had for the first time allowed his fired-up emotion to shift into the natural feeling of fear when he saw the man who had just shot him once more cock his revolver, especially realizing he had no avenue of escape. Now all he could do was shake and smile at his friend.

Seeing Buckshot had also dropped his left rein Ryan charged forward and grabbed them both from beneath the horse's neck, before heeling his own cayuse and leading the horse away from the fight on up the hill.

Once he felt they were out of pistol range he stopped and helped Buckshot from his horse. Then the two of them began pouring rifle fire back into the tents.

They were some two hundred yards away from the action, but the shouts and cries rushed up the slope into their young ears and it was terrifying and invigorating at the same time.

Soon Ryan pointed out to his friend the four riders headed in their direction and they both stopped shooting and grinned at each other, but their joy was a moment too soon.

Randal Rowe, known throughout Arizona and New Mexico as The Gila Drifter watched the men charging up the hill and he took deliberate aim, getting a sight alignment on the white snow and then moving ever so carefully over to where the top of his front sight touched the top of the big Stetson and then he squeezed his index finger.

The Merwin barked once and a long stream of fire erupted from its silver barrel with sparks scattering all around before they fell harmlessly into the trodden snow. But the 200-grain flat nose lead slug did not fall harmless into the snow, it found the small of Chris Morgan's back and he threw his arms high to either side and screamed at the unexpected pain.

Quigley had seen this same gesture many times and knew it could only mean a hard hit on Chris. Immediately he cut Apache back so he could side ride the boy and motioned for Laramie to do the same on his right.

Then they left, headed north away from the *WT* spread, yet not in the direction of the *K—S* either.

Chuck Bitler was outraged, not so much by the fact they had lost the large wall tent, or he had dead and wounded, but because he had been found napping and would have to explain that to Mr. Somerset.

Looking around he saw two of his new gunmen dead and another with a slight wound to one leg. Two of the old hands were dead; Bobo the cook was one of these.

"All of our mounts are scattered from here to gone and then some, and it could take a full day just to round them up," he shouted. Infuriated he turned and screamed, "Where the hell were you?" at the new men who now stood about looking at the mess left behind after the raiders rode away.

"Mr. Bitler, I'll take your orders. I'll take your gold. I'll take your disappointments with an understanding mind, but I will not take your shouting at me," Gila said. "And if you love life, you will never forget it."

He then opened his revolver and replaced the spent 44 WCF case with a live round before he added, "I hit one of them hard. He will not make it very far."

A cold chill ran up Bitler's spine when he looked into the eyes of the killer and he realized he might have a man here that was a greater threat than Quigley Hancock. In fact, he might just have a man who was Hancock's equal.

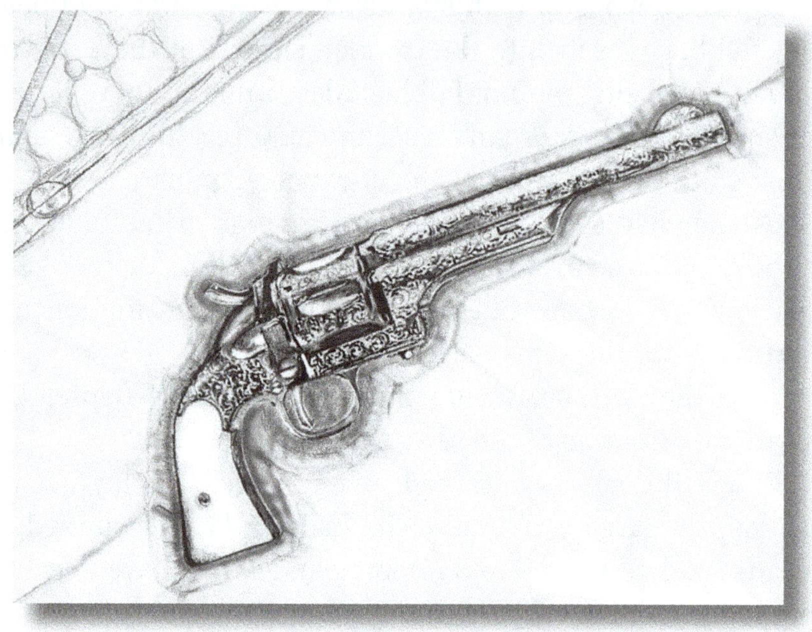

Merwin & Hulbert, Marked 'Caliber Winchester 1873'

Chapter Forty Five

Lurking Observers

The Gila Drifter was right about one thing, before they had ridden three miles Chris was dead. Realizing this, Quigley stopped and tied him over his saddle and then he did as his adversary had and sent his boys off in twos, each using a different trail back to the ranch, he alone led Chris' horse.

This was simply a routine maneuver, he was fully aware, with the return of the wind, their trail would soon be obliterated to a tracker by the ground blizzard, but he was training young men in the art of survival, and few things trained better than repetition.

The giant of a man also thought, *'There is one other element that trains well or at least alerts sobering attention to grave facts, and that is a man can get killed doing this work. They each had killed others and learned to find little remorse in it, and although other K—S hands have been killed, Chris is the first of their little group, of my special highly trained boys, to die.'*

Somehow before this night, being a member of this elite band seemed to carry a security that one rode within a protection ring in which bullets and arrows could not penetrate. No longer was that felt, and it was sad riders who returned to the *K—S* that night.

Unknown to Quigley Hancock or Chuck Bitler, Wiley Bass had also been at the *WT* that night.

After cutting a fresh trail leading from the *K—S*, which headed in the general direction of Somerset's spread, he suspected a raid was in the making, so he followed it.

Arriving just as Quigley split his forces, he stayed out of sight and watched. He could have put a stop to it easily enough, but he didn't for more than one reason. He wanted something he could use on Hancock. He also had heard Francis Wheeler and Art Linton were among the gun hawks Somerset had imported from Cheyenne and both of these he held papers on. But mostly he wanted to see the tactics Quigley would use to raid the *WT* outfit. Wanted to see if perhaps the rumors were true and in fact, Quigley Hancock was indeed his old elusive foe, *The Arkansas Avenger.*

He waited long after the firing had stopped, and he watched as the men below began recovering from the assault.

Finally, when one of the horses returned on its own, they used it to round up several more, and then seven men rode out. However, they did not follow the men who had stormed them. Instead they cut a trail straight to the *K—S*, at times tromping over the covered tracks left there only a few hours before. It was these men who Bass followed.

The difference between Hancock and Bitler was that Quigley anticipated a return attack and had scouts out watching for approaching riders from any point on the compass, something Bitler never thought of.

Dave Dawson had seen Laramie and Dusty long before they saw him and upon hearing the news about Chris his heart fell sad, but he never once thought of shucking his duty. It also was him who spotted the *WT* riders long before they were near enough to see him.

The sun was just rising, giving the advantage to the raiders as they came rushing down upon the *K—S*, but Quigley had anticipated that, and he ordered his men to hold their fire until Bitler and his men were amongst them.

He had also sent his boys out to the south with orders not to show themselves if possible until after they heard firing, and then come around and down the same hill as the *WT* riders had used. The sun would then be at their backs and very likely confuse those who were not expecting them.

Quigley knew men fought more fiercely when they had a cause, and nothing cultivated a cause more than a dead comrade. Thus, briefing them he said, "Boys, don't engage until you have them, and when you do, keep Chris Morgan's name on your lips."

Watching them ride off, he was satisfied his many hours of arduous training was about to pay off like never before.

Wiley Bass also watched the events as they played out that morning and saw first-hand that the *WT* men were out generaled as he had not witnessed since Irvin McDowell advanced against Little Joe Johnson at a stream near Manassas, Virginia back in July of '61.

Bitler had ordered everyone able to ride on this retaliation raid with only McCrery, in his condition, staying behind to give what relief to the wounded as he could until they could get Doc Smythe out there.

Wheeling their long rifles while riding at full speed down a slope caused one man to lose his balance and slide from his saddle, only to be overrun by the horse following closely behind him. This was the first sign of the impending disaster.

Their shots were wild and not all that rapid, as they had difficulty recharging the chambers at that speed. Also several of the men were not experienced riding hell-bent for leather in a group, nor were their mounts, and several of these became almost unruly.

The Gila Drifter and Donny Wadsworth were the only *WT* men who resorted to revolvers, and it was them who dropped the *K—S* men who fell that morning, save when Art Linton hit Nandres Hall in the back with his short-barreled shotgun.

However, he too fell moments later in like manner to Lucius Reed who let go with both barrels of his own lead seeder.

Unfortunately, Luscious made the fatal mistake of standing to reload, and the Merwin once more spit death and sent Reed to his reward. Wadsworth also put two rounds in Nandres Hall as he passed the wounded boy.

Had it not been so pathetic, Bass would have been amused.

Quigley had positioned his men in such a manner, if they stayed behind the cover he provided, they would be pretty well protected. He had instructed them not to shoot until the attackers had passed their positions and then cut into them from behind, and this had a murderous effect.

When the *K—S* men did open fire, it was like a slaughterhouse, with men falling over their mounts and from their mounts, in short order.

Finally, realizing he had ridden into a trap, Bitler turned and charged back up the hill, from where he came with only six of his men to follow. Unfortunately for him, they ran headlong into Laramie, Buckshot, and Dusty who cut down three of these.

The Gila Drifter himself, realizing they had ridden into a trap continued straight ahead, leaning over his saddle, charging on as fast as his horse could carry him, and soon was out of the action.

He alone saw the solitary rider sitting upon his mount observing the battle from afar, and he wondered as to the identity, but not enough to engage him.

Bass, being so engrossed in what was happening in the smoke covered yard below never noticed the single rider who made it through, coming out the other side unscathed.

Bitler rode east, followed by Christy King and Donny Wadsworth, all that remained of the twelve men who come with him that morning.

Wiley Bass waited until all the sounds of gunfire had ceased and the smoke cleared by the wind, before he eased his dun down the north slope towards the bloody yard of the *K—S* plaza.

Quigley saw him coming but considering the manner in which the approach was being made, did not consider him a threat until he recognized the zebra dun, and then he was not so sure.

"Well, you show up at the most unexpected times."

"Been doing some killing I see," Bass replied.

"Just defending ourselves."

"Mr. Quigley, they killed Nandres Hall and Lucius Reed," Buckshot suddenly ran up and reported.

"Get their personal effects, and we'll bury them along with the rest of these poor bastards."

"Yas, Sur," came the reply from the youngster.

"They all dead?" Bass inquired.

"All but one," Quigley replied. Nodding over his left shoulder to Daniel McIntyre, a young man who, because of his blacksmith qualities, had been hired shortly before Quigley had quit the *WT*.

The man was lying on the snow-covered ground behind Mrs. Seibold's buckboard, exactly where he had fallen after being hit with a single flyer from the same blast of Reed's shotgun that killed Linton. His wound was high on his right shoulder blade and was bleeding profusely, but if they could get the bleeding stopped, it would not be fatal.

Bass took his own neckerchief and made a compress and applied it to the hole in McIntyre's back. "What do you have to say for yourself about all this?"

Not knowing Bass, and not seeing the star hidden by his heavy coat, McIntyre assumed he was being questioned by a *K—S* man, and uncertain if they would let him live or not, he didn't want to provoke anyone. "I'm sorry about all this. Mr. Bitler just told all of us we had to come here and attack you. I didn't want to do it, but it were his orders and ________."

"Well, now you got your evidence," Quigley said looking down at Bass.

The lawman had to admit this would put Bitler behind bars and likely on the gallows, but he wasn't sure how bad it would affect Paul Somerset.

He knew for a fact Somerset was in Cheyenne meeting with the Governor, and it would be easy for him to claim he knew nothing of this, and Bass figured most likely he did not know.

This had been a retaliation raid because of what had happened the night before at the *WT*, not something that Somerset could have planned. Nonetheless, it would look bad on him and with his outfit shot all to hell, he would have to start over with new hands and a new foreman, and good men don't drift in with the wind.

Bitler's wrist wound had opened sometime during the last few hours and instead of returning to what was left of the *WT*, he turned north and headed for Poison Spider and Doc Smythe.

His intentions were, as soon as he had been taken care of, to send the Doc on to help with the wounded back at the ranch. However, he lost so much blood he was unconscious when they rode into town, and he could not give any such instructions.

Christy King was still so scared he never thought of anything but to get to a bottle and a table with his back to the wall where he could see Quigley Hancock if he came in.

Donny Wadsworth's only concern, now that Bitler was down and everyone else apparently dead, was how was he going to get paid for coming here in the first place, and he too walked over to the saloon.

As soon as he came in, he looked over at Zerelda and said, "Honey, get a bottle of the best this place has to offer and come over here."

Tomson stopped her with, "That'll be three dollars."

"Bitler said to set 'em up at Mr. Somerset's expense and he would be in later to cover it," Wadsworth replied in a kind but strong voice.

She looked at her boss, who took a deep breath and thought a second, *I sure don't want to get Bitler or Mr. Somerset mad at me _____*. Finally, he nodded his head to her as he said, "It's against my better judgment, but go ahead."

The bottle was half empty when they heard the heavy steps of boots approaching the door and a shadow of a large man pass the clouded window. Both of the men sitting there in a drunken state reached for their six-guns, but a cloud of relief swept over them when Gila walked in and looked around.

It was Wiley Bass who eventually sent Doc Smythe out to the *WT* and also sent word via stage to Rawlins, where the news could be wired to Paul Somerset as soon as possible. He then took a room at the hotel and waited for the next development.

Quigley Hancock saw to it that the wounds of his own men were tended to, as well as that of Daniel McIntyre. In fact, he wanted McIntyre in very good shape should any of this come before the court, and with Paul Somerset meeting with the governor, he would not be surprised if it did.

McIntyre not only freely admitted to them attacking the K—S, but also was willing to say that Bitler had been warned that the raiders on the *WT* might not be men from the K—S, and still he pursued his grudge against Hancock. He also told Bass that he had overheard Bitler discussing the hanging of Siebold and bragged about shooting that little spy Etta Williams.

With McIntyre in his camp, Quigley at times hoped Somerset would bring it before a court, but he also was no fool. He fully realized money could buy anything, including jurors. What he did not know was Wiley Bass had witnessed their raid on the *WT* and he could give disastrous testimony.

Several weeks passed before they were in need of supplies. This time, instead of sending a couple of men in, he decided it would be best if he and his boys went. Thus, on Friday morning, the thirteenth of May, Quigley Hancock and his four men rode into Poison Spider from the south.

The last snowstorm had been three days before and it was now mostly gone, leaving behind a muddy street in which few things maneuvered without difficulty.

The sight of three *K—S* riders and another driving a wagon did not go unnoticed by any of the inhabitants who were out that morning. Everyone had heard the rumors about how Hancock had shot the *WT* all to hell, leaving only a handful of the men alive, and most of the folks there didn't understand why arrests had not been made.

Chapter Forty Six

From Hotel To Livery

They tied up in front of the hotel, then Ryan stopped the wagon next door in front of the General Store, where they all went in.

Greg Searight's sister was behind the counter. Her husband was in the back tending to several bags of flour he had discovered damp from where snow had blown in through a crack created as the boards shrank during the extremely low temperatures they had experienced that winter.

Quigley noticed she displayed a slight expression of fright when she saw him, but he didn't understand it, as he had never given her cause, and assumed she had not recognized who he truly was.

Touching the brim of his hat he said, "Ma'am, we are in need of a few supplies before Mrs. Seibold gets home. I have the list here if it will help."

"Ah, yes. That will help Mr. Hancock. I'll have my husband fill it right away," she said, then turned and hurried through the door separating the storefront from the warehouse. "Honey," she called out as she disappeared from sight.

Both Buckshot and Ryan were gazing at the big jar containing long twists of licorice, but neither had remembered to bring any money with them, so look was all they could do.

Some say timing is everything and they would have enjoyed making that comment at that very moment. For unknown to Quigley or any of his men, the stage which stopped at the hotel that day contained four men sent there to meet Bitler, who was still lodging upstairs across the hall from Wadsworth and Rowe.

Bitler had spread the news Christy King had been murdered by Hancock and buried out somewhere on The Big Open where his body would never be found. However, in reality he had cut a shuck for Lander three days after the shootout, but only Bitler knew that.

Parker, Harris, Burton, and Joiner checked in and inquired as to the direction to the *WT* or the whereabouts of Chuck Bitler.

Joe Marquis looked them over and immediately recognized them as more trouble to Powder River valley.

Each wore exposed revolvers, three of which carried two. One of them had a Spencer Carbine lying over his shoulder while the other three each had a long gun of some kind in hand. *'Damn, will this never end?'* he wondered before saying, "Bitler is upstairs, room 2."

The oldest of the four nodded his head and looked up at the staircase, then back at Joe, "We'll need a couple of rooms ourselves at least for the night."

"I'll have the Misses put on sheets fur you."

"Obliged," was the only comment he got in return before the men started up the flight of stairs.

The Poison Spider Hotel was a tall two-story building with the eight rooms to let on the second floor. Each had a single window, save those located on the front and back, which were privileged with two each.

Paul Somerset kept room Number 1 always, for his personal use whenever he was in town, which had not been that often lately.

Deputy Bass had requested Marquis to reserve the room across the hall for him unless all the other rooms were occupied, and he needed to rent it.

Bass had not been seen for two weeks now, but Joe knew he came as often as he could, and he tried to accommodate the man when possible.

With the other two *WT* men in room 3, he told his wife to set up rooms 4 and 8 for the new men, reserving number 5 for Bass. After seeing the looks of those new men Somerset had imported, he thought perhaps the deputy would be needed soon.

Bitler also knew it was unlikely Somerset would be in town in the near future, as he had been staying in Cheyenne most of the time since the loss of his home at the *WT*. As a result, he often helped himself to Somerset's private stock of imported whiskeys kept there.

"I'll get right to the point, we have a problem with one man and a few boys he keeps with him. He is a sheepman and the foreman of the *K—S*, the only outfit in the whole region what has put up barbwire."

Bitler stopped and let his words sink in. Even though he knew these men were not cowhands they would not be in favor of anyone bringing sheep into cow country and everyone, be it cowhand or dove of the cyprian sisterhood[1] hated the thought of fencing in open range, especially with barbwire.

"Now, don't let the fact this is a lone man, give you little concern. He is a scraper in the first order from way back, and some say he is wanted back in Kansas as well as other places, so the law will be back a' us. Besides Mr. Somerset is a member of the Wyoming Stock Growers Association and personal friends with some mighty big wigs down to Cheyenne."

---

[1] Dove of the Cyprian sisterhood: Prostitutes.

Again, he stopped and this time he got out four additional glasses and poured two fingers in each glass, which emptied his bottle. "You have but one job here and that is to remove Quigley Hancock from this earth."

He offered another pause, but before he could continue, they heard a knock on the door.

"Yes?"

The door opened without a reply and in walked his other two gunmen.

"Oh good. I'm glad you are here. I want you all to get acquainted and work up a plan that will be a sure-fire success.

This gentleman is the famous Gila Drifter from down Arizona way, and with him is Donny Wadsworth a man who has no reason to apologize to anyone."

The men looked each other over, sizing the others up as they did.

"First we need to get Hancock away from his ranch. He has turned it into a fortress and to assault it is disastrous," Bitler said.

Rowe coughed upon hearing Bitler's excuse for not taking the *K—S*, thinking, *'Fortress my ass, he just outfoxed you, Bitler.'* But he didn't say anything or make any other gesture more than clearing his throat while looking over at the empty bottle and frowning.

Bitler seeing this, turned to Wadsworth and said, "Donny would you go next door and get a whiskey decanter from Mr. Somerset's room?"

The man didn't like being sent as an errand boy, but he did like the idea of top-of-the-line whiskey, so he nodded his head and left the room.

As soon as the door was closed so his comments would not be subject to anyone who might be in the hallway, Bitler continued. However, before he made another point Donny rushed back in the room. "He's here, right downstairs. I see'd him from the window. He's loading a wagon next door."

Chuck Bitler had rather the fight take place outside of town where there would be no witnesses. Unfortunately, before he could make the point, Rowe started for the door with full intentions of looking for himself. Sadly, for Bitler, the others took his exodus as a sign of intention to engage and followed him out the door.

Parker slid the dust cover back on his Winchester and lowered the lever slightly checking to make sure the chamber was loaded, satisfied he closed the bolt.

Joiner also checked his Spencer and the others loaded a final round in their revolvers.

Rowe observing the action of the others and remembering the $1000 bounty Mr. Somerset had placed on Hancock's head followed suit, but didn't bother checking his revolver, considering his was a double-action and he always kept it fully loaded.

Joe Marquis saw the six well-armed men descend the stairs followed by Bitler and suddenly felt sick to his stomach.

Ryan was once again on the spring seat ready to move out as soon as Laramie dropped the last bag of grain in the bed. The others were walking back towards the hitching post in front of the hotel, where they had left their horses when the gunmen came out of the hotel's front door.

Quigley immediately recognized the expression on The Gila Drifter's face and knew the time was upon them. His only thought, other than the task at hand, was for a split second he hoped his boys would survive.

Before any of the gun hawks had a chance to jerk a piece, he moved sideways one quick step to throw off his opponents and went for his short Colt, all in the same split second.

Rowe, too, recognized the man was making his play, and his hand dropped to the Merwin.

Ryan was twisted in the seat looking back over his right shoulder and suddenly his eyes locked on the silver revolver being grasped, and with a speed so quick as to make the scene seem a blur, it was up and out of the holster. But Rowe had just cleared leather when the 45 hit him full in the chest knocking him back inside into Bitler who was last in line.

It had all happened so fast none of the other players were prepared for it, and each looked surprised, some more than others.

This gave Quigley time to send another round into the man who was raising a hammerless shotgun. However as Burton fell backward, he discharged the Greener and the shot passed between Dusty and Quigley, each taking a single ball of buckshot to their legs.

Dusty dropped immediately when the 36 caliber round ball broke his shinbone, but Quigley was luckier. The shot entered his left thigh high and spent itself there in the big muscle missing the bone and the femoral artery, thus he was able to stand his ground.

Buckshot and Laramie were now both clearing leather with their own weapons and picking out targets of their own. Unfortunately, they both chose Wadsworth and each sent a round into his chest.

Parker had his Winchester up and got off a quick shot at the big man who he considered his main threat, but his shot was high and Quigley's hat went sailing up and away down the street taking a little of his black hair with it.

Unfortunately for the killer from Ellsworth, before he could work the lever again, Dusty fired a quick round into him from where the wounded boy had fallen to one knee, this was immediately followed by a 45 from Quigley's short Colt and in less than a heartbeat, Jimmy Parker lay dead in the muddy street.

Joiner now had the big hammer back on his Spencer and he swung it up and around at Quigley, but Buckshot's old Opentop sent a 44 Henry round into his right hand, knocking the rifle from his grasp.

At first, he was simply surprised, then realizing what had happened he went for the Remington on his left hip, but he wasn't fast enough, and Laramie dropped him with another 44 to his gut.

Harris now took deliberate aim with his rifle at Quigley and fired, but it snapped on a bad primer. It was a fatal piece of misfortune; for once again the two ole friends took the same target and sent 44 bullets into the rifleman's chest.

Burton had been hit in the lower rib on his left side and slowly began to rise from where he had fallen back just inside the hotel door. Looking around and seeing his companions were laying about in front of him, in various degrees of twisted and distorted forms, he suddenly realized he needed to get to work or he would be lying with them.

His shotgun was outside, discarded just off the boardwalk and he started for his Colt, but then spotted the Kennedy[2], dropped by Harris and immediately he lunged forward. He had it up, and as quick as a wisp of wind, he was squeezing off a round when the long skinny razor-sharp blade entered his side under his right arm burying itself to the hilt.

A strange expression suddenly swept over him and he fired the rifle into the air and the 44 round crashed into the sign across the street over *The Poison Spider Saloon.*

Looking about Quigley realized Bitler had not been among them, and this he didn't believe, so he started past the moaning gutshot Joiner and into the hotel lobby. There, laying on his back with his cold blue eyes staring at the ceiling twelve feet above him, was The Gila Drifter, but his engraved nickel-plated revolver was not in its holster nor anywhere in sight.

Joe Marquis was standing behind the Post Office cage with an expression that could be described falling somewhere between terror and panic. However, when Quigley looked straight at him, he quickly cut his eyes toward the backdoor as if to say, "He went that way."

---

2 Kennedy: The Whitney-Kennedy lever action rifle, based on an action designed by Andrew Burgess produced from 1880 to 1886.

Nodding his appreciation, the big man, now with his long barrel Colt in hand, started in the same direction, limping as he went.

Immediately through that door was a short corridor with additional doors, one to either side, then another directly at the end, which led outside.

Quigley first opened the door on his left and seeing it was the quarters of the proprietor and with a quick survey inside he dismissed this room. Next came the door across the hall and it, too, was quickly eliminated as being nothing more than a small room where Marquis kept the copper tub used in bathing.

He gently closed this door and then looked to the rear one. *'Yep, he went out back, but just how far did he then go?'*

Bitler had indeed gone out the backdoor before turning north, and on past, the store, corral and into the livery. There he saddled a large dapple gray that Carol Joiner had ridden to this dusty little camp only an hour or so before.

During the ride there, Joiner had tried to get a horse race going among the others but had no luck. Finally, seeing the sport was out of the question, he began bragging on his mount, proudly boasting that the big gelding's mother had been a Tennessee Quarter horse that was purposely bred to a Thoroughbred back in Kentucky. "He is both quick to get off and has the endurance to outlast any cowpony or cayuse put up, and he never fails to take the purse in a contest," Joiner claimed.

At this moment Chuck Bitler had but one thought and that was to get away from Poison Spider as fast as he could. Never had he witnessed such a one-sided fracas as had just taken place in front of Marquise' hotel. A single man and a bunch of kids had gunned down some of the most notorious gun-throwers on the open plains and now he was sure Quigley Hancock would be after him.

Wiley Bass had, at the first moment, heard a shot below, watched the fracas from the window. Then when he heard the sound of the backdoor slamming, he crossed the hall into Paul

Somerset's vacant room and from there he saw Bitler run up the back alley into the livery.

His attention was distracted from there when movement in the back alley flickered for a second in the peripheral view of his right eye, and now he watched as Quigley Hancock, with long barrel revolver in hand, moved cautiously along the same trail his quarry had so recently traveled.

The big man did not rush. He was in no particular hurry and he certainly did not want to pass the hiding place of his old adversary, for doing so would most likely result in a bullet in his own back. There was not a single doorway or whiskey barrel that went uninspected, not one building corner that was not checked before he moved on.

Upon reaching the corral Quigley saw fresh tracks in the mud proving a man in riding boots had recently stood there. The prints clearly revealed he had turned to check his backtrack before moving on into the barn just a few yards ahead.

Although it was well over a hundred yards from the hotel window where Wiley Bass stood, to the livery where Quigley was now moving ever so slowly through the corral, the deputy did nothing to interfere on the final outcome of this play.

Bass, in his heart, knew Bitler had brought on most of the pain suffered in this burg and the surrounding countryside. However, Bitler worked for one of the biggest men in The Big Open. A man who swung a lot of weight in Cheyenne, and after all was said and done, the weight of justice rarely swung to the right or wrong of things, rather to the strongest in politics, and in Wyoming during the last half of the nineteenth century, that was the men in the Wyoming Stock Growers Association.

He also knew Sheriff Dixon would likely recommend him as the appointed lawman if the men in Powder River country got their way and a new county was created. It would not be good for the governor to hear of him siding with a sheepman.

There was one more thing that kept the lawman from getting involved, and that also had to do with feelings buried deep in his heart. He had now become convinced Quigley Hancock was indeed *The Arkansas Avenger*, only after coming to know the man, Bass found him to be totally honest.

Without any qualms to the contrary, he knew Hancock was a killer without remorse when he had been wronged or another had been wronged, as in the case of the murder of Etta Williams. Nonetheless, from everything he had witnessed and in all the information he had gathered here, he could find not one move Quigley Hancock had done, resulted in any degree different than he would have done had he himself been faced with the same circumstances, and this fact caused him considerable heartburn.

Remembering the years he had hunted what he believed was a ruthless murderer of innocent people in the ghostly image of *The Arkansas Avenger*, he now questioned those tales that had led him in this pursuit to begin with.

Now, all he could recollect had come from the mouths of northern victors and not one complaint from those of the vanquished.

The war was long over, even reconstruction in the south had ceased shortly after Grant left the White House, and now more than half of the immigrants who had settled in the west were refugees from that devastated land. Mostly they had shown themselves, to be honest, hardworking people seeking a new life.

When Wiley Bass first pinned on a badge, he had given his oath to respect and enforce the law without personal feelings, and it was at times hard to do, especially in those early days, when most of the law he was enforcing was against the men who had worn the same color tunics he had worn in the great conflict.

Now, after so many years had come and gone and he no longer was the youthful man who had given his oath so strongly, he wondered about the extent his values had strengthened and how some of them had changed.

Deep inside, as he watched Bitler emerge from the top landing of the livery barn and take deliberate aim at the man who unknowingly moved below him, Wiley Bass wanted to get involved, wanted to do what he felt would be the right thing, but he did not make a move. *'Am I witnessing the end of the ghost that so long eluded me?'* he wondered, but he did not wonder long.

The report was louder than Bass had expected, and he felt mesmerized as the scene played out before him. Christopher Cotton Bitler discharged the revolver six times straight down before he rolled over and fell forward into the muddy street below.

The shiny revolver was knocked from his hand upon impact with the street, his neck broken in the fall, but it was of little concern to him. The 44 Winchester bullet had entered his left side, four inches below his armpit, and exited through his right collarbone, and he was dead before he began his last fall.

Buckshot and Laramie simultaneously turned to see a wisp of blue smoke curly upward from the muzzle of Quigley's '73 carbine, now in the hands of Ryan Rodriquez who had retrieved it from the scabbard on Apache.

Both saw an expression of satisfaction slowly sweep over his face and both were surprised at his statement, "He killed my dog."

Quigley holstered his Colt before he reached over and picked up the Merwin and Hulbert and cleaning the mud from it, he turned and started the long walk back to where his boys waited.

As he did, people began emerging from the few buildings along the only street in Poison Spider.

If they were speaking to one another, he was unaware of it, for his march back to the hotel was in silence as far as he was concerned.

Stopping and looking at Doc Smythe who was tending to Dusty, he looked questioningly.

Finally, Laramie realized his issue and said, "It was Ryan, with your rifle."

Quigley nodded his head a couple of times and then turning to the tall thin half breed, he stretched forth his hand and presented the highly engraved pistol to him. "You earned this; now learn how to shoot it."

"*Gracias,*" Ryan replied, taking the revolver and rubbing his hands over its etched finish.

Bass suddenly appeared in the doorway and stepping over the dead bodies, he looked at the bloodstain on Hancock's left pant leg. "You hit bad?"

"I'll live."

"That depends," the lawman said and then turning he spoke to the doctor. "You better get the blood stopped in Hancock's leg soon, or we will have another grave to dig."

It was the first time any of them really took notice he had been hit, and suddenly every eye there shot to the round hole in his chaps.

Quigley knew his strength was slowly slipping away, but until now, he had not had the consciousness to give the reason much thought. '*Yeah, I have lost considerable blood,*' he agreed with the statement, but he would not give Bass the satisfaction of knowing they were in agreement on anything, instead he asked, "How long you been here?"

"Got in some after midnight," Bass replied.

Quigley just nodded his head, knowing the man had probably witnessed the whole affair, but neither had he the inclination to give a reply; his thoughts were interrupted by Doc Smythe's hand on his leg causing a sharp pain to shoot through him.

"Better come inside so I can clean that. I think the balls still in there." Then as if in an afterthought he added, "Bring in the boy too, but be careful, his leg is broken."

Epilogue

Poison Spider would eventually die, and its actual location would be lost to the never-ending wind and the hardy sage of The Big Open.

Paul Somerset moved the hotel and saloon several miles to the southwest where a new town named in his behalf, was begun; it too died away. However, some old-timers claim its name was simply changed to Hiland when it became known as the highest point on the rails between Casper and Shoshone. Others dispute this, claiming Poison Spider was nearer Moneta and that Hiland and Somerset were two totally different towns altogether. It matters little, neither of these bergs was even an idea in the minds of the people who tried to survive along the lower edge of Powder River in the early eighties.

Wiley Bass never did achieve his goal of being the appointed top lawman when the new county of Natrona was created six years later. He had succumbed to a snake bite a year after he turned in his report of the shootout at Poison Spider, in which he exonerated Quigley Hancock and his boys of any wrongdoing.

Callie Seibold returned from Rawlins only to find life without Karl too lonely to endure after the trouble no longer dominated her mind. She eventually sold her holdings to Judge Carey and moved to Bismarck where she opened a fine hotel that catered to Euro-Americans.

John Carey's CY ranch, beginning with the flock he bought from Carrie Seibold, was soon the object of many a wager in the local saloons and around the campfires as to whether he ran more sheep or beeves.

Dusty Salser would recover from his wound and later became a famous lawman himself in Idaho.

Laramie Patay split trails with Buckshot and headed down to Fort Washakie trying to learn of any information about his mother. Eventually, at the age of twenty-six, he returned to his land in Montana with a Shoshone wife and two towheaded children.

Ryan partnered with Buckshot when he returned to Coulson only to find the town of Billings erupting across the river into a mad confusion of construction.

Eventually, Buckshot got another job on a riverboat, but the time of such travel on the Yellowstone and Missouri was to shortly come to an end as the Northern Pacific rails steadily crawled westward, stealing their trade.

Ryan went with him as far as Saint Louis, but the life aboard a boat was too confining to a boy who had been born on the high desert, and he departed the company of his pard there and hired on as a cook for an outfit that was hauling crossties for the Atchison, Topeka and Santa Fe Railroad as it moved west. Ryan left them in Sante Fe and eventually the man drifted back to the ranch of his birth where he became a top vaquero like his father. He took a young Mexican wife and before he was twenty-eight years old was supporting seven children.

Buckshot stayed with his trade and eventually rounded the horn on a tall sailor and stepped ashore in San Francisco Bay. He tried working there in the Wonder City for a season, but the lure of the water and the smell of the salt air had captured his soul and he eventually joined the United States Navy where he made a career as a professional seaman.

He was on shore leave in Havana the night the Maine went down, and finally mustered out in 1919.

After the big war, he returned to Madison County, Florida but not one of the people he remembered still lived there. Nonetheless, he used most of his savings to buy the decrepit old stage stop, that as a boy of ten he had helped build, and for the remainder of his life, he tended the little cemetery nearby. Although he often wondered, he never learned where Reb Brown was buried.

The weekly edition of the Coffeyville Sun's headlines announced the Armorists agreement in Europe on the eleventh Instant[1] and other war news on the front page, right next to a long editorial about the KKK in Kansas.

However, near the bottom of the backside of the single sheet was a small notation.

> Quigley Hancock long-time resident of Montgomery County passed away quietly on the 31st Ultimo[2] at his home near the old village of Verdigris. Doc Hollister reportedly said he succumb to pneumonia after being bedridden only three days.

The epitaph on his fine granite headstone reads;

Quigley Hancock
Born September 1, 1838,
Died November 1, 1918
A Quiet and Peaceful Giant
Now resting in the arms of the Lord

---

[1] Instant: Meaning it happened this month.

[2] Ultimo: Latest or last month.

The paper went on to say:

> Mr. Hancock is survived by his wife Mariah and two sons, Cater and Stanley, both Army Captains, serving in France.

-30-

Characters of The Big Open

Ranches
WT
K—S
CY
The Goose Egg

Owners
Paul Somerset (*WT*)
Karl Siebold (*K—S*)
Gayle Somerset (*WT*)
Camilla Gustav Siebold
(Callie) (*K—S*)
John Carey (*CY*)
Searight brothers (*The Goose Egg*)

Ranch Foremen
Chuck Butler
Miles Abbey
Quigley Hancock

Riders
Christy King
Effird Nelson
Blaine Sedgwick
Jacob Wells
Sidney McMullin
Lucius Reed
Paul Spalding
Martin Henry
Blaine Sedgwick
Nandres Hall
Stacy Beck

Sean Hennessey
Zeb Sapp
Perry Taylor
Terry Ellick
Hank, the cook

Dingus Rockland Mendoza Haeckel
Buford Gillyard, the shepherd
Shelly McCrery
Eddie Thorbs
Dakota
Dave Dawson
Curley Driggers
Wesley Bobo, the cook

WT's Hired Gun – Hawks

Quigley Hancock's Special Squad
Randal Rowe aka Gila Drifter
Buckshot Gunter
Francis Wheeler
Laramie Patay
Donny Wadsworth
Ryan Rodriguez
Art Linton
Dusty Salser
Jim Catron
Chris Morgan

Town Folk
Sunny Tomson: Owner of the Poison Spyder Saloon.
Marietta Williams (Miss Etta): Soiled Dove at the Poison
Spyder Saloon.
Ole Dave: Jehu of the Stageline.

Joe Marquis: Operated the Poison Spyder General Store and Hotel.

Zerelda: The new working girl from Cheyenne brought in to replace Etta. Archibald Smythe: Poison Spyder's Doctor. Wiley Bass: Carbon County Deputy Sheriff.

We hope you enjoyed TH Bear's novel, *The Big Open*. If you have not had the chance to read the Trilogy of *The Owl Hoot Trail*, you can order it directly from BluewaterPress LLC on the Internet at www.bluewaterpress.com.